ISBN: 978-0-9839069-1-9

Cover Concept, Artwork and Design: JH Glaze
Text Editing: Susan Grimm
First Printing December 2011
Published by MostCool Media Inc.
"Make it interesting. Make it MostCool."

Proudly printed in the United States of America.

Second Edition June 2012

11 10 9 8 7 6 5 4 3 2

Dedicated to my wife Susan, who continues to run down this crazy path with me and helps me keep focused on my work. Your tireless support and editing assistance enables me to keep moving forward. You will forever be my favorite cheerleader.

To all of my readers and reviewers, thank you for the awesome comments and encouragement. Without you, my stories are just words on paper.

Finally, thank you to Zack Parris - my first pass editor, April Holt - my copy proofer, and my story review team: James Swearengin (ISSO Productions), Catherine Barson, and all of the others who have to listen to me drone on about my latest story, day after day. Y'all are the best.

NorthWest

Feel your Fear !

NorthWest

"With lies you may get ahead in the world - but you can never go back."

~Russian proverb

One

Spring was late in coming to the northwestern forests this year. The animals were undoubtedly eager for the arrival of warmer weather and the abundance of food that would ultimately come. For now, they must settle for the early shoots of plants that had just begun to poke their heads out of the ground before the first big thaw of the season.

The chilled morning air seemed to amplify the sound of a healthy eight-point buck working his way through the striking shadows that littered the path in front of him as he found sustenance in the young plants. He stepped over a moss-covered log and continued moving through the clearing making tracks in the newly fallen snow with his hooves and his snout as he pushed the snow about looking for the next tender morsel.

He lifted his head often, alert to his surroundings. This being his seventh year of the mating season, he was more than aware of the smells and sounds around him lest he be surprised by another younger, more motivated buck, or worse a pack of wolves scouring the forest for breakfast.

As he gracefully bent his head downward to sniff the forest floor, he took a step forward and found his progress halted as he encountered a very solid object with his antlers. He was startled by the sudden collision since mere seconds ago he had scanned the forest around him and had noticed nothing to be alarmed about.

How could it be that he would find himself standing so close to another eight-point buck looking back at him? For a moment he was unsure how to react since he had not even a whiff of warning of another of his kind in this part of the forest. Surely there were no sounds to alert him. How could he have missed another male in his territory?

He took a cautious step back, lowering his rack into a defensive position and the intruder did the same. He brought his hoof up and slammed it to the ground, again as a challenge, and again the animal in front of him mirrored his actions. Now he was angry. His nostrils flared and he snorted his frustrations at the brazen trespasser who dared to confront him in his feeding grounds.

At this time of the year, contests were common among the bucks in the forest, usually for mating rights with a healthy young doe. However, it seemed this challenger wanted to fight for no apparent reason, and never one to resist the challenge, this strong male steadied himself for the charge. The moment had to be just right and he eyed his opponent who appeared to be waiting to make his move.

He was growing increasingly impatient, locked in a standoff with a worthy adversary, so he decided it was time to make the first move. Summoning all of his strength he surged forward, shaking his head side to side in an attempt to inflict the most damage to this stranger when he struck. With full force he hit with a loud 'Krrrack' as he made contact – but with what?

His right antler broke off at the crook of the first two points and tumbled to the ground as the force of his body caught up with him, pushing his neck into his shoulders with great energy. Stunned, he stumbled and went down on his front knees, struggling not to fall completely to the ground. He blew shafts of steam from his nostrils as he looked and saw that his opponent had suffered the same fate.

The injured buck rose again to his feet, preparing to charge. All at once there was a whirring sound above him and a blur of motion as something struck his shoulder, slicing it wide open. The hit created a foot long gash.

He bawled in pain as he was knocked off balance by the momentum of the strike, and blood shot straight out from the wound. His opponent disappeared as the blood struck some invisible object between them and cascaded down to the ground. He managed to turn his head a bit when he noticed the shadow from a moving object above him.

Just then another swift blow struck his neck and his half severed head dropped toward his chest as his legs gave out and he slumped to the ground. The world went dark around him as he wondered where he was, and what had just happened.

The creature dropped from its position in the tree to stand over its victim and began hacking off large chunks with a jagged appendage, greedily devouring the raw flesh. This was not a meal to be savored. It was only food – fuel – nothing more.

Six Hours Earlier

The panels of the radar screen lit up as the airman working in the Joint Tactical Ground Station was taking the second bite of the best turkey sandwich he had ever tasted. Warning alerts were blaring. Something was happening. An emergency appeared to be unfolding. "Shit!" he blurted out, blowing morsels of food from his overstuffed mouth.

A red flashing blip appeared to be shooting across the sky at an unheard of velocity. He was so startled that he dropped his sandwich to the floor as he jumped to grab the mouse at his computer. With a click, he brought up the Eagle View tracking detail screen.

He punched in a two digit speed dial number as he picked up the phone. The phone rang twice before the person on the other end answered. "I have a bogie over

California travelling at about twelve hundred miles an hour and…" He stopped talking as the unknown object disappeared from the screen. A voice replied, "Did you say twelve hundred?"

"Ah, well sir, it's gone now. Should I do anything?"

The man on the other end sounded tired and frustrated, "Listen, it was probably some kind of meteor. I don't want to wake anyone at command at three in the morning to report a meteor! Was the recorder running?"

"Yes sir. The system checks out. It's been documented."

"If you see it again, we'll scramble some fighters to check it out, but for now just stand down. We can review the recording in the morning."

"Yes sir." He heard the officer grumbling as he disconnected from the comm. He looked down at the remains of half his sandwich lying face open on the floor. "Damn, sometimes I hate this shit," he grumbled. He decided to clean up the mess just as soon as he finished the other half.

He rolled his chair forward over a slice of tomato, grabbed the rest of the sandwich and took a big bite. "Man, this is good!" he mumbled through a mouth full of bread and lettuce.

Meanwhile:

Somewhere in the forests of the Pacific Northwest, a strange ship landed hard, smashing trees and embedding itself partway in the damp, snow covered, still frozen ground. It was steaming from the heat of entry into our atmosphere. It had crashed more than fifty miles from the nearest populated area. Light snow was swirling and falling around it and there was no one there to see it, let alone hear it happen.

Two

The woman on the streetcar droned on and on, talking with a heavy accent, to her friend. Now and then, a word or two would merge into Spanglish, and then the pitch would go from dull to shrill and end in raucous laughter. Occasionally a baby would cry, breaking the rhythm of her rant, and she would glare at the baby and sigh loudly before continuing.

Most of the animated conversation went completely unnoticed. John Hazard sat staring out the window, lost in thoughts of the day ahead of him, and particularly of the days behind. It's strange where fate can lead. One day he was an up and coming detective in a small town police department with a promising career. The next he was living in the city taking classes at a community college and working on an entirely new career path for himself.

John was still amazed at the situation he had encountered on a case eight months earlier. It was an experience that changed the way he saw the world, the way he perceived things to be, not in the natural world, but in a supernatural sense.

He had moved with everything he owned to San Francisco to try to hide himself in the big city. He figured that this was a place where strange was the norm, a place where a freaked out detective might get his shit together after such a traumatic experience.

The incident had begun with a murder investigation, a double homicide to be exact. It quickly developed into a strange and complex case involving missing people and some maniac who was possessed by a box that stole people's spirits.

The whole thing was really insane, and he tried to get over it in the weeks that followed the conclusion of the investigation. Nightmares, panic attacks, and night sweats drove him to request a leave of absence. Rather than stay in that small Idaho town, he packed everything into an old, rusted out pickup truck and drove non-stop to San Francisco, stopping only when the Pacific Ocean got in the way of going further. At the time, it just made sense to make a change.

It took a week of searching to find a furnished efficiency apartment. After he moved in with his few boxes of belongings, he spent his days, maybe weeks, sitting on a sleeper sofa in his underwear. He frequently drank himself into a slow easy coma.

By sometime in the sixth week or so, as he was finishing off a bottle of Jack, he had a revelation. What if he just quit the police force and got himself a new career, something that he could work at from his new found perspective. Not the standard detective work dealing with the day to day horrors of criminal investigation, but taking on the unknown terrors of the supernatural world. A world that, only some months before, he would not have even realized existed.

John had always considered himself to be a logical person, a realist. It was a one of the requirements of the job in law enforcement. There was good and bad, right and wrong, black and white and sometimes a few shades of gray. Whatever he felt about it, he'd always trusted in the physical evidence that was before him. However, now he had been thrown a curve. Confronted with the supernatural, it scared the shit out of him to discover that the realm of the bizarre and paranormal actually existed. It really sucked to be so wrong about something so terrible, and often so inherently evil.

Sure, he had watched all of those late night movies with ghosts, witches, demons, vampires, werewolves, and such. There were zombies, hairy beasts with big teeth and other things that bumped in the night, but those were supposed to be figments of imagination, of superstition, right? Wrong. Really wrong it seemed. If the evil, antique spirit-sucking box he had encountered on that case could exist, how many of these other things existed as well?

His fate was sealed. He could not return to the days of innocence - those happy, carefree days (carefree? yeah right, maybe when he was three years old), days of believing there's no such thing as monsters because now he knew unequivocally that there really were monsters.

It was this one fact, this one little piece of information he had never really wanted to know, that overwhelmed him. It possessed him. It became the source of the only clear vision he had of where his life could go from here.

He would not return to small town America to work as a detective investigating robberies, assaults and old fashioned homicides. That was evil on a petty scale. Even murder between humans, mostly crimes of passion, couldn't compete with the heinous activity that came out of the supernatural realm.

Now his destiny stretched out before him along a much darker path than he ever would have followed before. He would still perform the duties of a detective, but officially his new title would be John Hazard P.I., Paranormal Investigator. That was exactly as it was to appear on the business cards he had ordered, if the fucking things would ever come in the mail.

Three

Emily thought it seemed a little cool for this time of year as she pulled her sweater around her shoulders. She was sitting out on the deck of the coffee shop checking for jobs online with her laptop. Her latest bout of unemployment had gone on too long although she had gotten a few contracting and temporary jobs over the past three months.

The problem was that temporary jobs caused interruptions in her unemployment checks, and there was not enough money to pay the bills. She had no choice. She scanned all of the major job sites in hopes that the right one would be hiding there, that perfect job that would both pay well and allow her some free time to continue to pursue her career goals. Maybe two jobs if that is what it took to get her finances straightened out.

After finishing her scan of the regular sites, Emily went to the free site where most people posted things for sale. She clicked on Oakland, then the link for jobs. It seemed like it was going to take a long time for the site to load, so she glanced around at the clientele who had wandered in while she had been occupied.

The guy behind the counter must be new because she had never seen him before and he had put more chocolate in her mocha than she liked. There was an old man at the counter who was trying to decide what he would order and grumbling about the prices and fancy coffee and something else she couldn't quite hear.

At one of the tables was a girl with cobalt blue hair and multiple piercings. She faced away from Emily, which allowed a view of the tattoos of dragons and snakes that extended from beneath the tank top she was wearing up her neck, to just below her earlobes where they would forever seem poised to strike. She chuckled silently, imagining thirty years in the future, as a grandmother explained to her granddaughter why she got the tattoos, and warning her never to do that to herself.

Aside from the two diverse customers and the jerk-wad behind the counter, she was alone, and she liked it that way. She returned to her screen, allowing her eyes to readjust and scanned the listings. More of the usual crap. They wanted insurance agents, financial advisors, work from home, envelope stuffers, all of the things she had already considered and been warned about, and then something new jumped out at her.

Videographer/Camera Operator needed for documentary project. Minimum requirement: Bachelor's Degree in communications and experience operating Steadicam and Final Cut video editing suite. Two week commitment required. Email resume to adventure@bay-uni.edu.

That sounded good except for the two week timeframe. It was going to take something more permanent to really get her bills straightened out. Still it would be nice to finally use her Communications degree for something other than a framed document on her bedroom wall. She hadn't worked with a Steadicam before, but she had friends who did, and she had been told it is 'just a heavier camera'. No big deal. She could fake it.

She bookmarked the website page and continued looking, but after a few minutes she found she was still thinking about the documentary project. She clicked on the bookmark and re-read the ad, then hovered the cursor over the link and clicked on it. Her email opened with a new message ready to send. She typed:

To whom it may concern,

My name is Emily Sparks. I live just outside of Oakland. I found your ad on the Internet and would like more information about the videographer position. I have a B.A. in Communication, with a minor in Film Editing. I am very interested in your project and would like to learn more of the details. Please contact me by replying to this email.

Thank you very much,
Emily Sparks

She clicked the 'send' button, waited until the message had cleared, closed her laptop and shoved it into her leather carry case.

She gathered her empty cup, stir stick, and used napkins and stood to walk to the trash can. She noticed the old man had left the counter and when she stepped into the aisle, she found herself face to face with a strange man.

"Excuse me, Miss." He muttered as he hobbled past her, the smell of stale alcohol and body odor almost overwhelming her. She held her breath and smiled, politely nodding, and quickly headed out the door and back toward her apartment to print out some résumés.

Walking briskly down the busy street, Emily looked up at the clear blue sky and smiled. As bad as things were for her right now, she was not even close to approaching the circumstances of that obviously destitute old man, and if things turned out as she expected, it might be a good day after all.

Four

It was a beautiful, quiet day at the community college. Many of the students were attending a rally at the stadium and most of the people left on campus were professors and students who were just not that involved in political issues. The atmosphere on campus had been charged for months now, and it was beginning to wear on the nerves of even the passive and uninvolved.

Professor Macy Renner was sitting in her cluttered office filling out a spreadsheet of expenses that had so far accumulated for her documentary field trip project, and her face revealed her frustration. Rays of afternoon sun spiked into the room illuminating specks of dust that floated through the air like snowflakes every time she lifted a sheet of paper.

She had made reservations for a private plane to fly her class up into the national forests of the Pacific Northwest, somewhere between the states of Washington and Oregon. She'd ordered supplies and rented equipment, and even covered accommodations for an overnight stay before heading off into the wilds of the forest.

This had stretched her budget to the limit and now she had to figure out how to pay a videographer to film the adventure. Without proper documentation, it wouldn't matter what they discovered if there was no proof of it to bring back.

The student who had volunteered to go for free backed out at the last minute and now she would actually have to pay someone to take his place. Macy was determined to make this field trip for her students happen, and she had personal reasons for doing so. That was why she had placed the ad.

She had been following a strange phenomenon for several months now. There were reports of missing aircraft, hikers and hunters in about a hundred square mile area of national forest. They had disappeared without a trace and all search and rescue operations had been abandoned in each incident. It was as though they had dropped off the planet.

Macy had analyzed all of the information she had gathered and found similarities to disappearances in the Bermuda Triangle. She figured if she could get some half decent footage, she could distribute the film. It could be a documentary on the case of the NorthWest Triangle, a place where things simply vanished forever. Maybe they'd call it "Renner's Triangle."

Just thinking about having the phenomenon named after her was enough to bring a smile to her face. It could finally be her chance to get some personal recognition and bring attention to her program. It might guarantee her funding at the university for years to come. Her career surely would benefit, but some of the details in the case reminded her of the horrible events that had occurred during her childhood.

The unexplained disappearance of her twin sister at the age of thirteen continued to haunt her. How could anyone shake the loss of a sister who would never be seen or heard from again? She was her twin, her other half, and the only real friend that Macy had ever had. Her loss had a chilling effect on everything in her life in the years that followed.

She picked up the framed photo of two little girls playing together, which sat at the corner of her desk. Gazing at her twin, she thought about all the secrets, the special 'twin signals,' and good times they had shared. What happened to you?

The involuntary cry from her heart reaffirmed why she had started this two-semester course in the first place. It wasn't because she thought it would be interesting to study paranormal phenomenon, though that was true enough. It was because she could still remember, in brief flashes of fragmented memories, the terrifying strangers that took her and her sister over a three-year span from ages ten to thirteen years old. "Fucking aliens," she said out loud.

It was something that no little girl should have to experience. The long cold gray fingers clenched around her legs as she was lifted from her bed, and silently, effortlessly carried upside down through her window and into an odd shaped doorway. She could hear the sounds of crying, and sometimes screaming humans, men, women and children all around her.

The brilliant flashing lights that seemed to shine right through her body burned like points of fire as she lay helpless on a transparent but solid glass table. It was all she could do to keep from sobbing as once again, in her tortured mind, she could hear the familiar screams of her sister from another chamber as the creatures worked over her with their unusual metal instruments.

A knock on her office door brought her back before she could recall what came next in this horrible flashback. "Yes?" She stood to answer it, steadying herself against the desk.

The girl opened the door and stuck her head in, "Professor Renner, sorry to bother you. I just wanted to let you know that I received an email a few minutes ago from someone regarding the online ad for videographer. Do you want me to schedule an appointment with her for tomorrow?"

"Oh, most definitely. Tell her to come in early in the morning so we can confirm our final team before lunchtime. We are down to less than forty eight hours to departure and we need to know if we are good to go or if we will need someone to pull double duty with the camera." She set the photo back in its corner instinctively turning the photo face down to hide it from inquisitive eyes.

"Is eight o'clock okay then?" The assistant watched Macy flip the photo over and made a mental note to check it out later.

"That would be lovely. Could you please close the door for me on the way out?" She sat down and spun her chair around to face the window so the tears that had begun to flow down her cheeks would not prompt any questions.

"Sure, sorry I interrupted…" The assistant was irritated by her cold behavior, but closed the door without any further comment.

"I'm not." Macy mumbled to herself as she stared out the window, her mind relieved for the moment from the terror of her memories.

Five

The last thing Rajesh Pradeep wanted to explain to his parents was how his engineering studies had been put on hold while he immersed himself in a half year of paranormal investigative studies. He decided it was best to keep it to himself rather than suffer the consequences. Had his father known what he was doing, it could mean the end of the cash flow that he needed to maintain his lifestyle.

He eyed the shelves in the sporting goods store trying to decide if there was anything he needed that was not on his list. Was there anything else that he might need on this trip to the wilderness? He had already invested a considerable amount in his tent, sleeping bag and mat, stainless steel dish and utensil set, flashlights, batteries, dehydrated food, canteen, and a box of condoms… just in case. Like he would really need them, but there were going to be women on the trip, and anything could happen. Secretly he wished that something would.

He looked again at his list and everything had been checked off except one thing, a hatchet. He had added the hatchet to the list because he realized they would need to have a fire to cook, and at night for light and communal discussions, but even the thought of carrying a hatchet went against his anti-violence stance. Not that he expected violence, but this was America and he had seen more violence in the two years since he had been attending school here, than he had his entire life before he came.

Still, he did want to eat and stay warm on this trip, and building a fire would be difficult without something to chop up the wood. There were various sizes and the one he chose was about as long as his arm from elbow to fingertips. He took the thing from the display rack. The rubber grip felt uncomfortable in his hand. He could have sworn that it was burning the skin ever so slightly as he held it. At that moment he rather resented his parents for instilling so many fears and foolish beliefs in him. After all, this was simply a tool, a piece of metal designed to cut wood or drive in tent stakes. It would only be a weapon in the hand of a man that intended to use it as such.

So while he was still convinced that it would be used only for good and practical purposes, he put the hatchet in his cart. After taking a few turns through the racks of sports clothes, he pushed his nearly empty cart to the front of the store and up to the checkout lane where an athletic looking type was working the register.

As he stood there waiting for the person in front of him to find his credit card, he picked up an Outdoorsman magazine from the rack and flipped through the pages. There was an article on solar powered generators, an ad for shotgun shells, an article about building a shelter with a poncho and some branches and one on how to survive an avalanche in the spring. Flipping past an ad for mountain boots, his worst fears were confirmed. He stared at the article about a person who had accidentally lopped off three fingers while chopping firewood.

He was stunned and stood staring in horror at the hatchet in his cart while the exasperated cashier repeated, "Next!" He began putting his few items on the conveyor belt and carefully picked up the hatchet, holding the wretched item between his thumb and pointer, and lifted it away from him. He set it on the energy drink display at the top of the counter. With obvious relief, he continued to empty his cart on the belt.

The cashier rang everything up and announced, "That will be twenty three dollars and eighty-five cents." After he swiped Rajesh's card, he pointed at the card reader and said, "Please press the green button."

The young cashier tore off the receipt, quickly glanced at it, and smiled. "You saved two dollars today. Thank you for shopping at Sports Mart!"

Rajesh took his receipt, shoved it in his pocket, and pushed his cart out the door and across the parking lot to his car. On the way home, he was thinking about his feelings about the whole hatchet thing. Was he being ridiculous? Shouldn't one live by their convictions? "You have to believe in something or your time here on earth will mean nothing," his father always said. Seeing things from that perspective, he felt proud that he had walked out without it, but somehow deep in his gut he had a feeling he would be sorry he had done so.

Six

Sherri Washington carefully reviewed her stack of documents wondering if she had forgotten anything that Dr. Renner had asked her to do. This had been referred to as a 'class assignment'. She had made the reservations, procured the maps, and hired the guide to take them up into the forest the first two days.

For some reason he had refused to travel beyond the Whitmore gap. When she inquired as to his reason, he simply replied, "Weird things going on up there lately. Can't do it." Weird things indeed, exactly what her class was going into the woods to investigate. She didn't even try to argue with him about it.

It looked like she had taken care of everything, everything except packing her clothes and a small bag for her son, Shandre. His grandmother, his father's mother, had agreed to keep him for the next two weeks while she was away. For this she was grateful since she needed to go on this trip to get a passing grade in her class.

Shandre was already six, and quite the little man, but he would always be her baby no matter how old he was. Being a single mother was no easy task and situations like this always pointed a wagging finger at her ability to manage, something she had been dealing with for some time now.

This trip was the pivot point of a life spent searching for answers, and she was truly looking forward to it. If she had not been able to make arrangements for her son, she might have not been able to go on this trip. Without these class credits, she wouldn't graduate and might miss the only chance she had for some kind of life for her and the boy, away from here.

There was no way that she could raise the money for more classes if she were unable to complete this course. This Paranormal Investigative career path was a total fit with the life she had been 'blessed with', as she put it.

When Sherri was fifteen years old, she developed an ability to hear voices of those who had passed from this world, in particular the voices of her grandmother and her great aunt who had both died years earlier. Throughout the years, they spoke to her whenever she was in danger, or if she was about to make a decision that would have a negative impact on her life. At those times her protectors would advise her on what was about to occur and what action to take to avoid peril.

Anyone could imagine how shocking it was when she heard them for the first time. It was an experience she rarely related to family, and definitely not to friends.

She was on a trip to Los Angeles with her high school marching band. They were scheduled to march in the Tournament of Roses Parade on New Year's Day. Their chartered bus made a stop at a truck stop along the highway for a thirty-minute break.

Like many highway truck stops, this one was a combination of gas stations and fast food restaurants. At this time of the day, it was a very busy place as families and truckers stopped to get something to eat.

The group piled out of the bus and most of the kids headed straight to the food court area. The number of band members inside of the building swelled the size of the crowd considerably and all of the talking, laughing, and carrying on added to the din and chaos.

Sherri and a few of her friends had gone into the restroom while the other band members got in line at the counter. After she finished using the toilet, she stood in front of the mirror washing her hands next to her friend. She casually smoothed her hair with her fingers as she stepped away from the sink when she heard a voice saying, "Don't go out yet. Stay here for a few more minutes."

"Did you say something, Annie?" She looked at her friend in the mirror.

"No, but I was thinking about Max. You must have been reading my mind. You didn't read my mind, did you?" she blushed. "I mean, like that would really creep me out if you did!"

"No, of course not! I must be hearing things."

"Right, I'm glad you can't read my mind because I think Max is so totally hot!" Annie was gushing with evident passion for the guy.

"Max? Really? Isn't he kind of a geek? Like, he reads those comics all the time and hangs out with those programmers. They're always talking about video games and stuff like that."

"Yeah, I know, but Max is different. He just seems to really 'see' me, right? Hey, come on. Let's get out there and get some food before we have to go. I'm starving!"

"Don't go Sherri. Stay here. There's something you need to know." It was that voice again. It seemed louder this time and more insistent.

Sherri turned to face Annie, "So-o-o, you didn't just tell me to stay here? You want to tell me something?"

"Girl, were you smokin' something in that stall? Nobody said anything!" Annie checked her hair to make sure every strand was perfect, moving her head from side to side to fix her part.

"Something strange is going on. You go ahead. I'll be out in a minute. I need to... uh... check something." And she leaned in closer to the mirror and pretended to look at one of her eyes as if to remove something from it.

"Are you sure? You're acting kind of funny. I can check that for you if you want." Annie moved closer.

"No, really, I'll be right out."

Annie looked at her quizzically, wondering for a moment what was going on. "Ok then, I'll go see if Max is in line. Maybe he'll give me cuts!" She turned on her heels and walked out of the bathroom.

Did she look strange? Sherri examined her face to look for any sign of illness. She didn't know for sure what she was looking for, but there had to be some reason she would start hearing voices.

"Don't worry, baby. You hear us now because you need us." It was her grandmother's voice, she remembered her well enough.

"But why, Gran? How? You're not really here. I mean, you're..." She looked around the restroom expecting to see someone.

The familiar voice finished her sentence, "Dead, honey?"

Just then gunshots rang out and she heard a scream. Without hesitation she ran to the door catching herself before she opened it. She had no idea what might be happening out there, and she wasn't sure she wanted to find out. However, curiosity got the best of her and she cracked the door so she could try to see what was going on.

Out in the food court area where the rest of the band members were waiting to get some lunch, three armed robbers were holding up the restaurant and the customers.

She couldn't see most of what was happening, but she could hear it all.

"Everybody get your wallets out and throw them in this bag." A white pillowcase was being passed from person to person and wallets and loose money were being tossed into it as it went by. Across the room at the gas station counter, the cash register was being emptied into a similar bag, and Sherri could see that the barrel of a gun was being pressed against the cashier's forehead.

At one of the tables in the food court, two police officers had just finished their lunch. Until now they had remained hidden behind the group of teens. Quietly, they whispered and used hand signs to coordinate their next move and rose from the table. Pulling their weapons, they stood and took aim at two of the gunmen, yelling, "Police – drop your weapons!"

The trigger happy robbers opened fire on the crowd. As the deluge of bullets rained upon them, the teenagers who had been standing in lines at the counter fell to the floor. Some had been hit and were on the floor screaming, while others ducked or scrambled for cover. The police had positioned themselves in a way that blocked both front exits so no one could run for the door. They had hoped to surprise the thugs into giving themselves up, however, the automatic weapons continued to fire round after round and there was nothing they could do to stop them.

The punks worked their way to the doors, stepping over bodies and grabbing up kids to use as human shields until their bullet ridden bodies could no longer be supported. Stray bullets slammed into tables and walls and ricocheted off the tile. When a napkin dispenser was hit, bits of paper floated like giant snowflakes in the air.

Time warped to a slowed pace before the police, who had each been hit several times, got off a few lucky shots. Amidst the screaming and chaos, the killers dropped to the floor. The third punk had taken advantage of the confusion and ran out a back door. He was two blocks down the street when the shooting ended.

As the smoke cleared from the building, thirteen students, including Annie and the two policemen, lay dead on the floor and eleven more were critically wounded. The screaming and wailing of the injured rang in Sherri's ears for weeks afterward. The scenes of death invaded her dreams, leaving her screaming in the dark night after night. Had she not received the warning, she may have been killed and at times she felt the guilt of having survived.

Now many years and dozens of similar spiritual warnings later, Sherri was about to become part of a team where others knew of her gift and respected her for it. In fact, they were counting on her to help them discover the secrets behind what was happening up in the wilderness of the Pacific Northwest. For once in her life, her gift could make a real difference for something beyond self preservation.

Seven

John checked his email messages around seven-thirty that evening. He found the message from Dr. Renner concerning the interview in the morning amongst all of the aggravating spam. She wrote to ask him to come, sit in on the interview and offer his opinion on a possible videographer named Emily Sparks.

It was a little late in the evening to answer Macy by phone seeing that it was past normal office hours, so he hit 'Reply', and typed his answer to let her know he would be there. After sending his response, he sat back in his chair and closed his eyes. He had been through a lot of shit in the last couple of years, and in this quiet moment, he thanked God that he had survived.

Since he had come here, he had spent a lot of time alone. Quiet, uninterrupted days left him with a lot of time for personal reflection, and he often questioned his decision. Sometimes, he even missed parts of the life he'd led as a detective, at least the social aspect of it.

He had made some friends in that life, real friends, people who seemed to care about him and leaving them behind was one of the most difficult things to come to grips with. The damn shame of it was that, after what had happened, he just couldn't stay there.

In small towns, people talk. If the story ever got out about what had happened on that case, they would have talked a lot. The last thing he wanted to do was try to answer a shitload of questions. He couldn't really explain everything, especially the supernatural stuff. If there had been further investigation he might have to tell them why he'd failed to do things by the book - again.

Even in the military, he would try to follow orders, do what he was told, but often it took too long. He would end up getting his ass in trouble when expedience seemed to trump decorum and he'd break the rules. He didn't try to figure out why he was that way; he just knew that he was.

So a career move to paranormal investigation held promise for him. When dealing with things that most people don't understand or even believe exist, he'd have many opportunities to make things up as he went. As long as nobody got killed, what kind of trouble could he possibly get into?

With nothing else to do tonight, he went back to surfing the web. He looked at personal ads and came up empty, so he navigated to the Paranormal News Central website. That was a place where he could always find things related to his new career, and the people involved in that were possible clients if he could find a way to contact them. All of that prospecting for clients had to wait until after this trip though. He needed to get his certificate in order to get some kind of a Paranormal Investigation business license.

John took his time looking through every article and listing. After reading all the recent posts and coming up dry, he decided to crash for the night. Maybe if he got some sleep, he would be on time in the morning.

However, it seemed no sooner had he crawled onto his uncovered mattress, closed his eyes and started to dream, then the sun had risen and light was breaking through his windows in direct aim at his eyes. He rolled out of bed, showered and shaved. Before long he was dressed, and with a defrosted bagel in hand, he left the apartment.

He arrived early enough to get a cup of 'good' coffee and stood in line at the Panama Star coffee shop just off campus. He was definitely needing his morning coffee boost and his bagel needed a chaser. He'd wanted to get to the faculty building a bit early if possible to check out the résumé of this Sparks chick and prepare any questions he might ask as part of the interview. Rarely did he get the opportunity to participate in such activities, and he wanted at least to appear to be professional.

As he stepped up to the counter the barrister asked him, "What'll it be sir?"

"I'll have a regular coffee with an extra shot."

John was crazy about that extra shot, it was like a nitrous power boost on a race car for him, and it was just what he needed to get the party started this early in the morning. He pulled a couple of bucks from his pocket and paid for the coffee, then threw the change in the tip cup. He couldn't afford to be more generous at the moment, and he honestly didn't see why someone pouring him an outrageously expensive cup of coffee needed more than that anyway.

He picked up his coffee and headed out the door. As he was adjusting the sleeve that had been placed on the cup to keep him from burning his hands, he nearly ran down a woman on her way in who was clearly not paying attention any more than he was.

"Excuse me," she said smiling at him.

"No worries." He didn't stop as he continued down the sidewalk, but he did look to see if the rearview matched the front, since she was kind of attractive. He continued across the street and onto the campus grounds, heading over to the faculty building where the interviews had been previously held. There had been several others who had been considered to shoot the video for this excursion but either did not make the grade, or didn't want to 'intern' on the project, or maybe they just weren't available for the two week period that it required.

He didn't know why but today he had a good feeling about the outcome of the interview. Maybe he was developing a sixth sense, maybe that part of his brain was beginning to wake up to extrasensory input. Whatever it was, since he had begun this class on Paranormal Investigation, it seemed his senses had sharpened and his ability to feel a situation, good or bad, had been improved to a much higher degree.

By the time he arrived at room 224, he had finished his coffee. Everyone else was already seated around a conference table and waiting for Ms. Emily Sparks. Dr. Renner had asked the core of the team to attend to get a feel for Emily. They were not there to simply qualify her résumé and skills as a videographer, but to judge whether or not she would be a good member of the team. The low rumble of chit-chat stopped when he entered the room and everyone sat looking at him.

"Good morning. How's everybody today?" John addressed the group including Dr. Renner, Rajesh, or Raj, as he preferred to be called, and Sherri. Heads nodded and affirmations were grumbled.

"Shit, were we supposed to bring something to take notes with?" He noticed that the three of them had a pad and pen sitting on the table in front of them.

"No, John," Macy said reaching into a bag sitting on the floor. "I brought writing materials for everyone. Have a seat." As John sat at his place at the table, Macy began instructing the group on her protocol for this interview.

"Previously I've interviewed applicants for this very important position on our team in the privacy of my office.

The interviews were conducted in a professional manner – a standard question and answer session. Now, I'm not so sure that it was the best way to operate, so today we are going to conduct an experiment as a part of this interview."

She reached her hands up to her head and touched her temples with the tips of her fingers. "In this format, I want each of you to relax and allow yourselves to feel the answers as opposed to just listening to them." She closed her eyes as if concentrating on the vibrations in the room, then opened them again suddenly.

"Are we allowed to ask any questions?" Raj inquired as he scratched his head through his mop of black hair.

"I was just about to say that questions are not limited to the standard talk about job experience, where the interviewee sees herself in five years, or what does she think she can contribute to our project."

She pushed her glasses up with her middle finger. "I want you to ask any question that comes to your mind, Raj. No matter how ridiculous it may seem at the time. I believe we have to go beyond the norm in this situation. We need to sense what this woman is about... can you do that for me?"

As Raj and Sherri nodded in unison, Macy smiled. She couldn't help but think what good little sheep they were. They were good followers and always performed as expected. She glanced over at John. Then there's Mr. Unpredictable.

"So this is an experiment within an experiment, right?" John looked around at the others for approval. He was grinning and feeling very proud that he was the first to come up with that observation, but no one was nodding in response.

"Exactly, John! We should use the skills we have been learning and developing throughout our classes and practice them in all aspects of our project. So when Ms. Sparks arrives, feel free to get involved. Go ahead and take a minute, while we wait, to write down some opening questions." After everyone nodded in agreement, there was silence while notes were jotted down on paper.

At exactly seven fifty-nine, Emily Sparks blew into the room like an umbrella in a windstorm. She was carrying a small shoulder bag and a file folder. "Oh hi... uh... good morning everyone, my name is..."

Macy finished her sentence as she held out her hand to invite a handshake. "Emily Sparks. Yes, very pleased to meet you. I am Dr. Renner." She motioned at each individual as she introduced them, "and this is Rajesh Pradeep, he prefers to be called Raj..."

Raj nodded and stood to shake her hand. "Very nice to meet you, indeed."

"Hello Raj. Yes, you too." Emily replied.

Macy continued, "And this is Sherri Washington, the intuitive on our team."

"A pleasure to finally meet you," said Sherri. Emily just stared back at her wondering what she meant by 'finally.'

Then Sherri said, "Oh, I meant that it's good that we could get our camera girl." She laughed a little. "I didn't foresee you coming or anything."

Emily smiled and shook her hand. "Well, I hope I can be an asset to your team for this adventure. It looks like you are just about ready to go." She looked over at a couple of backpacks that were leaning against the wall.

"Ragin' like a bull in a rodeo with the bleachers full of clowns is more like it." She turned to see John grinning at her from his end of the table.

"Emily, I'd like you to meet John Hazard. He was once a police detective in small town Idaho, but he is here with us now to add his investigative skills to our group."

John stood and looked Emily in the eyes. He could sense a quiet urgency in those eyes, but he smiled again and said, "I hope you will be able to come with us. It would be a shame if we had to film this thing ourselves. It would probably end up looking like somebody's bad home movie if I had to hold a camera."

"Oh, it's nice to meet you too, Mr. Hazard, or should I call you Detective?"

"John will work."

"Okay then, John. I know what you mean about footage looking like home movies, and believe me, if you allow me to come along on this trip, there won't be any jittery shots unless the project calls for them."

"That sounds good, exactly what we are looking for. Have a seat, Emily, let's get started." Macy motioned to a chair and Emily sat down.

Eight

The helicopter was flying toward the ravine around a hundred feet above the tree line. The pilot planned to make a wide turn, then a pass through the ravine before calling off the search for the day.

Below the canopy of trees, dressed in camouflage, a hunter lay immobilized. Clinging to consciousness and missing the lower half of his leg, he screamed as he tightened his belt on the bleeding stump in a desperate attempt to stop the blood loss.

He looked up as he heard the sound of a helicopter approaching and tried to drag himself toward a clearing. He could see no more than twenty feet in front of him. He tried to pull himself up, but the pain was too intense and he lost his balance falling face-first into the pine needles.

He rolled over on his back hoping to see the chopper as it flew over to catch a glimmer of hope. He watched to see if it moved in any way to indicate that he had been spotted. He tried to wave, but the effort used up whatever was left of his strength. He lay there feeling life drain from his body. The thump of the helicopter blades was loud as it passed over without hesitation.

He smiled at the ridiculous thought that anyone might see him below these trees. He would have laughed out loud if he'd had the strength. Sobering, he thought of his wife. She'd be waiting and worrying.

Some ten yards behind him, his partner had stopped screaming as the creature devoured what was left of him. The sound of ripping flesh and gurgling of blood and gore was maddening. He did everything he could, not to think about his friend in that moment or what lay ahead for him.

He caught sight of an arrow that had been tossed from its case when he had been attacked. It was only about a yard from him and if he could get to it the odds would be slightly increased in his favor. When that thing attacked, maybe he could shove the arrow through its eye straight into its brain.

With every bit of strength he had left in him, he pulled himself through the pine needles and moss toward his only hope. The ringing in his ears prevented him from realizing that the sounds of carnage behind him had ceased.

The creature sat for a moment watching him as he strained to reach his objective. It tilted its head like a dog, tensed its body and leapt into the air, landing on the hunter's back effectively pinning him to the spot where he lay.

Rearing its head back, the creature roared a sound more terrible than any he had ever heard. It shoved a bony protrusion from one of its arms between the hunter's ribs and jerked back with a cutting motion. The hunter, still pinned to the ground struggled and screamed, blood spurting from his mouth. The world around him went dark as he heard the sound of his ribs cracking.

The monster paid no attention to the final gasp of its victim as it plunged its jaws into the wide gash on the hunter's back. With bone cracking precision, it ripped a lung out from the lifeless carcass, savoring the taste as it chewed the organ, blood drooling from its mouth. Pausing only a brief moment, it bent over the remains of the hunter once more, ripping and pulling, continuing the bloody feast while entrails oozed between its grinding jaws.

Nine

Emily felt hopeful as she walked off the campus. She had been told that the job was hers if she wanted it, and she did want it, kind of. Her only concern was that they were going to be gone for two weeks in the forests of the Pacific Northwest and, when she returned, she would be right back where she started, unemployed and desperate. Granted, she might have a little more cash in her pocket, but she really wanted to find a permanent job and this gig was far from permanent.

They must have really wanted her to go with them. She had voiced her hesitation during the interview, saying a bit timidly, "I would love to go with you, but..." and they raised the offer from twenty-five hundred dollars to five thousand with all expenses paid. Just like that! She was so surprised she almost accepted on the spot. She figured it would cover two months rent and give her time to find something else when she got back.

Still, there were a lot of things to arrange before she could leave. One important matter was her cat, Ralph. He would need to be boarded somewhere. She didn't like to think of him caged up like that. There was also a list of necessary camping gear with very little time and no money to get some. Oh, and her landlord would want some kind of payment since he had already warned her about eviction. She ticked through her list of concerns, and the thought of it overwhelmed her.

She'd better see about the other two interviews she had arranged before she could agree to go on a trip for two weeks. One was a dental receptionist job and the other for a bartender assistant position at a nightclub, both jobs that had the potential to generate a good stream of income. Or not.

Still, she had been offered this videographer job and it would give her the chance to use her education, the one she had gone in debt for, and maybe sweeten her résumé. Also, the subject matter, supernatural phenomenon, was something she had always had a fascination with and it would be a chance to get some first-hand experience in that realm. It could be an awesome two weeks if she decided to go.

She got to the Caltrain station and waved her commuter pass over the gatepost. After a few minutes the train pulled in and unloaded its passengers. Emily stepped into a car and took a seat next to a window. As she sat there waiting for the train to move on, she noticed a stench wafting throughout the car and wondered where it could be coming from. She saw a guy who appeared to be homeless sitting in the middle of the car and people all around getting up and walking out to get into another car.

About a minute later, her gag reflex was beginning to kick in, so she followed the other people out into the fresh air and into the next car. It was a bit more crowded and as she stepped through the door, it closed behind her. The train pulled out of the station while she was finding her seat and she almost fell into it when she sat down.

As the train rocked and clacked down the tracks, she sat and looked out the window comparing three different scenarios in her head. There was the future where she went on the trip, filmed and edited the documentary, the Science Channel picks up the documentary, she wins an award, and becomes a famous producer of documentaries. She closed her eyes and enjoyed the applause.

Next was her future as a dental receptionist. She saw herself sitting behind the counter, answering the phone, greeting people who looked like they were in severe pain, maybe even getting her teeth cleaned for free, dealing with kids day after day... "Fuck that!" abruptly speaking out before she saw the little old lady in the seat across from her glaring over her glasses directly in her direction. She gave a little wave, and sheepishly mouthed, "Sorry!"

Emily leaned back in her seat and closed her eyes again. The bartender assistant, on the other hand, now that could be more exciting. She'd meet lots of interesting people, everyone having a story to tell... the drama, the excitement, the tips... especially the drama. This interview had potential and she decided to prepare herself mentally for the volley of questions. "What do you think makes you stand out from those we have already interviewed for this position?" She would be ready. "I really have a way with people, you'll see!" she might answer.

Nearby there was cacophony of rap music streaming from quite a few cell phone speakers. She pulled one of her résumés from the folder she was carrying and studied it looking for anything she might improve on. All of a sudden some guy started yelling something she couldn't understand. He seemed to be speaking English because every couple of words made sense, but she just couldn't make out the rest.

She was startled but she couldn't assess whether it was a threatening situation or not. She looked around but no one else appeared to think anything unusual was going on, and most of the people who rode the train on a regular basis would know if any shit were about to hit the fan. Wouldn't they?

Emily convinced herself to relax a bit and she strained to hear what he was saying. "It will all end in a flash of blazing glory, the Lord will come and take me and all of his believers, and the rest of you will be left to be eaten by the monsters, your bones crunching in the jaws of hell beasts, then you will know that I am not crazy, yes crazy like a fox is crazy..." he took a breath, "yes...when they surround you in your white pants country club, drinking your drinks and playing pool and ping-pong, the end will fall on you like graffiti from the spray can. It will!" He stopped to wipe the spit from his beard.

Sighing with relief when she saw they were pulling into her station, she jumped up and moved to the door as it slowed to a stop. Two steps out of the car and moving toward the stairs, she could hear the tirade continue behind her as the doors slid shut.

She exited the station at street level and she closed her eyes and tilted her head skyward letting the brightly shining sun warm her face. It was a great day to be alive, and she was planning to enjoy the rest of it just as soon as she got these other two interviews out of the way.

The Players Lounge had advertised for an assistant bartender, but had not set any particular time to come in for an interview. She had decided to simply drop in and see if she could talk to the manager. Since it was late morning, they might be cleaning and getting the bar stocked for later. It could be a good time to get a face-to-face.

As she glanced at the crumpled paper in her hand and walked toward the address she had written there, she began to notice that the neighborhood looked a little dicey. Not really ghetto, but more of an industrial-type area. There really weren't a lot of shops after the first block from the station. After passing a couple of boarded up store fronts covered with graffiti, she saw the relatively new neon sign for the Players Lounge.

It seemed like a nice enough building and it was larger than she expected for this part of town. Obviously the clientele came from the warehouse and manufacturing district surrounding the place. That could be a good thing with regular customers who would tip well, if they were treated right.

There were a few cars in the parking lot and a couple of black SUV's with gold wheels. There was no doubt that folks had money here, but just what kind of money? Maybe this club was one of those dives where celebrity rappers hung out. If that were the case this could be a really good job, and her spirits lifted at that.

She walked up and opened the red door. It looked like a nice place so far, with its plush red carpet and a very well stocked bar. Softly curved sofas lined the border of the room behind black enameled tables situated to face a small dance floor directly in the center. The lights in the main area were dimmed and she could see that it would be an interesting place to work to say the least... that is if she actually got the job.

There appeared to be several adjoining rooms off the main area. She assumed they might be V.I.P. or private rooms. If that were true, big money could be made taking care of the clientele in those rooms if a girl could get that assignment. But then, she thought, what would taking care of those customers involve? She tried to push those thoughts out of her mind. "That would be so gross!" she said softly, but she quickly regained composure and turned her negatives into positives. "Focus, Positive, Focus," she repeated to herself quietly.

From one of the other rooms, she could hear voices, occasionally loud, perhaps angry or upset. Maybe someone was getting written up, or fired? Emily considered whether she should just head back out and forget about interviewing here for today. Since she really needed to consider what to do about the video work for the documentary, she quelled the urge to go and mustered up her courage.

Guessing that the only other people in the place were employees and maybe one of the managers, she figured she should follow the sound of the voices to find someone to talk to. As she stepped through the doorway, she expected to see a few people at most. "Excuse me…" was all she could manage to say before suddenly becoming aware of what was actually happening in the room.

There were about five men, two older men sitting at a table, and two other younger and very large men standing behind a man who was on his knees and half mumbling, half screaming something through the bloody foam pouring from his mouth.

"Excuse…" was all that left her lips before there was a loud report. A gun was fired into the back of the man's head blowing skull fragments and brain bits all over the tile floor. The impact threw him face forward into the bloody debris. "…Me!" All heads turned in her direction as she squeaked out the word before her hand came up to stifle her scream.

Then, as she turned to run from the room, she saw the man with the gun raising it toward her. She was determined not to stay long enough to see what happened next. She ran toward the front door, which seemed a much longer distance than when she had first entered the building. The room seemed to stretch out before her as she ran, taking forever to reach the exit. She launched herself through the doorway just as a slug from the big guy's gun slammed into the doorframe beside her sending splinters flying.

Emily's feet hit the street and she knew full well she was running for her life. As two large men burst from the building, she ducked down an alley. They stood there for a moment looking both ways, their eyes adjusting to the sunlight. They scanned as far as they could see but there was no sign of her. They could see no place for her to hide, no dumpsters or fences in the immediate area around the building, so they ran full out in the direction of the alley.

When Emily had come to the end of the alley, she headed off in the direction of the train station using every ounce of strength she could manage. As she ran down the street, she could hear the footsteps of the two thugs running behind her, clomping the pavement in their three hundred dollar Italian dress shoes. She did the only thing she could think of, run faster.

The thugs were catching up to her and Emily was terrified that they might succeed, and then the worst thing that could happen, happened. The folder she was carrying, which contained her résumés, slipped out from under her arm. She was running so fast by the time she was aware of it, all of the papers were scattered far behind her. Reflexively, she stopped to go back and get them. Shit! She knew she didn't have a chance.

The men were gaining on her and the papers dotted the street ahead of them. By the time she could get to them, the men would get to her. Even if she could somehow get to the mess before they did, there was no chance of picking up every last sheet of paper. So she turned and ran again toward the train station.

As she rounded the corner of the last block to the station, she glanced back over her shoulder. The men had stopped and were holding up one of the résumés. Her heart sank as she realized that her home address and phone number was at the top of the page in bold letters. She could see one of them pointing at it, and then at her, while one was bent over laughing and trying to catch his breath.

Ten

Mark Woo sat in his apartment with a bag of ice resting in the crook of his arm while holding another on the side of his head in an attempt to take the swelling down. He tried to recall the details from the previous night. Though he ached from head to toe, he felt confident that he would be feeling better in a couple of days.

He had a scheduled flight to make tomorrow but did not expect it to be a problem to fly the group from the university up to Seattle. He had chartered the fifteen passenger plane over a month ago and had to go to the local airstrip later in the day to check the plane out, review its maintenance records and create his flight plan.

The weather for tomorrow was supposed to be clear all the way up the coast so he was grateful that this flight, his twenty-first this year, was likely to be uneventful. He had information about the purpose of the trip, the date, and the destination but he hadn't really paid much attention to any of the other details. When that girl had sat down across from him at the restaurant where they met to finalize the deal, most of his attention was distracted by her amazing, perfectly shaped breasts.

The conversation as he remembered it went something like, "Taking some students, blah, blah, blah, will be staying for two weeks, then flying back, blah, blah, blah..." In fact the only thing he really heard was his payment for the job.

While most commercial pilots these days came from a military background, Mark had begun his flying career when he was only sixteen years old. His friends were working on getting their drivers licenses but he thought it would be a lot cooler, and more impressive to the ladies to get a pilots license instead. While his friends would be taking their dates out to a movie at the local Cineplex, he would be able to take his date out to some other, more exciting destination.

It seemed like a good idea at the time. Mark had a problem with thinking things through. He hadn't even considered that a lot of parents of teenaged girls might frown upon their daughters flying to Denver with their date for a weekend romp in a ski lodge.

By the time he figured it out, he already had his pilot's license, and a small four-seater that his dad let him borrow from the company hangar whenever he wanted. What followed were a few flights a year just to stay in practice, and twice he flew a few of his buddies to the beach for spring break.

Ultimately, he got a convertible sports car to go with his new driver's license. However, even with all of these enticements, relationships with the fairer sex did not come easy. When he managed to get a girl on the hook, it only lasted a few weeks at a time.

It ate at him that most of his intimate moments involved money changing hands. Maybe it was the friends he hung with. Perhaps he wore the wrong clothes? The truth was that the problem with Mark was his attitude, the all consuming desire he had to kick the shit out of anyone who even dared to look at him for more than a few seconds. He had decided that he just might be a fighter, not a lover and had become quite fond of that idea.

Last night had been a lot like other nights. Mark had sat on the sofa drinking shots of cheap tequila, playing video games and waiting for the bars to fill up. He didn't have to worry about going to work the next morning like most folks, because he didn't have to work. He lived his life like a lot of his rich kid friends, sleeping all day and partying all night.

Actually, Mark did not really party all night. He would quit drinking just before leaving the house, then switch to club soda when he got to the bar. This tactic enabled him to overcome his social difficulties early in the evening, then take advantage of others who were drunk in the early morning hours after the bars had closed. For Mark, this method worked out very well. Around midnight he would start to sober up and his attitude would begin to shift, making him more aggressive and more likely to start a fight.

Of course, he didn't get into a fight every night. No one could do that and survive. Usually he just sat and looked for the right 'victim' as he called them. They had to be at least a foot taller than Mark and physically built like someone who went to the gym a lot. Most importantly, the guy had to have at least two gorgeous women hanging on his arms.

It was that last requirement that kept Mark out of trouble and allowed him to spend many a night in the clubs without any confrontation. He saw a lot of big guys in the bars where he would hang out that fit the profile, but typically they'd be there with just one woman.

Almost by accident, Mark had discovered that when a man had two women with him, one could be vulnerable to the offers of another interested party. Likely, at least one of them was in love with the guy. The other resented the favored one and was glad that someone else could intervene, cause a disturbance, or maybe even kick his ass for being so stupid and selfish.

Often, if things went as planned, Mark could talk one or even both of the girls into going home with him. This usually happened when he really poured it on thick. If he was having a good night, he might even get laid.

Last night when he was out, he thought he had hit the jackpot. There was a guy who had three women with him. They were so hot he thought he was going to have a boner before he had time to start some shit. So he waited a bit longer than usual to make his move on the girls and gave himself time to deal with his uncontrollable urges and raging hormones.

Mark always began his approach by staring, not so subtly, at the women for a long time. He paid close attention to their every move. He did not try to hide that he was watching because that always got the guy pissed off, making him easier to beat. A man who fights with emotion makes mistakes because he allows his passion to make the decisions. Mark had learned that during his martial arts studies, and he used it to his advantage.

He found a seat within about ten feet of their table. The music was thumping and, though he could see them talking, he had no idea what they were saying. Next he began looking at the women, staring until he had eye contact with each of them. He would smile, like he was glad he'd been caught, which of course he was. As usual, the guy ignored him for the first hour or so, and Mark waited for him to ask that golden question, "What the fuck are you lookin' at?"

A guy with two babes often has a bit more self-confidence than the guy sitting there with his wife. It takes a lot of money or a lot of mental control to land two fish, but how awesome that this guy had three! This had to be the Super Bowl of all women wrangling events, and Mark was ready to earn the ring.

Problem was, the other team appeared to be a real pro. This guy seemed to not give much of a shit who was staring at him or his ladies. In fact, he would look at Mark, smile, grab a breast, suck some face, or just plain thrust his hand into a crotch to piss him off. So Mark bided his time. He was waiting for his chance to exercise the restroom maneuver.

The restroom maneuver meant waiting until the girls went to the ladies room together, then he could intercept and proposition. Around midnight, two of the girls started to gather their small club handbags as though they were ready to make a move. Mark saw his opportunity and headed to the hallway where the restrooms were located. As the girls approached, he made his move.

"It's a beautiful moonlit night out there, and you two girls look like thrill seekers. Wouldn't it be awesome to fly to Vegas, check out that moon from above the clouds, hit some casinos, have a few laughs, and then head back at dawn?"

The girls looked at each other and the blonde spoke first, "Are you smoking something, asshole?" She said in a husky voice. The brunette interjected, "Oh hell, yeah! Vegas, baby! I'm in. We'll fly down there, get a hotel room, do some gambling, and you can suck our dicks till the sun comes up!!!" Her voice was not quite right.

Mark realized what was wrong as the two 'girls' stepped into the men's restroom. "Dicks?" he said aloud as his mind processed the words. "Oh shit!" he muttered under his breath as he came to the full realization he had just hit on two guys. "Fucking San Francisco!"

He just stood there somewhat stunned. He could feel the heat spread across his face, as he turned red with anger and embarrassment. He didn't realize how long he had been standing there, and by the time he started to move toward the rear exit, it was too late.

As the two came out of the restroom, they saw Mark slowly heading toward the back of the club. They walked over and grabbed him, each one by an arm, escorting him back toward their table. Had his reflexes been just a little sharper, he would have broken their grip right there in the somewhat secluded part of the club, but by the time he came to his senses, they were about to cross the dance floor. "Fucking let go of me!" He tried to yell louder than the thumping music the DJ was playing.

"What? Come on baby, come and meet Mitch and Candy, they are just gonna eat you alive." The blonde yelled over the music while doggedly dragging him as he tried to wrench himself free. It was then that Mark had a near out of body experience and he realized what was happening. Everyone in the club could see two dudes dressed like really hot chicks hauling him across the dance floor.

Were his feet really dragging as they pulled him? Were they thinking he was looking forward to some hide the popsicle session? He had thrown out the invitation and volunteered his plane to take them to Vegas! "Oh, hell no!" He felt the surge of adrenalin as his inner animal began to emerge.

"Fuck this shit!" he yelled, sweeping his right leg out and knocking the blond off his heels, sending him slamming and skidding face-first into the parquet wood dance floor. At the same time he brought his left fist up connecting with the nose of the brunette putting the guy on his knees as the lights went dim before him. The scream went unnoticed as it melted into the thump-thump of the music, but the dancers were becoming aware that something was wrong and began to clear an area around the action that was unfolding in their midst.

Two people were writhing and bleeding on the floor and more and more dancers had stopped and were standing there looking at them in shock. Right about then was when Candy stood up. The fierce look of an assassin shot across her face as she stepped out of her 6-inch spiked heels, reducing her to about five feet and one inch of lethal female aggression.

Mark was busy kicking the blonde who was now lying on the floor in a fetal position with his arms wrapped around his head. With each kick, he screamed profanities. "You.. (kick) fuckin'.. (kick) think.. (kick)." He was so involved that he didn't see Candy coming up from his left side. He finally noticed that the stunned crowd around him was looking in that direction.

Candy was moving with the grace of a ballerina as she crossed the floor, each foot methodically placed in her dance of destruction, the crowd seeming to part like the Red Sea before her. She wore a bright red silk top and a glittering silver miniskirt that shimmered in the shafts of light reflecting off of the disco ball that hung from the ceiling. Her full breasts bounced as she came towards him and the crowd was fixated on her as the music suddenly stopped. You could have heard a pin drop except for a few people gasping and muttering their outrage. They were quietly urging Candy to kick his ass.

That was when his mind finally comprehended the style of her movements. She was swaying from side to side as she walked toward him, her arms making definite patterns, her eyes focused like lasers on him as she covered the distance between the table and him in a flash. Mark had just enough time to say three words before she made her move at him. "Fucking Kung Fu?"

As she leapt into the air, her leg flashed out and her foot caught Mark on the side of the head. He heard his jaw crack as the kick dropped him to the floor. He was really hurting now, the world was spinning and he regretted the choice he had made in attacking the two girly-boys. Helpless to move, he laid on his back, trying to get up. Hell, trying just to breathe.

He looked up from his position on the floor and the gorgeous, badass bitch was straddling him, intentionally showing him her panty-less crotch. This one was definitely a she, and was waiting for a sign that he got that message. As soon as she saw the look of surprise on his face, and she knew that he knew a woman was about to kick his ass, she proceeded to stomp his lights out.

Eleven

Emily burst through the gate at the station, rushed onto the train, and headed straight for home. She was out of breath and sweating profusely as she took a seat so upset that she almost sat on the little old lady who was sitting there.

"I'm so sorry." She said, but the woman just looked at her with tired eyes. Embarrassed and blushing, she moved to a different seat. Once she was seated, she tried to plan her next move. She knew that it would take two or three times as long to drive across town than it took by train. She tried to calculate the distance of the walk from the station to her apartment and how long it would take to get home. She figured she might have about thirty minutes from the time she got to her apartment, to get some clothes and things together. The thugs would be driving and dealing with traffic. It would take them longer to get there.

She wondered if they would actually come after her. It would be easy since they had her address from the résumé, but was it really worth it to them to follow through? Kill her? Probably, since she was the only real witness to the murder. The only thing she could do now was run. Run and try somehow to get someone to help.

Leaving the station, she briskly walked down the street toward home. She looked in every direction for parked cars that might look unfamiliar, suspicious, or had people sitting in them, but all was clear.

Arriving home, she crossed the street and walked up the front steps of the old apartment building sliding her key into the lock of the lower entry door. Before going in, she looked around again to verify that all was clear. She checked her mailbox and found a few late bill notices as usual. Tucking them under her arm, she climbed the stairs to her apartment.

When she got to the landing on the second floor, she stood outside the door and carefully pressed her ear to it to see if she could hear anything inside the apartment. It was quiet. She inserted her key into the lock, turned the doorknob carefully and slowly opened the door.

Ralph leapt at her from behind the door and she screamed, scaring him. The large orange tabby ran for the bedroom. "Ralphie, I'm sorry baby. You scared mommy." She closed the door and followed him to the bedroom and reached under the bed to get him. He always hid under the bed when he was nervous or when she was angry with him for scratching the furniture or eating the houseplants.

She picked him up and sat down on the bed. "Mommy has to go away for a while, but we're going to get someone to take care of you..." She stroked his short fur and he purred loudly pushing himself into her hand. "But who are we going to get right now? Shit!" and Ralph cringed again in her arms.

She reached into her pocket and pulled out her phone, scrolling through her directory until she came to Diane, her neighbor. She pushed the call button and waited. After two rings, Diane answered. "Hello?"

"Hey Diane, it's Em. Thank God you're home! I have a big, big favor to ask."

"Yeah, honey? What's that? You sound upset." Diane was from the South, born and raised. Along with her slight drawl, she called everyone 'honey', a real giveaway.

"Well, I'm going to be out of town for a couple of weeks and I was wondering if you could take care of Ralph while I'm gone."

"Ralph? Oh, you mean your kitty cat. Sure thing, honey. He's no trouble at all, but if you're gonna to be gone for a couple a weeks, I should probably bring his supplies on over here, instead of leavin him up in there all by his little self. He's gonna miss his mama, bless his heart."

"Thanks, Diane. That's perfect. Can you come and get him?'

"Sure, honey. When'd you want me to stop on by?"

"Well, now would be a good time."

"Ya mean, right now?"

"Yeah, right now, I don't have much time." She looked at the clock. She had already wasted ten minutes. "I hope you can come and get him now. I promise I'll make this up to you when I get back, Diane."

"Are you sure you're alright, Emily? You sound mighty upset."

"I'll be just fine when I know Ralphie is in good hands." She carried the phone under her chin and pulled a small suitcase out of the closet. She lifted it up on the bed and opened it.

"Well, okay then, dear. I'll be right on over. Have his things ready, and I'll see ya in a minute." The phone disconnected just before the words passed through Emily's lips, "Bye…"

She looked utterly confused as she rifled through her dresser drawers trying to decide what to take. Jeans. Shorts. Sweatshirt. Thong? No! She kept grabbing onto something else as she dug in the drawer only to grab hold of it, then leave it lying there.

Since this trip was going to the northern woods, it would be warm during the day, but it could be cool or even cold at night. It might even rain for two weeks straight. What the hell! How do you pack for that in one suitcase?

She took the jeans, a couple of sweaters, underwear, a couple of concert t-shirts, a pair of sneakers, and stuffed all of it into the suitcase. Next she needed her deodorant, so she headed for the bathroom with a small plastic carry bag.

The bathroom was a mess, towels draped over everything. Dirty clothes, q-tips, powders, creams, and used tissues with traces of makeup were strewn everywhere. "Mental note to self... clean the fuckin' bathroom if you live through this," she muttered to herself.

She was staring into the open door of the medicine cabinet when a knock came at the door. She ran out of the bathroom to the kitchen area of her apartment. She was looking for some kind of a weapon. She opened the drawers frantically until she found it.

She grabbed the largest knife she owned out of the drawer, and went to the door. She boosted herself up on her toes and carefully looked through the peephole. It was Diane, and she was looking up at something above the door as she waited for Emily to answer it.

Opening the door, Emily said, "Hurry in so I can close the door!" She took Diane by the wrist, pulling her into the room.

"Okay now, Em. Now I know something is goin' on here." She nodded at the knife in Emily's hand. "Please, honey, what is it?"

Shutting the door and double locking it, Emily set the knife on the table and spoke nervously, "I'll tell you if you help me get Ralph's things together while I finish packing." She was already walking into the bathroom.

"Hon, now I guess his litter box and food are still in the same place as always?" Diane waited for an answer. "Emily?"

Emily stuck her head out through the doorway, "Yeah, please hurry, Diane! I don't think I have much more time!"

"Now, you promised to tell me…" she said, walking toward the bathroom where Emily was rifling through the medicine cabinet. "Wow, honey, your place is trashed. Did someone break in here?"

Emily looked at her, as if to say, you really wanna go there? She tilted her head and took a deep breath. "Okay, Diane. This is going to sound crazy, and forgive me for continuing to pack while I tell you this, but I have about fifteen," she looked at her watch, "…oh shit, maybe ten minutes before some really bad guys get here, and I'm afraid that if I'm here when they arrive they are going to kill me. Maybe you and Ralph, too, if you're still here."

"What?? We gotta call the police right now!"

"You know how long it takes the police to respond in this city, Diane! They'll get here just in time to find our bullet riddled bodies! I don't think we have that kind of time." She threw a couple more items into the carry bag along with a toothbrush and some pink soap that was resting on the top of the sink by the faucet.

The phone was ringing. "Diane, just get Ralph and go! Buy him some supplies, and I'll pay you when I get back. Please? Hurry!"

"I hate leavin ya this way. It just doesn't seem right." She scooped Ralph up in her arms and called over her shoulder, "You call me when you get where you're goin and let me know you're okay. Promise now, honey?" She turned toward Emily and crossed her heart, "Cross your heart?"

"Promise! Now go!" She rushed over to answer the phone and the voice on the other end said, "Hello, is this Emily?"

"Yes, who's…" Then she realized how foolish she was to answer the phone.

"It's John, John Hazard. I was just calling to see if you had decided to join us on the…"

"Yes!"

"Great, will you need someone to pick you up in the morning?"

"I need someone to pick me up right fuckin' now!" she screamed at the cell phone she had dropped on the bed while she tried to zip the over-stuffed suitcase.

"Give me your address. I think I might be in your area right now. Are you okay? You don't sound so good." He started to pull over to look for the address on her résumé. He remembered the street name, but not the number.

She had to think. "225 Rockland… Apartment 2C, but you better hurry cuz I gotta get out of here in the next five minutes or I'm dead!"

"Seriously?"

"Fuck, John! Some seriously bad people are on their way here to kill me." She picked the phone up from the bed and put it to her ear.

John knew better than to ask what was going on. His cop reflexes were kicking in. "Is there a back exit out of the building?"

"No, just a fire escape," she said looking out the window across the room.

"Look, if someone is coming to kill you they will probably come in hard. You need to watch out your window for them, wait until they get inside the building, and then get your ass down that fire escape. I should be there any minute and I'll meet you at the bottom. You got it? If you are not there waiting, I'll blow the horn to let you know I'm out there." He felt the rush of adrenalin now. John began scanning all the people he could see along the way. Maybe he could spot something suspicious.

Emily picked up the suitcase and walked toward the window that opened to the fire escape. "Right, fire escape... Shit!"

Shoving the phone in her pocket, she bent over and unlocked the window, grabbing the top latch and tried to pull it open. It was stuck! She tried several times, until finally it broke loose nearly throwing her to the floor.

She was just sticking her head out the window when she heard the slamming of car doors outside on the street. She leaned out and peeked over the rusted cast iron railing and caught a glimpse of two very large men dressed in black walking from the SUV to her apartment entrance.

"Fuck!" she whispered and began to feel more panicked as she grabbed the stuffed suitcase and hoisted it through the window onto the landing of the fire escape. She was certain that she had triple-locked her door, but unsure if it would hold up if someone was determined to break in. As she stepped through the window she prayed.

"You better be there, John. Please, God. Hurry!"

On the street below, the two thugs broke the glass on the security door and reached in to unlock it.

"Yo, what apartment was that?" one asked the other.

"2C, second floor."

"Yeah, I know, I know! Second floor! You think I'm some kinda mook?" He turned his back to the open door and faced his alleged heckler.

"Nah, I didn't mean..."

"Fuck you! I should pop one in ya like they did to Bobby." He started to raise his gun.

"Come on, man. Let's do this and get out of here. I'll buy you a beer on the way back." The guy held his hands out defensively.

"Beer sounds good, but I should still kick yo' ass," he said, turning to step through the door. They hurried up the steps and looked down the hall to find apartment 2C.

Meanwhile, John was beginning to be concerned that he might not make it to Emily in time, so he started running the red traffic lights as much as he dared, without putting anyone in danger. Even so, he hoped he wasn't being played for a fool.

How could he know what she might be involved in? Did he really want to get mixed up in something that could make him an accomplice? Emily Sparks is an attractive woman, but attractive enough to risk doing time?

He made up his mind to chance it. If it was really bad shit, he could always throw her out of the car, right? His thoughts wandered to a previous case he'd been assigned.

A very attractive woman had killed two people with a nasty kitchen knife. The female victim's head was completely severed, and the male was viciously stabbed through his lower jaw. After witnessing such a crime scene, he had decided that people were capable of most anything. The perpetrator in that case was a gorgeous redhead.

It only made sense to get his gun out of the glove box and put it on the seat under his leg where he could get to it quickly if necessary. This way, if he had to stop suddenly it wouldn't slide to the floor. Now he was ready for anything.

Out in the open air of the landing, Emily struggled with the ladder and could not figure out why it wouldn't move. She even tried standing on it. Suddenly she heard a sound from inside the apartment. Someone was trying to open the door!

Out in the hall, one of the men was on his knees staring at the lock on the door. The other pushed him, said, "Come on, man! Let's just kick it in, for fuck's sake!"

"Man, just give me a second!"

He stuck the shaft of the pick into the lock just as John rounded the corner onto Rockland.

As he pulled into the alley next to the building, the stark black hulk of the SUV caught his eye immediately. He could see the bottom of the old fire escape system but there was no one standing there when he arrived. He parked close to where he thought the ladder might drop, pulled the lever to pop the trunk lid and blew his horn. Then he rolled down the window, leaned out as the warm air rushed in, and looked up.

Emily was frantically trying to drop the ladder for the fire escape. He got out of the car and called up to her, just loud enough for her to hear, "There's a latch right by your feet. Pull it!"

The ladder broke loose and dropped straight down. He cringed as it clanged to a stop about six inches from the concrete and right in front of him. Flakes of rust rained down on him. He shielded his eyes from it as he watched.

"Throw me your bags!" he hissed up at her. She was trying to manage them while climbing down the ladder.

She dropped the bag over the side of the railing and he caught it as a smaller plastic one fell out of the pocket it had been stuffed into and hit the street with a thud. As she scrambled down, he opened the trunk and threw in the bag.

Upstairs, the would-be lock picker was having no luck. "Fuck this fancy shit!" yelled the gruffer, more impatient one and kicked at the door. Bang! Again, bang! The third kick finally pulled the inner doorframe off and the thugs ran through the doorway into the apartment. Guns drawn, they checked the bedroom and the bathroom, then stood in the living room area and looked at each other, shaking their heads silently.

Finally, they noticed the breeze blowing in through the curtains and realized the window was open to the fire escape. The door kicker ran over, pushed a small table off to the side to make more room for his hulking body, and stepped through the window. He looked up through the rusted stairs, no movement. Then he leaned over the railing. The girl was in the car!

John had just put it in gear as the thug opened fire. Now, he stomped down hard on the gas and the tires screeched in response. Bullets whirred as they bounced off the pavement, ricocheting into walls and trashcans lining the alleyway.

"Shit, they're shooting at us!" John looked down the alley as the bullets rained down around his accelerating car. "What kind of trouble are you in?" He heard a crunching sort of a sound as a slug smashed his taillight and penetrated the trunk. He reached the next street and turned sharply onto it.

A car swerved away from them as John took the corner wide, cutting into the other lane. They could hear the driver yelling as he mowed down a line of trashcans sitting on the curb awaiting pickup.

"Why is that guy trying to kill you?" John asked her after he had regained control of the car. He was focused on her and ran the red traffic light at the next intersection. He could feel his heart thumping in his chest.

"Get us out of here, and I'll tell you every detail!" she plead with him.

"I don't think this is over yet." He looked in the rearview mirror as the thug's SUV shot out of the alley a block behind them, and slammed into a wall on the opposite side of the street. "Wait a sec... yeah, it's over for now."

Twelve

Eddie smiled wide and leaned closer to the stage clutching a five dollar bill in his hand. He was getting ready to shove it in Karla's garter when she got around to him. He felt a heady rush of pleasure as she grabbed the pole and pressed her self against it while sliding down to squat close to the floor. He knew this was the song that would reveal her perfect double D's, and he wanted to soak up every last drop of her gorgeous body before she left the stage after her set.

Karla was glad that Eddie had finally arrived. She had not been having a good day with tips. At most, she figured she would have about fifty bucks left after giving the club owner and the DJ their cut of the day's earnings. If she played him just right, she knew Eddie would easily make up about another fifty bucks all by himself. The psychology of the gentlemen's club almost guaranteed it.

A good tipper at the stage almost always generated a sort of competition in the audience. It was like seed money to a group of guys vying for her attention, guys who might drop a hundred bucks during three songs if she could play them right. So she intended to pull out all the stops.

She crawled toward him on her hands and knees like the feline she imagined herself to be and, when she was directly in front of him, she moved quickly to her knees. She looked Eddie directly in the eyes, gently licking her lips while she gyrated slowly up and down as if she were straddling him.

He was so predictable. She knew he would lean up and put some money in her garter, although she was never sure just how much. If she could get him really hot, she might be able to motivate him to donate everything he had in his pockets.

It was time to push him.

Right on cue, the five-dollar bill he had intended to give her was joined by a twenty. With twenty-five bucks safely tucked in her garter, she winked and blew him a kiss. She reached around behind and let the 'girls' loose, what Eddie called 'the most beautiful melons ever grown in California'. Truth be told they were more manufactured than grown and were quite firm from the stretching. Eddie could have bounced a quarter off of them if he could get her naked and make her lay still.

Eddie didn't care. He was really hot for her today and, before he knew it, he was instinctively reaching for his wallet again. Her plan, beautifully executed, was working its magic. She had him, so she did what she knew would really make him sweat. She moved on to the next guy standing next to the stage waving a twenty at her.

Karla had a way of staring into a man's eyes when she was taking their money. It seemed to ease their minds, or at least that was her intention. Maybe she didn't realize that as the twenty-dollar bill slid into her garter, her eyes were the last things this guy was looking at. She was on the stage, he was on the floor. From his angle he could take in everything, meaning everything that he was paying for.

She smiled and gave him about a minute of the song in exchange for his generosity, and then as smoothly as possible worked her way around the stage collecting various tips from the other fans who were waiting to pay tribute to her body and the way she made them feel when she moved the way she did.

When things were slow, she always asked the DJ to play a dance remix song, usually at least five to eight minutes long. This one was seven minutes and forty-six seconds and she knew by the guitar riff that she was about four and half minutes into it. She had collected almost a hundred bucks in that short time, and now she was ready for the grand finale.

She grabbed the snap on one side of what could barely be referred to as her panties and released it. Then, holding on to the clasp, she used her other hand to unsnap the other side. Now she could slowly, seductively reveal the glory of her perfectly trimmed treasure in one smooth motion. She held up the fancy bit of fabric and lace for a few seconds before dropping it to the floor behind her.

By now Karla had worked her way back to Eddie and she swayed in front of him, letting him drink from her naked beauty. Then she knelt down while leaning back and put her hands on the floor behind her, arching high and slowly spreading her long supple legs. Eddie felt the hormonal rush he had been waiting for. This was the feeling, a kind of high, that kept him coming back to this place night after night to give away his money… to her!

Sooner than Eddie was ready for and before Karla had the opportunity to extract all of the cash from the wallets of the fools scattered around the stage, the song came to an end. The DJ cut in for a moment as he led up to the next song.

"That was Destiny, Gentlemen. She is available for private dances and VIP. And remember, gentlemen, these beautiful ladies work for tips only, so be sure to take care of them. Keep in mind your tips bring out that 'special smile.' Next up, Tiffany."

Destiny, as Karla was known here in the club, grabbed her scant clothes from the floor of the stage and dressed herself as she walked to the steps. By the time she got off the stage, Tiffany was already swinging on the pole.

Eddie did as expected and moved to a table in a corner of the room. A waitress met him at the table, "Can I get you something, baby?" she cooed as best she could, almost drowned out by the loud music.

"I'll have a tall glass of beer, and it doesn't matter what kind." She nodded and started to walk away. Just then he thought of Karla, "Make that two." He shouted after her.

Karla had motioned to Eddie to give her a minute and had disappeared into the back where the dressing room was located. Minutes later she reappeared and walked over to the DJ. She stood in the booth talking to him, then handed him something as he nodded his head. Karla strolled over to Eddie's table and sat down.

"What's up baby? Is this mine?" She pointed at one of the beers that had been delivered by the waitress. He had been so busy watching Karla's coming and goings, he hadn't even noticed that the drinks had been delivered.

"Huh? Oh, yeah." He raised his glass as if initiating a toast. "Here to us, to the adventure we are about to take together, and the completion of this class so we can get back to a normal life."

She touched her glass to his and began to drink as he continued, "I got the rest of the gear today, and I think we're ready for this trip. How're you feeling?"

"I'm excited, baby. This trip is going to help me finish the class and then maybe I can finally get out of this place. Like Macy said, we can't fail this final exam. As long as we're there, it's a guaranteed A!" She giggled. "I can't remember if I ever got an A in anything before!"

"Maybe we should celebrate that. Your first A!" He reached over and grabbed the front of the seat on her chair with both hands and slid it closer to him.

"Champagne?" she asked as she raised her hand to summon the waitress.

Eddie gently pulled her arm down to stop the call, "No, baby, not that hundred and fifty dollar a bottle crap in the VIP room. I meant let's go out for a nice dinner later and really celebrate." He looked into her eyes, "After all we're gonna be in the woods for two weeks after tomorrow. It might be nice to have a going away dinner – with real food."

"Oh, you mean like that." Some of her enthusiasm faded as she saw her cut of the hundred and fifty bucks disappearing in a puff of smoke. "I guess so."

Karla had enrolled in the Paranormal Investigation class in an attempt to get out of the exotic dancer business. Sure, she loved the money she made here, and the power she seemed to wield when she was on stage, but she also was well aware that as women in this profession got older their attraction faded and she could be left without work.

Someday the gravy train would pull into the station and she'd have to get off. When that day arrived, she'd have to find some other source of income. Exotic dancing didn't necessarily qualify as solid employment experience. So unless she wanted to end up in a mobile home park up in the woods with some guy named Zipper or Bubba, she'd better have a backup plan.

Originally, she had intended to take some classes to get certified as a paralegal or medical assistant. Then she discovered that those courses took up to two years to complete, and she'd have to meet the prerequisites. Instead she opted for the class with no special requirements. One of the best reasons for choosing the PI class, as it was called, was that it could be completed in less than a year.

Eddie, on the other hand, had a great job and made tons of money, which was Karla's only attraction to him. No matter how much she tried to convince herself otherwise, he barely qualified as more than just another wallet full of cash. She had invited him into her world even so, and now that he was there, a mutual addiction held them together. Her addiction to money was fed by Eddie's addiction to her body.

When Eddie had discovered that she was going to take the PI class, he signed up as well. He figured it would be a chance to spend time with her away from the club. She seemed to work all the time and, if she wasn't working, he often had no way of knowing where she was. That made it difficult for him to pretend to have some kind of normal relationship with her, which is what he really wanted.

His plan had worked out well so far, and he was looking forward to spending two whole weeks with her on this trip. Away from the club and other distractions, she may be able to finally see why he's the right guy for her.

Wishful thinking it was, indeed. Karla's intentions were more along the lines of turning her certification into a moneymaking enterprise. She figured as soon as she got her business going and her office set up with an investment from Eddie, of course, she could break the news to him that she was not interested in anything more than a business arrangement. Until then, she'd have to keep his hope alive, and continue to collect the benefits of her deception.

Things were going well, and they would graduate soon. They had been looking at affordable office spaces, researching marketing and advertising costs, and short of ordering the business cards, the plan was right on track.

"So we are all ready to go then? You got the rest of the supplies." She tried to get a feel for his state of mind and forced a smile to put him at ease.

"Yes, I think I got everything on the list."

"Did you get my sleeping pad, baby?"

"Honey, I got you the most expensive, top of the line sleeping pad they make. You could lay that thing on a bed of sharp rocks and it would feel like a feather mattress resting on a fluffy cloud." He smiled back at her.

It always made her cringe when he called her honey. It wasn't like a southern style 'Honey' or a casual kind of usage like 'Dude'. It oozed over her like some kind of possessive tentacle when he said it. It just didn't fit her idea of the nature of their relationship and gave her a chill.

"I am so lucky to have you, Eddie. You take such good care of me." It wasn't exactly a lie. She forced a girlish giggle and hugged him. Indeed she was lucky, and indeed he did take care good of her.

Thirteen

John was filling up the tea kettle over a sink full of dirty dishes. He usually cleaned his apartment once a week and it was three days since the last time. Emily was sitting at the dining table, staring out the window. Her thoughts kept running over and over the horror of what she had witnessed. She wasn't paying attention to anything John was doing until he asked, "What kind of tea do you like? I have regular tea and green tea."

Emily turned to look at him. "You're joking, right? You don't have something stronger?"

"Coffee?" He reached for the can of coffee he kept on the shelf above the sink.

"No, not coffee. I'm talking like Wild Turkey, or something from my uncle, Jack Daniels. Tea is not going to get it right now. I need something to numb my brain."

"Sorry, I should have guessed you'd want something to calm your nerves." He reached for the doors below the sink and, opening one of them, he pulled out a new bottle of Jack and set it on the table. He got out the last two clean water glasses from the cabinet and carried them over to the table.

"You got any Valium?"

"No, I don't keep…" He paused as he cracked the seal on the bottle, poured himself a quarter glass, and then tipped the bottle over the second glass. "Uh… drugs in the house," he finished.

When he reached a quarter glass, she stretched over the table and touched the neck of the bottle, pressing it down to keep him pouring. When it was almost half full, she let him set it upright as she sat back in her chair.

"Just kidding, John. Right now I don't even know if that could help me relax."

He slid the glass to her across the table like a bartender in an old western movie before lifting his glass. He took a big gulp and set the drink down, holding on to it as he watched her. He wanted to look her in the eyes as she told him her story.

"So, you were pretty quiet all the way here. You gonna tell me what happened?" He strained to get the words out as the fumes from the drink were catching in his throat.

"Yeah, I've been trying to get my shit together, John." She shook her head. "I'm wondering if I was dreaming or something. Stuff like this just doesn't happen to good people, does it? I'm so freaked out."

"I was a detective for about four years, Emily, and that was after I got out of the military. You'd be surprised what happens to people. Shit, usually always good people. You wouldn't believe me if I told you some of the things I've seen."

"Well, when you say it that way, I can only imagine what you've experienced. You've probably seen the worst of people and all kinds of violence. And John, please call me Em. All my friends do."

"Okay, Em. My friends call me John, or Hazard, depending on how pissed they are at the moment." He laughed and took another sip from his glass. "So, if you want to call me something else, I guess you'll have to make it up."

"How about John then?" She was smiling.

"Good, suits me I guess. And a smile suits you. You feel like talking now?"

She nodded and took a long drink from her glass before starting. "Well... I left the interview this morning, you know, at the college, and headed over to a nightclub called the Players Lounge for another interview. You know, I need some permanent type work."

"I've heard about that place. Caters to factory workers and gangbangers..." He rubbed an itch on his nose and crossed his eyes to try and see what was causing it.

"That's the place." She watched him for a second to see if he was really paying attention before continuing, "When I walked in the door no one was in the main area of the bar, but I heard voices in a room kind of off to the back. I didn't think they were yelling. I just thought they were talking loudly, you know, how people do when they're in a group. When I got to the doorway, it was like everything happened so fast but took so long to end."

She rubbed her eyes and the bridge of her nose. The stress was taking its toll. "I saw maybe six or seven guys, several of them dressed in dark suits. One of them was on his knees on the floor and he was wailing and saying something like, 'you don't have to do this, I have kids, man, I'll pay it back.' " She paused and swallowed hard.

"Then there was a loud cracking pop and his brains sprayed out the front of his head onto the floor and he fell forward into that mess. That's when I saw the gun in the hand of one of the two guys standing behind him. Then, before I could stop myself, I screamed..."

"Oh shit!" John finished her sentence for her.

"Yeah. How did you know that's what I said?"

"Well, I've been around death more times than I care to say. Not actually when it happens so much, but afterwards to investigate. I've always heard that the most common last words people say before they die in an accident, or a surprise encounter is 'oh shit' or something to that effect. But go on, I didn't mean to interrupt."

"Weird, but I believe it. So anyway, I screamed, 'Oh shit!' and just like somebody was turning a crank somewhere, all heads turned to face me. That's when I ran like hell out of there, and headed for the train."

"So they got a good look at you?"

"I don't know, I think so. I don't even know how long it was I stood there before I ran. It seemed like forever, but by the time I got outside the place, I had a good lead on the guys who were chasing me."

"You're lucky you even got out of the building. They must have been pretty surprised that someone walked in on them." John took another swallow from his glass.

"Like I said, I ran like hell. I thought I'd make it to the train and get away, but remember I just came for my interview? So I still had that damn folder full of résumés. I dropped it all over the road while I was running."

"It had your address on it, didn't it?" John shook his head.

"Yeah, and that's how they found my place. I saw them pick up the folder, and I knew I was screwed. I figured I had just enough lead on them, by taking the train, to get home and pack some things before they got to my apartment. Plus I had to find a place for Ralph." She saw his eyes narrow and a disappointed look spread across his face. "Oh! Ralph's my cat. He's staying at my neighbor, Diane's."

"And that's what you were doing when I called."

"Exactly! And maybe I haven't said it yet, but you saved my life, and I will never be able to thank you enough." She stood up and leaned over the table and kissed him on the forehead. "Thank you, John."

His heart fluttered for a second, "No problem. Might say I was in the neighborhood anyway. I guess we need to call the locals and report this before all the evidence goes missing."

"No, John. I don't want to do that. If I report it I'll be tied up for days answering questions and probably end up getting killed anyway."

"I don't think they'll be able to get at you. The police would put you in some kind of protective custody or something." He swallowed the last drops of liquor in his glass and poured another couple of ounces into it.

"Either way, I'd be screwed. I'm way behind on my rent and about to be evicted. I'd figured with a bartender's job I could probably get some cash in tips right away and be able to give the landlord enough to hold him over. I guess that doesn't really matter anymore after all of this shit."

He reached out across the table and held on to her hand. "Don't worry, Em. I was once a detective back in Idaho. I know the drill. They'll probably find the body dumped along the side of the road. Scumbag probably deserved what he got, but the thing that bothers me is how you've got yourself all mixed up in all of it now. A case will be opened, but without a witness, they won't have anything to go on."

"That isn't making me feel better, John." She shot him a stern look.

"Sorry, I guess that's the best reason for you to go with us. It'll get you out of town 'til things cool down. When we get back from the trip, you can stay with me for a couple of days until you get things sorted out. I can help you with that. I have some favors to call in. It'll be alright."

"So you were a detective in Idaho, huh? Why'd you quit? What in the world brought you to San Francisco?"

"Long story, and I wouldn't want to bore you with it." John sighed and looked away from her trying to keep the memories from racing through his mind.

"Boring might be nice for a couple of hours after what I've been through today. Please."

"You are not going to give me a pass on this are you? Are you sure you're not some kind of reporter, or something?"

"It's your place, John. I'm your guest. You can tell me about it or not. You can even toss me out if you feel like it. It's completely up to you. Besides, maybe it would be therapeutic in a way to tell someone about it. I'm not a reporter, for sure, and I am certainly not a shrink, but I get the feeling you keep things to yourself a lot."

"You might be right, but I gotta tell you it's some weird shit, which is exactly why I prefer not to talk about it."

"First you say boring – but weird is okay, John. I've seen and heard a lot of strange things at this point in my life, especially living here in this crazy town. You go ahead. I'll just listen. If it pushes my insanity meter into the red zone, I'll let you know." She looked into his eyes with an understanding that melted his defenses.

"Promise you won't ask me to explain the details? I mean I'll give you most of it, but I won't answer any questions, okay?"

"Okay, John, I promise. Go on with the story."

He took a deep breath and let it out slow. He was feeling the alcohol now, and hoped he wasn't slurring his words. He leaned back in his chair and began, "Well, one night I got a call to investigate a double homicide, which was way out of the ordinary where I'm from. I went, checked out the scene, but something didn't feel right."

"As I was digging into it, you know the usual investigation, interviews of friends and all, people in the town started turning up missing. Now don't forget, I was in a small town in Idaho. Missing people are few and far between, but over a period of about a week and a half, not only did I have two murders, I had four missing people."

Emily smiled her encouragement. "Pretty strange, I guess. It probably seems like a slow night around here compared to that action." She smiled again, "Continue, please."

"Right, well I finally identified a suspect and planned to put him under surveillance. That's when he decided to kidnap a baby." He held his hands about twenty inches apart, "From the maternity ward at the hospital no less!"

"A baby?"

"Not just a baby, a newborn! How fucking crazy is that? I didn't even know he'd done it, but I had a hunch and went to his apartment hoping to find something when he showed up with it."

"Wow, sounds intense. Did you catch him getting out of the car with it?"

"Well no, not exactly. I had to break into his apartment and then all hell broke loose."

"You broke into his apartment? That doesn't sound like standard procedure." She tilted her head a bit and pursed her lips. "Sounds kinda strange for a police detective." She purposely said slowly.

John hesitated. He wasn't sure why he was telling her all of this, but he really wanted to tell her more. For most of his life, he'd kept his feelings and emotions under wraps. Emily was one of the few people he'd ever met who seemed to understand something about him, like she really knew him, although he couldn't figure out why he felt he could trust her that way.

"Em, you'll think I'm crazy if I tell you all of it."

"No, John. Crazy is what my day was today. Crazy is the shit storm you saved me from. I don't, and won't think you're crazy."

"This is totally different from that, and that is exactly my point. Your experience was... I hate to call it normal criminal activity. This was...", he looked away from her and toward the window. "What I saw that night, I simply can't explain and the others who were there couldn't either."

"So you had witnesses? What did you see John?"

"You promised, remember? No questions I might not want to answer? I don't know you well enough to tell you all the details. Maybe someday. I can tell you that I had to take a leave of absence after that. Ultimately, I quit the force, moved here and enrolled in the Paranormal Investigation program at the college."

"So you saw ghosts?" She moved a bit closer to him.

"Maybe I saw a pink elephant playing a trumpet. You promised not to ask questions." He reached out and tapped her on the nose as though she were a child. She could sense that he was getting a little frustrated, so she changed the subject.

"Okay then, tell me about this trip we are taking, this wilderness adventure. What's at the bottom of it?"

"Well there's some kind of phenomenon that has been manifesting up there in the forests of the Pacific Northwest for the past couple of months somewhere near the border of Washington and Oregon." He had a map of the area laying on his coffee table, and he gestured for her to follow him to the sofa. He leaned forward and circled a place on the map with his finger.

"A number of small aircraft, hunters, hikers and campers have gone missing without a trace. The officials don't have any idea what is happening and, aside from posting warnings to the public, they have put their investigation on hold because of budgetary problems."

"Then we're going there to investigate this so called phenomenon?" Emily sounded as nervous as she felt.

"That's the plan, and you'll be filming every minute of it." He gave her a big toothy smile. From the looks of the girl, she was going to need some rest.

"You know what," he said. "We have to get an early start tomorrow, and I'm really buzzed. We should get some rest. I'll get some blankets and sleep on the couch." He crossed the room and she followed as he opened a closet door and reached to the top shelf for the blanket and pillow he kept there for friends who might crash on the couch once in a while.

"John, I'm not a shy person, and I really have the creeps now. If you don't mind, I'd rather share the bed with you." She put her hand on his arm.

He turned to look at her and her eyes seemed to look right through him. He felt a rush of warmth through his body, something he hadn't felt for a long time. He hesitated for a second, and then replied, "Uh, sure, that's okay with me if that's what you want."

"Yes, it's what I want but I'd rather wait a while, it's only seven-thirty or so, and the sun is still shining. I hate to sleep in daylight. Does that TV work?" She brushed her hair from her face with her hand.

John nodded, "It sure does. Uh, but I don't have satellite." He picked up the remote control off the table and pressed the power button.

Fourteen

Marcus Strand (Ho-tep, as he called himself, since he believed he was really a reincarnated Egyptian king) took another long hit off his bong, held the pungent smoke in his lungs for as long as he could take it, then coughed violently before resuming his conversation. He was talking on his cell with Taneisha, the girlfriend he had tried to break up with earlier. "Girl, I tried to tell you, you don't be feeling my long wave spiritual vibes. Ho-tep needs more from you. How can I be tied to one woman when I gotta glorious harem surroundin' me when I'm out in the kingdom? A man needs his freedom to be a man! You know how it is."

Taneisha was screaming into the phone. Even when he held the phone away from his ear, his friend Lamont could hear her from across the room. The words were muffled, but it seemed the cursing was quite clear. To him, it sounded like, "screech, screech, motherfucker! screech, piece of shit! screech," from where he was sitting.

"Fuck you and your Ho-tep Egyptian king bullshit, Marcus. It's over!" The volume of the words pierced his eardrum. "Don't bother to ever call me again. I am putting you on call fuckin' block, forever! GOODBYE!" He heard the sound of the line disconnecting as she hung up on him.

He sat stunned for a moment, then held the phone away from his face and looked into it. "You too bitch!" and he pushed the button as if to end the call that had already ended long before he yelled.

He smiled at Lamont, "And that's motherfuckin' that!"

Lamont smiled back, "It sure sounded like it, Yo' You the man, Ho! I can't believe ya put up with her shit for so long, the whinin' bitch!"

"Man what are you talkin' about? That girl is smooth like chocolate candy cream. I like it when she comes back around." He smiled slyly. "And she will."

"Huh? Yeah, candy with a hard center that'll bust ya fuckin' teeth when you bite into it!"

"You know she's special, man." Marcus looked at the phone in his hand.

"Well, her special ass just dumped your stupid ass." He poked him as he said it, and Marcus pulled his hand back as if to swing, then busted up laughing.

"Oh, she'll be comin' around. Ain't nobody walk away from the King... and you know Ho-tep got the hoodoo mojo magic!" Marcus wagged his head and pursed his face as he spoke.

"Right." Lamont motioned to the remains of the bag of weed on the table. "Say, King, how 'bout repackin' that bowl?"

Marcus lifted the bong from the table and held it out in front of him. "For the good of my kingdom and my subjects, let it be done." They both started laughing as he reached for the bag.

Fifteen

Macy Renner was sitting on her bed in a tank top and some cotton workout shorts. She had a very large backpack lying next to her. She had spent the past several hours carefully rolling her clothes and sealing various supplies in zip-lock bags in preparation for the trip. She had carefully loaded each item into the pack and zipped it shut.

Next to the bed and across from her sat her mother's old dresser. She and her sister used to enjoy brushing each other's hair in front of the mirror hung behind it on the wall. She looked over at it now and imagined her sister staring back at her. She wondered if they would have still been as close all these years later, the way they say that twins are. Would they still look alike as they did when they were children?

She imagined that she might not be making this trip if her sister were still around. She very well could be visiting her sister instead right now, sitting in a coffee shop somewhere, enjoying her friendship.

"I know we did everything we could to explain to mom and dad what was happening to us. The doctors were just ignorant and I blame them for everything that happened after that." She spoke to her reflection and she could see the pain in her eyes.

She had a sense that the reflection was speaking back to her. "Macy, you've been blaming yourself for what happened to me for all these years since that night. It's time to let it go. Move on with your life."

"But you never knew how much I loved you, Mary. I never really told you. I never had the chance before you were gone, and we were just kids then. What's love to a kid?" Tears began to fill the reservoirs of her lower eyelids.

"Do you really think you had to tell me? We could finish each other's sentences, remember? I knew how you felt and I felt the same way about you. I wish I could reach out and hug you right now, but I'm too far away."

Tears were streaming down Macy's face, and she could see that Mary was crying as well. Macy reached over and picked up the .38 revolver that was lying on the bed next to her. "Mary, after you were gone I could still feel you, sense you for months. I felt your sadness, and sometimes pain. I didn't understand. Mom and Dad kept talking about taking me some place where I could get better. I think they wanted to have me put away, but I convinced them that I would be fine."

"I'm glad you told them not to worry. You might have been locked up for years if you told them the things we saw, what those creatures did to us." Her sister was right. They did think she was crazy.

"Maybe this trip will give me a chance to get things straightened out. Maybe I'll find you up there in the woods when we find them." She shifted the pistol to see if there were bullets in the cylinder.

"You mean the aliens? Honey, you know you're not gonna find me. You knew it as soon as you stopped feeling me. By then, there was nothing left of me. When they finally ejected my body out somewhere in the universe, there wasn't much left of me." The image of Mary in the mirror began to shimmer like waves in a pool of water.

"I won't believe that. I can't give up hope that I can find some sign of what happened to you."

"Well, don't believe you can kill those things with that gun, Macy. I think you will need a lot more than that."

"I won't be alone. There'll be eight of us, Sis, and most of my team will be armed in some way. I've got a diverse group each with some special skill. Besides, even if I can just get some kind of proof that the fuckers exist, I'll be in a better position to stop them."

With that, Macy stretched out her arm, lifting her gun to take aim at the corner of the room as though to shoot an alien just then. She made the sound of a shot firing and motioned her gun in imaginary recoil.

"I see. So your people have special skills. Tell me, Macy, what special skill does that stripper have?" The image of Mary was fading.

"She calls herself an exotic dancer, Mary. She is important to my plan."

"And what role do you see her playing?" The fading image of Mary was merging with Macy now.

Macy hesitated as she popped the side of the revolver open and inspected the six shells in their chambers. As she flipped her wrist sideways to slam the cylinder back in place, she answered her own question. "Bait."

Sixteen

John and Emily had been sitting on the couch watching television for some time. It was near nine o'clock, and John was scrolling through the list of upcoming shows. None seemed interesting. "Oh, the joys of local television," John opined.

"Try PBS. There's always something unusual on PBS, unless of course they are holding a fundraiser, which they usually are." Emily settled back in her seat as John clicked through to public television.

"...Now remember for those of you at the fifty dollar donor level, you will receive a copy of the show you just finished watching, 'The Haunted Castles of Hollywood,' and a 'Support Real Programming' t-shirt. There are just a few phones open so call and make your pledge right now to keep quality programming on the air..."

"I knew it, change the ch... no wait! Let's check this out."

The title of the show was "Predators of America's National Forests." During the opening credits, there was video of a very large grizzly bear attacking a camper. The footage was shot using someone's cell phone camera. Next, a moose chased some guy through the woods and he scrambled up a tree. Lastly, a mountain lion dragged a bleeding goat down the cliff of a steep ravine as the opening credits rolled.

Just then, there was a knock at the door. Emily looked at John and asked, "Were you expecting company?"

"No, I hardly ever have guests over. I mean look at this place. You can tell I wasn't expecting anybody." He made a sweeping motion with his arm as he stood and walked toward the door. He looked through the peephole and then unlocked the two deadbolts and swung the door open.

"Sherri, this is unexpected. Come on in." John motioned for her to come into the room. "You remember Emily Sparks, from the interview?"

Sherri walked through the doorway and stood in the middle of the room looking at John. She looked very pale. "Hey babe, you feeling okay?" he asked.

She looked right past him as she answered in a monotone voice, "John."

Emily rose from the sofa and, walking toward them, held her hand out to Sherri. "Hi Sherri…"

"There will be pain and darkness," Sherri interrupted. "I see them screaming." She raised her arm and pointed at the wall across the room.

"What? Sherri, what are you talking about? Are you okay? Come on over here and sit down for a minute." He reached for her hand and as he touched it, his hand passed right through. "Oh, shit!" Sherri faded away and was gone.

"What the hell just happened?" Emily gasped as she rushed to where Sherri had been standing only seconds before. She passed her hands through the air where she'd stood and looked around.

"I'm not quite sure." John was reaching into his pocket. "I'd better call her." He pulled out his phone and hit the button for directory. He scrolled through to Sherri's number and waited while the phone rang, once, twice. "This is the kind of shit I'm talking about, Em. Why I'm taking this class!"

He redirected his attention to the phone as it connected, "Hello?" Sherri sounded as though she'd been in a deep sleep.

"Where are you right now, Sherri? What were you doing just before I called?"

"What? John? Is this John? I was asleep in a chair. What's wrong? Why do you sound like you're freaking out?" She coughed and excused herself.

"Because I am freaked out, Sherri. Do you realize you were just here in my apartment?" John was pacing now. Meanwhile, Emily was peering through the peephole to see if someone was out in the hall playing some kind of joke.

"That's crazy, John. I was right here. I fell asleep in the chair watching some show on TV. What are you talking about? Have you been drinking?"

"Look, I was just sitting here when you knocked on my door, and I let you in. I thought you looked kind of pale, you know, like sick, and you were saying some crazy shit about pain, darkness and people screaming. Then, when I reached out to touch you, you just vanished. Emily was here, remember her, the camera girl from the interview? She saw it too. I know I'm not just seeing things."

"Really? I feel kind of tired, but I know I didn't leave the house. I'm in my pajamas for pity's sake. Was I wearing my pajamas?"

"Well, you were here. I don't know what you were wearing. If you weren't here, then who was?"

"I'm not sure, John. Can we talk about this tomorrow? I think I need to go to bed now. I feel really tired."

"Alright, we can tell Macy about it tomorrow too. I'm sure she'll have some insight. See you in the morning."

"Yeah, okay. Goodnight then."

"Hey, don't be wandering around anymore tonight! Bye," he said and ended the call.

Still holding the phone, he dropped his hand to his side.

"Is this normal? I mean, is it like this every day around here?" Emily asked, squinting at John and walking back over to sit down on the sofa.

"This?" he shrugged. "This is nothing. Hang around a while and you'll see shit you never even dreamed existed."

"Really?"

"Really." And John sat down beside her.

Seventeen

Marcus and Lamont were half in the bucket after several hits from the bong and a couple of glasses of really good cognac. They had settled into a game of Grand Theft ATM, a spinoff of a popular video game. The whole purpose of the game was to steal cars, trucks, and construction equipment, and drive them through the windows of stores to steal the cash machines. Controversial for sure, but a very popular game.

Marcus had just gotten a very large haul of cash. He'd heisted a bulldozer and used it to break through the drive-through window at First Green National Bank. Back at the garage that was 'home base,' his crew was cracking the boxes open while they discussed the amount of pussy they could buy with that much cash. That was the reason the box on the game carried a warning for parents – Violence, Language, and Sexual Situations.

Marcus turned to Lamont, "So dawg, who's the King? Ho-tep gonna party with my bitches tonight." He waved his arms in a seated victory dance. "Yeah booyyzz!"

"Bitch, ya think yo' ass got somethin' now, but when ya' leave here tomorrow, the kingdom is mine!" Lamont was grinning from ear to ear.

"Fuck that! My people will kick your fat hairy ass if ya' even try movin' on 'em." Marcus looked serious for a second and then grinned. "Besides, Lamont, you don't got the hoodoo magic to make it work."

"I might not have ya' hoodoo voodoo, Marcus, but I gotta plan." Lamont said slowly, deliberately baiting him.

"Say what? You serious? You movin' on my shit, and my bitches? You think your gonna jump onto my porch an' fight with the big dog?" He waved his arm as if the apartment was his porch.

"No, serious, Marcus. It sounds like some dangerous shit livin' up in them woods for two weeks, yo! I seen Survivor Man on TV, an' I can't see ya'll eatin' no scorpions and bugs just to survive."

"Ain't no scorpions up in them woods, man! Your thinkin' 'bout the desert. And bugs ain't so bad if you pull the legs off first."

"That's what ya'll gonna eat then if somebody steals ya' food an' shit!"

"Listen, Lamont. All we gotta worry about is bears and wolves and shit. Well I got something for them if they even think of sniffin' round..." He reached under the cushion of the sofa and pulled out a very large pistol. "See. Me an' Dirty Harry here got the Magnum Force, dawg!"

"Daaaamn, Marcus! A fo'ty-five? That'll make a bear shit in the woods!

"Yeah and then fall in it's shit face first when I blow his fuckin' balls off!" He held the gun up as if he was aiming the pistol and shooting, and they both started laughing.

"Hells, yeah! That's what I'm talkin' about!" Lamont turned back to the game on the television screen. "Let's take the money from this ATM an' go celebrate at the strip bar!"

"I gotta finish packin', man, but you go ahead. Getta lap dance from Crystal for me." He stood and walked toward the bedroom with the gun still in his hand.

"You know it! Get ready, my bitches-s-s!" Lamont hissed as he worked the game controller.

Eighteen

It was just past dark and the streetlights cast a shifting shadow as Rajesh walked down the darkened road. His thoughts were occupied with his wilderness adventure that would begin tomorrow morning. He wondered what Taya, his betrothed back home, might say about it if she knew. It had been a long time since he had seen her, but he thought about her often.

When they were children, his mother and Taya's had arranged their marriage, as was the custom in his home village. Spending time with Taya was so enjoyable during those innocent years that he had wanted the arrangement as much as his mother did.

Years passed and, as they began to mature, they grew apart as their interests led them to travel separate paths. Shortly after his sixteenth birthday, he went with his father on a journey to Bombay. For his father, it had been a typical business trip, but for Raj, his first great adventure.

Raj longed to see and experience more from life and the world before settling down and starting his family. When it came to tradition, he had begun to question most of the things he had been taught in his short life. He felt he wanted to have a choice when it came to selecting his wife. Taya had been an entertaining friend when he was younger, but she was becoming more and more serious over time. By the age of fourteen, she had already planned their wedding ceremony complete with a guest list.

His raging hormones combined with his fascination for the big city reinforced his growing doubt about his future as planned. The many beautiful women he saw in Bombay solidified this in his heart and in his mind. But that was only one of the revelations that came to him on this trip.

His father had booked a room in a grand hotel where the halls were trimmed in gold, and the housekeeping team put chocolate mints on the pillows each night. He was quite fascinated by this kind of opulence and caused him to wonder what other things he might be missing in his small world back home.

Still, the experience may not have been enough to prompt his wanderlust until something happened that would open his mind to the possibility of phenomena in this world that simply defied explanation. It had occurred on the second night as they were returning to the hotel from dinner. His father had encountered an old friend along the way and became involved in a very deep political discussion, which seemed as though it would continue for some time.

While Raj waited patiently, he noticed an eerie quiet had settled around them and a bright golden light shining at the end of the alley. He was determined to slip away and get a closer look at the source of the light, even if only for a moment. While his father was in the middle of a long diatribe, he saw his opportunity and made his move.

The cobbled pavement was wet and the stone walls on either side of the narrow street were grimy and old. The aroma of sour garbage overwhelmed him as he slowly walked toward the light. He focused his mental energy to overcome the urge to empty his stomach and add to the oppressive atmosphere.

As he neared the end of the alley, there was a turn to the right. He edged closer to the wall and cautiously looked around the corner. There was a large courtyard-like clearing with a large fire at its center and eight men sitting, cross-legged, encircling the bright flames. The men wore nothing at all from the waist up and only a dhoti, the large white cloth wrapped around their lower torsos.

The gray tone of their skin seemed to come from some type of ash or clay smeared on their bodies and their hair was matted in long, gray dreadlocks that hung down across their backs. Their beards, as long and gray as their hair, were accentuated by the licking firelight and shadow. Large black circles around their eyes gave the appearance of hollow empty sockets in the dim light.

Raj shivered as he stood watching the men rocking forward and back as they stared into the fire. "Nagas, ramas, rengas," they chanted, repeating it over and over again. One of the men turned and opened a small pottery urn and scooped a handful of powder from it. Then with a slow sweeping motion, he tossed the handful of powder into the fire as the chanting increased in volume.

A fountain of multicolored sparks burst upward out of the flames. Raj retreated in fear as the image of a very large cobra seemed to spring from the fire and rise above the men. It's head swayed back and forth slowly to the rhythm of the chant. It wound around in a complete circle eyeing each one as it passed by.

Suddenly, with a whip-like motion, it jerked, and the single head became two. With another snap, two became four, and on the third, eight heads extended from the body of the cobra. The snake was now much larger and arranged each of the eight heads to face one of the men.

Raj became aware that he was standing in a puddle where he had wet himself from the shock. He was overcome with shame and turned away hoping to leave unnoticed. This can't really be happening, he thought to himself.

A loud sound came from behind and he turned back to see what had happened. The snake was growing larger and towered high over the men. Without warning, it struck. The eight mouths openied at once and shot down in a blur. Instantly, each man was swallowed whole.

Raj screamed out loud, and finally found the strength to move his legs and run away from the horrible scene. Behind him only silence, the pounding of his shoes against the cobblestones seemed to echo all the more loudly. As he neared the entrance of the alley, he found his father waiting for him with his arms crossed in consternation.

"So my son, you have decided to assert your independence in this great city. You have the look of one with a new, yet terrible knowledge, and have you wet yourself? Share with me what has happened."

Raj struggled to catch his breath, embarrassed that his father had noticed how he had shamed himself. He tried to put into words what he had seen. He finally found his voice and, when he had finished his tale, his father looked at him for a moment and then roared with laughter.

"My son, your imagination makes me laugh. The men of the Nagas worship the snake, but the master never eats his servant. Come, we have much to prepare for morning. Let's retire to our room."

Raj was stunned by his father's lack of interest or concern for what he had witnessed. He wondered whether the men had actually sacrificed themselves in the ritual they performed. Was it a grand trick to scare him because he had dared to spy on them?

The next day, when his father's business was complete, they returned home. Afterward, Raj spent many hours researching the various religious cults and sects of his homeland. Although he rejected most of the religious beliefs he had read about, he had witnessed one of the rituals. It was this single experience, and his studies, that led to his interest in paranormal phenomena.

He believed that this trip would prove to be fruitful. He hoped some secret regarding the phenomenon in the Northwest Triangle might be revealed. Perhaps it would be him who unraveled it. Even so, if his parents ever discovered what he was doing, they would undoubtedly force him to return to India before he was prepared to do so.

Nineteen

"I guess you've never seen anything like that before." John reached for the remote control to turn off the television as he sat on the couch to face Emily.

"No, and I admit I'm a little freaked out right now." Emily shifted in her seat and pulled the hair back from her face with both hands before letting it fall to her shoulders again.

"Well, it's like I said earlier, I've experienced some weird shit before and that's how I ended up in the P.I. class. That kind of phenomenon is why we're going on this trip."

Now that she'd had a taste of what could be expected, she wasn't so sure she wanted to go, and it showed all over her face.

John noticed her expression of doubt and felt he should try to put her at ease. "Don't worry. You'll get used to the weirdness. With the kind of people we have in our group, there's bound to be a lot more weird experiences before we're finished." Thinking back to Sherri's ghostly prediction, he added quietly, "Maybe a hell of a lot more."

"Yeah, but when I decided to come on this trip it seemed a lot safer than dealing with those thugs who were trying to kill me earlier." Her eyes showed the anxious frustration she felt.

"Look, Em, did Sherri's apparition, or whatever it was, try to shoot you or anything? Did she approach you in any kind of menacing way?" He sounded calm as he questioned her. "I think this trip will be just what the doctor ordered. Two weeks in the great outdoors. Just think about all that fresh, clean air, bluer than blue skies... and the company of more good people than you've known in a while. Well maybe, I guess I really wouldn't know about that." He was more than stretching the truth but, for some reason, he really wanted her to go.

"I know she wasn't here to hurt us, but…" Emily was twisting and untwisting a piece of her hair with her finger. "So you really don't think there's anything dangerous about going on this trip?"

"Statistics show, Em, that most paranormal experiences are devoid of danger. Ghosts, hauntings, cold spots, and things like that are usually quite benign. I've heard that dealing with shit like exorcisms and demons and dark matter can get a bit dicey, but I don't expect there will be any of that where we're going."

"Really? You're shittin' me! You mess with demons?" Emily's eyes went wide and she turned a bit pale.

"Well, I've never experienced the dark stuff, at least not lately. I'm not really looking for that kind of trouble." He hoped that he wasn't making her nervous again.

"The thing is, we stumble on things when we aren't looking for them. The worst experience I ever had with this wasn't something I was looking for at all, and I sure didn't expect to find anything like it." He hesitated trying to think of a way to say what he needed to say without revealing the whole story.

Finally he continued, "It did show me that bogeymen definitely exist out there, and it's best to be prepared rather than get a surprise in a dark alley." He watched her and awaited her response.

Emily was waiting for him to tell the rest of the story, but eventually she broke the silence. "I'd prefer to avoid that kind of… well, drama," she said looking John in the eyes.

"How can you protect yourself from that kind of thing? How do you prepare for it?"

"Well, you know those stories about witches and vampires and werewolves and such, and how they use things like silver bullets, crucifixes, garlic and all that? A lot of that stuff is just plain bullshit. Like holy water. From what I've read, a vampire can drink holy water if they're thirsty, and the worst that could happen is they might get heartburn or a bad case of diarrhea.

On the other hand, some things do work: talismans and the like, ancient runes and a lot of various protections have been passed down through time, since man was created."

Had he just mentioned vampires and werewolves as though they were real? Emily didn't go there. Instead, she addressed another issue that had captured her attention. "Created? So you do believe in God then?" Emily wasn't too sure about God. She never really had an inclination toward any religious beliefs.

"You don't? All you have to do is look around. You think all of this was an accident? I mean, how could there be just some explosion, or some kind of 'Big Bang'..." John made air apostrophes as he continued, "...that resulted in the world as we know it?"

"There had to be a design or some Creator, don't you think?" John went on, "And if spirits, ghosts and demons are real, why not God? If the only supernatural, unseen things out there are evil, well, then where would we be?"

"I guess you have a point there, John. I mean, if there really are supernatural things... I mean, aside from the Sherri visitation... cuz that was really strange for sure. If they do exist, it only makes sense that God could be real too. I guess we're going to have more than a few days to talk about this stuff. Let me try to digest everything you've told me so far."

She was holding her palm to her forehead as if holding back a headache.

"Sure, I get it. It's a lot to take in. Talking about religion and the supernatural in the same context is one of those conversation killers, right? Kind of like if I suddenly started talking about politics. Most people would rather not discuss it… that's way too controversial. But I'm not really talking about religion. It's more like spirituality."

He didn't look up to see the expression on Emily's face as he continued rambling, "Because religion is about rules and every religion has their own rulebook. Spirituality, on the other hand, can be as simple as a belief in a higher power."

At last he paused and looked at Emily, who was looking at him as though he were some kind of alien with three eyes or something. He took the cue and changed the subject.

"Anyway, I've been thinking. You have all your stuff packed in suitcases, and that's going to be pretty difficult to carry through the woods. I have an extra backpack with some well-padded shoulder straps. What do you say we load all of your stuff into it and see if I can scrounge up some extra food supplies to get you through this trip? I promise not to talk about the 'S' or 'R' words anymore tonight. Deal?"

"An excellent idea, John. Deal. You know, I threw everything together so fast I don't even know what I packed." She looked at the bulging suitcase sitting next to the wall.

"I'll be right back." He went into the bedroom and, in such a small apartment, she could hear as he crashed around in his closet and scraped things across the floor. Emily thought it sounded like he was tearing the room apart.

While waiting, she took the opportunity to walk slowly around the room. She looked, touched and snooped her way through his things. John had a bookshelf filled with books that ranged from science fiction, to textbooks, and other books on topics related to paranormal experiences and investigations.

She was reading the titles of each one when she noticed a piece of paper sticking out of a large hardbound book on the lowest shelf. She pulled the book out, and lifted it up to open it. It was immediately obvious that the piece of paper wasn't a piece of paper at all. It was a dog-eared photo of an attractive red-haired woman in a bikini with a piece of tape holding a strip of paper over part of the picture.

Carefully she lifted the strip and saw the man standing beside the woman. The photo looked as though it had been through a fire or something. She turned it over to see if there was anything written on the back just as John came back into the room.

"Find anything interesting?" He set the large backpack on the sofa.

"Uh, sorry. I didn't mean to be nosy." She blushed as she lied. "I was just looking at your books and this photo fell out." She held up the photo. "An old girlfriend?"

"Not exactly," John walked over and took the photo from her hand, placed it back in the book and put the book back on the shelf. "She was the murder suspect in the case I spoke about earlier. Back when I was a detective of plain old normal crimes."

"She's very attractive for a killer."

"Well, I never quite figured out if she was the perpetrator or not, to tell ya the truth. She didn't live long enough for me to even question her. It's a long story. Maybe we can add that to the list of things to talk about up in the woods. For now, we should get your stuff into that backpack, and then we should think about getting some sleep."

"Sounds reasonable to me," she said, lifting her suitcase from the floor and laying it on the sofa next to the backpack. She opened it and a mouse-shaped cat toy fell out onto the floor.

John picked it up, looked at it carefully and handed it to her. "An old boyfriend?" he inquired, smiling.

She smiled back at him. "Really, John. It was nothing like that. Just a minor fling, although we did sleep together frequently!" She laughed. "He was a bit furrier than I like my men to be."

She laughed again, and he began to appreciate how attractive she was. He was still smiling as he opened the pack.

Twenty

It was one o'clock in the morning and Eddie was lying in bed beside Karla watching her sleep. He felt so lucky to be there in that moment. He thought about how all the decisions he had made in his career had enabled him to earn enough money so he could afford the finer things in life. If you asked any of Eddie's friends, they'd agree that Karla was one of the finer things indeed.

Tomorrow, he would leave with her on one of the biggest adventures he'd ever undertaken. They'd go together into the national forests of the Northwest, sharing a tent, the excitement of the wilderness and the unknown. He was looking forward to two entire weeks of exclusive access to the girl of his dreams. The thought of it made it difficult for him to fall asleep.

Suddenly Karla snorted loudly and rolled over onto her back. The movement left the sheet pulled down to her waist completely exposing her perfect breasts. Eddie felt the tightening in his boxers as an erection sprang up.

He wasn't sure if it was normal for breasts that size to point straight at the ceiling or not. He'd never been fortunate enough before to be with someone who was so beautifully endowed. The girls he'd been with before were much closer to average size.

Karla was definitely not average. Had he looked just a bit closer, he'd see the tiny scars from her implant surgery and he would know why the 'girls,' as she called them, always stood at attention. Not that it would have mattered to him if they were real or not.

Eddie stretched out and stared at the ceiling. This was the first time she had allowed him to sleep with her. She had insisted he keep his underwear on, "to keep things respectable," and she had slept in her skimpy little panties as well.

Eddie had whined about her "being naked at the club in front of all those other guys," but she had shut him down with a logical statement. "Yeah, but if they try to touch me, the bouncers will toss them out on their ass. There's no bouncer here, Eddie. And who knows? If you're gentle with me, maybe your dreams really will come true." How could he argue with her when she was batting those eyes and flashing that smile?

Like so many of her other promises, his dreams had not come true. Here he was in bed with the object of his desire, his greatest obsession, and he was no better off than he was in the club. He could look, but not touch and it was driving him crazy.

He rolled back over to look at her again. Now, he was multiplying those dreams with every moment he spent studying every inch of her. He was so deep inside his fantasies that he didn't even notice when she opened her eyes. "See anything you like, baby?"

Eddie's face reddened. "You know how I feel about those gorgeous twins of yours. I don't think I've ever been so near to them in such an up close and private kind of way. You know, it makes me want to..." He closed his eyes and moved in closer to her as he reached for one of her breasts, hand outstretched.

"Get hold of yourself Eddie," she said, taking hold of his arm and moving it back to lay it down along his side. "We need to get some rest for tomorrow. We're going to be carrying those backpacks fully loaded for the first time, and we're gonna need our strength." She nodded her head toward the backpacks leaning against the wall.

She was right about that. Over the past few days, she had been carefully sorting her 'supplies' by weight. The heavy things went in one pile and the lightest things in the other. When she had finished sorting hers, she went to work on Eddie's.

She spent hours, filling her pack with items from the lightweight pile, mixing her and Eddie's things carefully together so she would be able to find them quickly if necessary. When her pack was nearly full she had tested the weight by trying it on. Since she had put almost everything that was heavy into Eddie's pile, she felt hers was light enough to carry, at least for short distances.

Meanwhile Eddie had been packing the heavy things into his backpack. When he had stuffed in the last item, he fastened the buckles on the pack's flaps and tried it on. He groaned and bent his knees as he lifted it into place. The hardest part of the lift was getting it up high enough to adjust the straps. Once it was in place, it wasn't so bad, but it was like having the weight of another person on his back.

He wasn't too happy with the prospect of a long haul carrying that much, but figured he'd get used to it after a couple of days, and they'd be eating their way through some of it. Anyway, it was a sacrifice he was willing to make if it meant he could finally be with Karla, and maybe get into her pants and relieve all his pent up passion.

Just now, lying in the bed beside her, his back was still a little sore. When Karla was gesturing toward the packs, he'd looked over at them with apprehension. Carrying that thing was going to be hell and she knew it. She had watched him as he eyed the packs and she could sense he was having second thoughts about carrying all of the heavy stuff.

This trip was the final part of her grade, and she needed it to graduate the class. If Eddie backed out now, she would be forced to carry all of her own stuff. There was no fucking way she could carry that much weight, not for two weeks. She needed a mule, and there was no time to find a substitute. She was going to have to do something to give him incentive to carry out their plan.

"Lay on your back, baby. Momma's gonna give you a little present." She used her most sultry club voice, and looked straight into his eyes as she quite affectively diverted his attention.

"Really?" Eddie sounded surprised, but the expression on his face transformed to one of happy surprise.

Karla didn't answer him as she moved into position. Instead she forced a very large, seductive stripper's smile and slid her hand under the blanket where the full force of Eddie's desire was screaming for attention. As far as Eddie was concerned, this was the moment he'd been waiting for, and he was more than ready.

Twenty-One

Macy's eyes were already open when the alarm went off at 6 a.m. She lay in her bed with her eyes closed, thinking. She had been so focused on her own mission for this trip. Now she was experiencing the anxiety of wondering if she had forgotten any small detail that could prove fatal while they were in the wilderness.

It had been a restless night indeed. Every time she had fallen asleep, she had begun dreaming, and each time, she would wake up in a cold sweat, screaming. The dreams had most likely sprung from her earlier encounter with her sister's apparition. She had been left awash in a wave of memories from childhood.

Once during the night she had relived the terror of being lifted out of her childhood bed by her ankles. It wasn't the first time she'd dreamt about it. It was the same every time and real enough to feel the cold rough skin of an alien hand scraping against her while she dangled in the darkness. She was afraid of what was coming next, unable to move or resist what was happening to her.

She could feel the cool breeze as she floated out the window and into the glimmering silver pod-like craft that was hovering just outside her family's house. Macy remembered hearing the futile attempts to speak and muffled sobs of her equally terrified sister as she was being carried behind her.

Aside from the obvious effects of fright, Macy often wondered if their inability to call out might have been caused by some partial paralysis of their vocal chords. Not only that, she hadn't dared to scream for fear of letting all the air escape from her lungs. She remembered feeling that she might not be able to take another breath and would suffocate in her state of immobility.

She had smelled the stench of rotting flesh as they carried her through hallways that had been used for such a purpose for many years. She recalled seeing evidence of fellow captives who possibly had not survived. Those who met their demise were either ejected into space or left to rot in some cavity within the ship.

The aliens had carried her into the dark interior of the ship where they laid her on a platform, which was unusually warm given the low temperature of the dimly lit room. It seemed to quiver and move beneath the weight of her small body. It had seemed to form around her to create snug contours that held her in place. She had lain immobilized as her eyes darted from side to side watching several glowing objects that had drifted into place, hovering above her for a moment before ropelike tentacles shot out and burrowed themselves painfully into her skin in several places.

Macy winced as she remembered the screaming. It was as though her cries had come from deep inside a great pit of darkness, clawing their way to the surface, and finally breaking through to an opening in a room that was stark and brightly lit. It was at that point, she had suddenly awakened back in her bedroom, shaken and wet with sweat, but free of the terror of the night.

These were no mere dreams that had interrupted her sleep. This was her reality, and had been for many years. This morning, the sounding of the alarm clock had released her from the futile attempts to get some rest. It was the starting bell for a journey she had been anticipating in some way or another for many years.

Macy burst out from under the sheets as she sat up and swung her legs over the side of the bed. She took a deep breath and dangled her feet there for just a moment, allowing them to hover just above the floor. Then she slid off the mattress and walked into the bathroom to begin her morning routine.

Fresh from her nice warm shower, Macy felt ready to conquer the world as she stepped into the kitchen to prepare her last bowl of cornflakes. No morning routine, no cornflakes, for the next two weeks. She had saved a nice ripe banana just for the occasion. Humming the theme song from Snakes on a Plane, she got everything out, lining up the utensils and ingredients on the counter. With everything in its place, she put her breakfast together just as she always had every day for the last twenty years though maybe with a bit more attitude than usual.

She sat down at the table and shoveled large spoonfuls of cereal into her mouth. While savoring her flakes, she grabbed the remote control lying on the table and turned on the television. The local news anchor was spewing out reports of robberies and murders as she typically did every morning about this time, but one report caught Macy's attention.

"A body of a man has been discovered in the warehouse district. He appears to have been shot execution style, in the back of the head. As yet his identity is unknown and police have no clues, but gang activity is suspected."

As terrible as it was, Macy had no clue why that particular report would jump out at her, but she didn't really give it much thought. A very loud commercial came on for a furniture company who was having a big sale over the weekend with the manager of a store yelling about the great deals. It grated on Macy's nerves so she pressed the power button on the remote and turned it off.

"I fucking hate loud, screaming people." She mumbled to herself through a mouthful of cereal, but the truth was, she just hated people. Period.

Twenty-Two

John rolled over to turn off his alarm clock and rolled right into Emily. She seemed oblivious to the wake up music as she continued to snore. He always kept the alarm on the opposite side of the bed from where he slept. That way he would have to move out of his warm, comfortable spot to shut it off. It helped wake him up and made it easier to get on with his day.

This morning he would have to get out of bed and walk around, which didn't sound too appealing. He decided to try to crawl over Emily and shut it off. It was the bumping and cover pulling as he went over that woke her up.

"Good morning." She smiled up at him as he was halfway to the alarm and he froze. "You know you look pretty good in the morning with that beard stubble, kind of that 80's TV detective look." She reached up and touched his jaw with the back of her hand.

"Oh yeah?" He smiled back at her. "Let me get this alarm turned off and I'll put my handcuffs on you for some in-depth interrogation." He reached over and hit the off button, then lay down beside her.

"I don't know what got into us last night, but I'm glad it did," he started.

"Me too. Yesterday was such a stressful day, it was great to release all that tension." She was still smiling as she spoke.

"Anytime, ma'am." He chuckled. "I haven't been with anyone like that since…" He tried to remember the last time he had slept with someone. "Since…"

She cut him off again. "Shouldn't we be getting ready? I wanted to get a shower before we leave. It sounds like it will be my last chance for a couple of weeks."

"Yeah, I guess I should be doing the same," he said, hoping he might be able to share the shower with her and have a little fun before they left.

"I'll go first!" she said, leaping out of the bed and running into the bathroom, her naked butt a flash of tan line and lightly browned skin as she slammed the door behind her. He heard her turn on the shower to let the water warm up and he figured if he waited a few minutes, maybe he could slip into the bathroom and join her. He sat up on the edge of the bed, feet on the floor, and prepared to make his move until he heard the 'click' of the lock on the door and his hopes were dashed to hell. "Damn!"

Emily was starting to hum a tune as he got up and headed into his tiny kitchen area. He wondered where things would stand with her after two weeks together in the wilderness. After all, she didn't have a tent or a sleeping bag, so she'd need to bunk with somebody once they got up into the woods. What better bunk mate than a strapping ex-marine, ex-military, ex-police detective who could protect her fragile self if a big ole badass bear came wandering into their camp looking for a snack in the middle of the night?

Well, out of the group that was going, the obvious answer was 'nobody but me.' He was sure he could convince her to share his tent, but he had to be careful how he handled this. Her obvious determination to shower alone this morning let him know that it was not a done deal. So the question at the moment was where to start? The answer was staring him in the face, start by making her breakfast.

He stood like a zombie looking into his refrigerator. Unlike most single men he knew, John actually had food.

Most of his friends might have a couple of twelve packs and a bottle of ketchup, but John had an absolute feast waiting to happen: fresh eggs, bacon, bread, butter, jelly, orange juice, and to top it all off, a couple of strawberries to add color to the plate.

Getting right to work, he put the bacon on the stove, the bread in the toaster, and set two places at the table. He walked quietly over and leaned up to the bathroom door to hear whether or not Emily was finished. Sounded like he had just enough time to get everything ready for her. She would step out of the bathroom with a towel wrapped around her hair and one around her body, and voilà! sit down to a wonderful spread.

When the bacon was brown and crisp, he put the strips on a paper towel to drain and placed them in the oven to keep warm. He poured the grease out of the pan and cracked the eggs on the countertop and poured them in carefully. While they sizzled, he took the toast from the toaster and buttered each slice, put them together and cut them diagonally. Then he flipped the eggs, let them cook for a second and grabbed a plate from the strainer on the sink.

The apartment smelled like good country cooking as he took the bacon from the oven, arranged the toast, eggs, and bacon on the plate, added the strawberries as a colorful garnish. He poured some orange juice into a clean glass, and set Emily's breakfast on the table.

He heard the water pipes thump as Emily turned the shower off, and he hurried to set the silverware on the table, adding a large paper napkin. He was careful to set the jelly within reach, and was just finishing up as she opened the door and came walking into the kitchen area.

Just as he had expected, her hair and body were wrapped up in towels, and she was rubbing her hair to dry it. He flashed a big grin and proudly announced, "I made you a nice, big, country breakfast." He pulled the chair out for her to sit down.

"Really? That was sweet of you, but I usually don't eat breakfast, John. Got any coffee?" She sat down in the chair and pushed the plate away from her.

John wilted like a cut flower lying on hot pavement in the heat of summer. "Uh, yeah, I think I have some," came the answer from the suddenly glum host. He looked in the cabinet next to the coffee maker.

"You didn't make some breakfast for yourself? Why don't you go ahead and eat mine. It looks really delicious, John. If I was going to eat something this early in the day, that breakfast would be exactly right." She was lying through her teeth, she hated bacon, but she wanted him to know she appreciated his effort.

He was making the coffee with his back turned to her, but it was obvious that she had hurt his feelings. She felt bad about that, after all, he had saved her life yesterday. "John, I'm sorry about breakfast. Really. I want you to know that I'm really grateful that you saved my life yesterday. And what happened last night, well that was especially nice. I don't make a habit of saying thank you all that often, just so you know."

He smiled weakly. "Oh sure, no problem!"

He picked up the food and moved it to the other side of the table, then sat down and started to eat. "Let me know when you're done with the bathroom, I'd like to get my shower before we leave."

"Okay, baby," she said and walked into the bathroom.

He stopped with a fork full of food just shy of reaching his mouth, and asked himself out loud, "Did she just call me baby?" Now he was grinning again.

Twenty-Three

Mark Woo arrived at the airport precisely at seven a.m. and checked in at the desk. He needed to prepare his flight plan and get the plane fueled and checked for the trip to Seattle. As he looked over the map, he searched for Whitmore Gap. Dr. Renner had requested that he fly them over that area. It was where they would be filming their documentary. If he wanted to receive the customary gratuity for a chartered flight, he figured he should try to make her happy.

When he completed mapping out the flight path, he entered the coordinates into the computer and waited for an acknowledgement. It was nearly instantaneous. He stepped over to the printer, which had already begun to spit out the maps and other documents he would need.

He had prepared an invoice to present to the doctor as soon as she arrived. She'd pay half up front, in cash, for the round trip flight. Then all he had to do was fly them up there. He'd party with his friends in Seattle for a couple of weeks, and then fly them back. Easy.

There was a girl up in Seattle that he particularly looked forward to seeing again. He had met her there on a weekend the previous summer, and they had kept in touch via occasional emails, text messages or, less frequently, a phone call. Only a couple of weeks earlier, he had contacted her and they planned their meeting. It was a date he intended to keep, no matter what might happen to prevent it from coming together.

For now, he had to focus on prepping the plane. He checked the tires and, as he did the walk around, it was painfully obvious to him just how badly he had been beaten the other night. Each step, each twist of his body sent sharp pains through his muscles, and his blackened eye throbbed each time he bent over to check or pick something up.

The bruises on his body could be hidden beneath jeans and a long sleeved shirt, and he had tried to cover some of the bruises on his face with cheap makeup he kept around for just such situations, but there was not much he could do about the eye. Since his passengers were mostly college students, he figured they might be bold enough to ask questions about it. Fucking punks!

Even two days later, it seemed like there was scarcely a place on his body where the girl had not hit him or kicked him. It was possible that he had a cracked rib or two since he was experiencing sharp pains whenever he took a deep breath.

Everything would be cool in a couple of days, most of the bruises would fade, and he could get on with being the scoundrel that 'would make his daddy proud.' For now though, he was starting to sweat and, when he wiped his face, quite a lot of his makeup wiped off on his shirtsleeve. He wanted to touch it up, but he needed to get the checklist completed. Besides, the swelling could not be hidden with make up. He'd just have to live with it.

When he finished his flight prep and returned to the hangar to wait for his clients to arrive. He looked in a small mirror hanging there to see what his face needed. "Oh shit," he said out loud as he realized it needed a lot of work.

Twenty-Four

Macy pulled into the parking lot and heard the gravel crunch under her tires as she found a space. She shut off the engine and sat for a few minutes staring out the window. This was her last chance for reflection. She could call everything off right here, right now. She could prevent any possible risk to her class if she just said the word.

"Fuck that!" She said out loud, striking the steering wheel with the palm of her hand. For her, there was no turning back. This trip was going to happen and she was going to confront her past head on, no matter what.

This was a small local airport. It was the one she preferred, since it would have been difficult for her students to board a commercial flight with anything that remotely resembled a weapon. Because of all of the restrictions, a hatchet would be a violation even if packed in a suitcase.

More important to her was the .38 she had hidden in her handbag. Without that little bit of security, she was not sure she could go through with the trip. She was almost certain that there would be no problems for her here, no screening or scanning to go through.

She felt confident as she went through the main gate and into the small terminal. She was carrying her large backpack, her handbag and another large canvas tote bag. She was not used to the weight of carrying all of these at once and struggled a bit under the load. The girl at the desk greeted her cheerily, "Welcome to Golden Community Flight Center, how may I help you this morning?"

Macy hated perky. "I'm Dr. Macy Renner, and I have a reservation for a chartered flight this morning with…"

"Pilot Mark Woo? He said there would be several people in the party. Will they be arriving soon?" Her smile widened.

"There will be eight to be precise. I'm sure they will be here soon. Do I have to wait for them to get here before I go to the hangar?" Was that really a piece of spinach in that girl's teeth at this hour of the morning?

"Oh no, you can go on ahead to Hangar 18 where the plane is being readied. I just need to see your ID and have you sign in before you go. Oh, and will you be leaving the country? If you are, I need to look at your passport."

Another spinach smile, was that from her breakfast? Macy sighed and dropped her cargo to the floor. She fished her wallet from her handbag and handed it to the clerk. As she set it on the counter, it rolled to one side and the barrel of her gun popped out of the top. The girl seemed oblivious as Macy pushed it back inside and removed the bag from the counter. Her heart was pounding in her throat as she waited for her ID to be returned.

"Thank you, Dr. Renner. Please sign here."

Macy pulled the pen from the holder and quickly scratched her name on the designated line. "And here…" the girl pointed at the paper. Again Macy signed. The clerk turned the page and was about to ask her to sign again when Macy interrupted. "Excuse me, but this looks like a contract. I wasn't told anything about signing any contracts." Her tone was becoming terse.

"Oh no, Dr. Renner. It's not a contract. It's a release form. Ever since 9/11 we have our clients sign this form. It simply releases us from all obligation in the event of a…" The smile disappeared and the spinach was hidden from view.

"Crash!?" Macy interrupted.

"Well, I'm not sure about that. I mean, it releases us from any liability in the event that you might have other plans... you know, other than traveling. It is just a formality, I'm sure." With that, the piece of spinach dislodged itself and flew in Macy's direction.

Dodging the green projectile, Macy began to rant. "That's pretty stupid when you consider that if I were a terrorist, and I was planning to use a plane as a missile, I wouldn't discuss it with you in advance and a 'release' form sure would not stop me from doing so."

"I am sorry, Doctor. I'm just doing as instructed. I don't get to make the rules. Please?" Macy shook her head and signed the last line of the document.

"Do I get a copy of that?" Macy was starting to pick up her gear.

"Uh, no one has ever asked for one before. I guess so. I mean it's really more for our use in case of any trouble." The girl's frustration was beginning to show and the perky attitude had left the building.

"There's a first time for everything," Macy said, preparing to lift the weight of the backpack. "I'll wait."

The girl took the paper and went into a back room. The copier was very noisy, but accomplished the deed. A minute later, Macy was holding her copy of the document. "Thank you. Now, which way did you say to the hangar?"

The girl didn't speak, she just pointed at the door leading to the hangars, and then returned to her work. Macy lifted, then shifted the weight of the backpack and headed out the door. There was a concrete walkway that led down the front of the hangars and she looked into each one as she passed. Finally, she came to the hangar where Mark was sitting at a desk playing a video game on his computer. A large number 18 was painted above the open roll-up door.

"Mark Woo?" She called through the door. He put down the game controller and turned to look at her. "I believe we have a reservation, Mr. Woo, for a flight to Seattle?"

Mark stood and walked over to her, his hand extended to shake hers, and she obliged.

"Dr. Renner, I presume?"

Macy nodded.

"Mark Woo," he continued. "Very nice to meet you. Bring your gear right over here, and we'll stow it with the others when everyone arrives."

Without a word, Macy carried her bags to the place he had indicated.

"Has anyone been added to your party since we spoke last?" Mark talked to her back as she walked toward the plane.

"What did you say?" She looked back over her shoulder at him.

"I said, 'has anyone else been added to the passenger list since we spoke last?' "

"When was the last time we spoke?" She struggled to remove the pack and set it on the floor.

"I'm pretty sure it was last Friday."

"Oh, if it was last Friday, then yes we have added one more, our camera operator or should I say videographer? Other than that, the team has not changed."

"So that brings the total to eight? Did your assistant convey my payment terms?" He waited as she reached into her tote bag and pulled out a fat envelope.

"Yes, eight, that's correct. I have the first half of your payment here, just as you requested. Could you give me a receipt please?" She held the envelope just out of his reach.

He stepped forward and took the envelope from her hand. Walking back to the desk, he opened the envelope and flipped through the twenty-dollar bills pretending to count them, then bent down over the desk and tore a piece of paper off of a pad.

"Do you want this made out to you or the university?" He held the pen over the paper.

"Make it out to me, please. Dr. Macy Renner."

She watched as he wrote something on the paper. He dropped the pen and handed her the note.

"Uh, Mark, you don't have something more official, like a receipt with your company info on it?"

"Here let me see it," he said reaching for the paper. He opened a desk drawer and grabbed a rubber stamp and an inkpad. He slammed the stamp onto the pad, then on the paper. Holding it up to his mouth, he blew on it and handed it back to Macy. "Good enough?"

"I guess, if that's all you have." She looked at the paper with the stamp on it. The stamp did not seem like it was made for a transport company, but she couldn't really make it out. Just then, she heard the muffled sounds of a conversation and turned to see Raj and Marcus carrying their gear through the large open doorway. They crossed the concrete floor toward the plane.

"We flyin' in this bucket?" Marcus asked, dropping his gear on the floor next to Macy's.

"Excuse me, but it's not a bucket. These prop planes are much safer for flying up around the Northwest. Nothing worse than having a fat goose sucked into a jet engine to ruin your day. These props just make paté out of 'em if there's an encounter." Mark came up beside them.

"Whoa dawg! What happened to you? Your face looks like shit, man!" Marcus was chuckling as he checked out the swelling bruises on Mark's face.

"Actually, it is none of your business… Dog" Mark's tone was sharp, but as sore as he was, he really did not want another conflict.

Macy stepped forward to interrupt, "I'm sorry, Mark. Allow me to introduce you. This is Marcus and Raj, members of my team, and guys, this is Mark. He'll be our pilot for the round trip." The two men nodded in acknowledgement.

Unable to prevent himself from talking shit, Mark went on, "It's none of your business, Marcus, but if you must know, I was up in the city the other night and two of your bro's jumped me."

Even though he was making it up, he pushed it further. "If you think I look bad, you should have seen those guys when I was finished with 'em." He finished his lie by glaring at Marcus until he spoke.

"Oh, and I bet your puny Chinese ass fucked 'em up real good." Marcus replied sarcastically. "What did you do use? Some Kung Fu movie shit on 'em, Bruce Lee?" Now he was grinning wide, and he could see Mark's face turning red.

For a moment, no one said anything. It was Raj who broke the silence. "Come on guys, what are you going to do? Fight it out right here? This is not a time for violence. It will prove nothing, and then we have to travel together. I am not asking you to abandon your testosterone forever, just tone it down for the next couple of hours."

"Ho-tep can handle it if Bruce Lee here can pull his panties out of his crack." Marcus was still grinning as he swaggered a little.

"Come on guys. Marcus, Mark, how about if we just stay in our own corners for the rest of this trip? Then when we get back, you two can meet up somewhere and discuss this?" Macy was standing between them now, making her case and hoping it would tone things down.

"Hey guys, we made it!" Eddie yelled as he and Karla came in through the large hangar doors. "We saw Sherri pulling up just as we were leaving the... uh... office."

As they walked toward the small group, they sensed something was not right. It might have been the way that everyone turned and looked at them without saying hello, but more likely the telling was in the glare of Marcus' eyes and Mark's reddened face.

"So what's wrong anyway?" Karla set her large carry bag on the floor as Eddie, her virtual pack mule struggled with both of their backpacks. He had one on his back and one was carried as dead weight in front of him.

"It's nothing. Just a little glitch in the program, but everything is fine now, isn't it guys?" Macy gave Marcus the look of death.

"What? I was just playin'." Marcus answered the look. "It was Bruce over there that lost it." He tried to assume the look of innocence.

By now Eddie had freed himself from his burden and he stepped closer to the group. Macy made the introductions, "Mark, this is Eddie and Karla. Karla, Eddie, this is Mark."

No sooner did the words leave her lips than Eddie exclaimed, "I thought his name was Bruce." He shot a quick glance over at Marcus before turning his attention back to the pilot. "Wow, dude those are some serious bruises. It looks like somebody really kicked the shit out of you!"

"That's what I'm sayin!" Marcus interjected. "Bruce here had a tussle with some of the boys, but we're not supposed to talk about it. Right, Macy?" He looked at her with an mock expression of alarm, then smiled again.

Macy looked back at him in disbelief. He really was pushing her buttons, and she was just waiting for Mark to jump on him when the pilot spoke up, "Hey, that's okay. I'm over it. I know the truth and really, Eddie, it's a long story. Right now, we'd better get the gear loaded. Maybe you could give me a hand, Rick James."

"Rick James? I'll give you Rick James, bitch!" Marcus picked up one of the backpacks. "Where we taking it?"

Twenty-Five

Except for the soft chattering of the birds, the forest was quiet in the morning light. A variety of trees, mostly tall pines, surrounded the area allowing only brief shimmering thin rays of sunlight to cut through the canopy overhead.

The female creature rested against the disabled ship. Her mate was busy constructing a nesting site in the large circular clearing nearby. Such clearings were rare in these parts, but the aliens were unaware of their good fortune. They were focused entirely on the task at hand.

Spider-like, the male was extruding a ropey material from somewhere in the middle of his abdomen. He worked quietly with single-minded determination, connecting the sticky web-like material from tree to tree, spanning the width of the clearing and then weaving a circular pattern from cross brace to cross brace. The nest had to be strong enough to support the weight that would hang there.

The creatures had already spent several days collecting animals from the surrounding forest to feed their offspring during the initial stage of development. He hoped to store enough food to prevent them from engaging in the horrible cannibalism that he had witnessed at home in his world. The ensuing chaos was still vividly etched in his memory.

Now, as a sexually mature adult, he would embark on his first and last reproductive experience. It was the natural order of life for adult couples of his kind to offer themselves to their hatchlings as nourishment, a nutrient-rich feast to give them the best possible start in life. When the hatchlings emerged from their eggs, they would have no other option but to begin eating immediately or die of starvation. Eat or die, eat or be eaten, it was the way of their world.

Despite the fact that their advanced intelligence passed genetically from generation to generation, they were still creatures bound to primordial instincts when it came to such procreative practices. The alien creatures never questioned the cycle of life as they knew it. They willingly accepted that their own existence would end in order to give life to the offspring they spawned.

Each generation possessed nearly all the knowledge of the parents that came before. Intelligence and reasoning were programmed directly into their genetic material. Any new knowledge or understanding would be added to the code which would be passed on throughout the generations, a fortunate trait considering the short lifespan of these creatures. Though this intelligence was passed through DNA, it wasn't an instantaneous awareness. The newborns had only the knowledge at birth to know that they must eat or die. The more they ate, the greater the level of their intelligence. In the same way a bud on a rose turns into a flower, at maximum growth the creatures would bloom into their full intellectual awareness.

There was no time for compassion for others. To them every other living creature was a potential meal, including others of their kind if need be. In their world no greater predator existed and, in the end, as food sources dwindled this would put the survival of their species at risk.

Now as the male continued to work diligently to create a fresh start for his offspring in this strange land, a deep-seated sense of dread came over him slowing his movements as he forced himself to complete the task. With everything he had already provided for them, he could not be sure how many of the young would hatch in this environment and time was running out. He must carry on building up their food supply before the hatch began.

As he labored on, the female was feeding on the fresh kill of the morning pausing to rest now and then to aid her digestion. Scattered about the edge of the clearing were the bones of many animals that she had consumed over the past month. Some of the gruesome remains were human, the bones of those who had happened upon her mate as he was hunting. He did not make any distinction between humans and other animals except for the strange loose and multicolored 'skins' that covered their meat, and the great deal of noise they made while being prepared or eaten.

The male creature had come to savor human meat, however, and to such a degree that several of the victims he had captured had served as a feast for him alone. The female knew no different as long as he saved some prize to present to her when he returned from his hunt. He was always careful to clean himself thoroughly after such a feast. He was well aware that an angry female could just as easily eat him while she was 'in waiting' to expel her matured clutch of eggs.

After many days, various animals, including several deer, wolves, and rabbits, were stored in the clearing. They were strategically arranged several yards from the spot where the eggs would hang to draw out the hatchlings as soon as they would fall to the ground. Though the young aliens would be left to fend for themselves, they came into life fully equipped for survival. Their bodies fully formed and functional at birth, nevertheless it would be necessary for them to eat massive amounts of fresh meat to achieve their adult size. The more they ate, the faster they would grow. If a plentiful supply of food were available, a newborn might reach full adult size in a matter of forty-eight hours.

As the female closed her eyes again, she wondered what her offspring would discover here in this new world, and if they would ever return to their home. At the moment, she decided, it did not matter. This world seemed quite amenable, and she was not overly concerned about their future. If they found this world unsuitable, the ship contained the tools and materials for repair. Once they reached full size and intellectual maturity, they could leave here if they chose, and with an adequate food supply, this could be accomplished within two or three cycles of this planets star.

She looked up as her mate ambled toward her. Everything had been prepared, and he had come to assist her as she made her way to the nesting site. He carefully attached the appendages that extended from her abdomen, stretching them slightly to reach the center of the web, and then prepared the area where he would need to position himself in order to assist as she attempted to expel the fully developed eggs from her body. Judging by her size at this stage, he was expecting a difficult time. It seemed as though she could be carrying hundreds of eggs.

Twenty-Six

Sherri, Emily and John came strolling in through the giant hangar portal about fifteen minutes after Eddie and Karla arrived. Sherri waved as she caught the eye of Marcus who was handing the last backpack from the pile up to Mark.

"Hey Sweet Cocoa, glad you could make it." His smile was wide as he walked over to her and wrapped his arms around her. He lifted her off the floor in a huge bear hug. "Are you ready for the adventure?" he asked as he gently set her on her feet.

"I certainly am," she chirped. "I'm as ready as I'll ever be to walk into the wilderness without the comforts of civilization for two weeks." She picked up her backpack again and handed it to him.

John and Emily were right behind her waiting to load their gear. John held a smaller case in his left hand as he handed his pack to Marcus. "You want that in the storage compartment, or is that a carry on, Sherlock?" asked Marcus as he passed the pack to Mark who was struggling to arrange the near full cargo compartment.

"I think I'll hang onto this one. I want to show the team the new tools I got for this trip," said John as he turned toward the rest of the group. "Come on, Emily. Let me help you get to know everybody right away so you'll feel more at home during the flight."

"More at home? Oh, sure, John," she said ironically, recalling what her home had been like just before she left. "I think I'd rather feel more at your home. Last time I saw mine, the door was being kicked in."

"Oh yeah. Sorry." He felt sympathy for what she had been through.

Macy was standing nearby and pressed Emily for more information. "I'm sorry, did you say your door was being kicked in? Is there anything I should know about?"

John was quick to reply, "No, Macy. Everything's cool. It's a long story. How about we save it for later? It will make good drama when we tell it around the campfire in the dark."

Macy still looked concerned. "Are you sure?"

Emily chimed in, "Yes, it's not that important. We'll tell you the whole story after we get where we're going." She forced a smile in hopes of reassuring her employer.

In the lull that followed, Macy took the opportunity to get everyone's attention. "Hey, guys! Let's grab some chairs and sit down. I have a couple of things to say before we leave." Everyone grabbed one of the chairs that lined a wall of the hangar and pulled them over to form a circle. Marcus carried his over to sit next to Sherri.

"Okay. About five weeks ago, when I first decided to put this field trip together, I considered the possibility that we might be walking into some danger. Therefore, I instructed each of you to bring protection as you felt necessary to preserve your own safety. We are going into a national forest where there are wolves, bears, and other dangerous animals roaming freely, and we must be alert to that fact every minute of the day and night."

Macy began handing out booklet printouts as she continued, "I also instructed you to research and review basic wilderness survival techniques. In the event that you were not as thorough as you could have been, I have printed some information for each of you. Even if you plan on spending all of your time in the presence of the group, there is still the chance that we could become separated or one of you may be lost."

Marcus interrupted, "Anything come to mess with Hotep gonna be chompin' on the barrel of my .45." He nodded and gestured as he looked around at the group. "That's what I'm sayin'."

Macy continued, "That's good, Marcus, but we need all individuals carrying weapons to be strategically located when we set up camp. Raise your hand if you have packed a weapon, please."

Five hands were raised, among them John, Marcus, Eddie, Macy, and Sherri. "My sweet girl is packing iron? Yeah, baby!" Marcus exclaimed when Sherri's hand went up.

Macy continued, "I'm hoping that everyone had the sense to pack these in with their other gear and not give Mark a reason to be concerned about his safety as our pilot."

Everyone nodded except John, who raised his hand then spoke out. "Hey, I kept my knife out of the pack cuz it has a nice sheath that fits right on the belt. That's cool isn't it?" He patted the large buck knife on his hip.

"Sure, John. Just keep it sheathed in case we hit some turbulence up there. I wouldn't want you to put your eye out." She smiled at him and he returned a blank stare.

Macy spent a few minutes going over some basic information about what should be expected when they set up camp. When she was finished, she looked around to see that everyone was on the same page. "Now unless someone has to go to the bathroom, I guess we can get this party started. Anybody need to use the can?" Three of the girls raised their hands and Raj sheepishly joined them. "Okay then, take care of business and we're out of here." The four of them scurried off toward the bathrooms.

After they walked away, Macy turned and asked John, "Is that what I think it is?" She was pointing at the case sitting at his feet.

John nodded, "Yes, ma'am! If you were thinking that it's my new Paranormal Investigation Super-Secret Toolkit, you would be a winner!" He grinned, proud that he was the only one with the forethought to bring some actual paranormal investigation tools.

"After we get in the air, and everybody is finished reading that document, I'll pass these awesome some tools around and let everybody see how they work. I think everybody will agree, this is some really cool shit."

"That's what I like about you, John. You always think of everything." Macy smiled at him, and he replied, "Not a big deal, Mace. Used to be a Boy Scout, and you know the Boy Scout motto?"

"Uh, be prepared?" she answered.

John showed his approval with a hearty "Hoo rah!"

"Hoo rah? Isn't that marine talk, Boy Scout?" Macy shook her head and walked over to talk to Mark.

A few minutes later, the others returned from the bathrooms and Emily walked up to John. "Um... I was wondering... I know I'm supposed to be the camera girl on this trip, but I haven't really seen any sign of equipment. Seems kind of strange, don't you think?"

"You know, I didn't either. I think we should ask about it." He started walking toward Macy, "Hey Macy, got a sec before we get going?"

"Sure." She looked up from the map she was studying, "What is it?"

"Emily here had a good question. Uh... what about the video equipment?"

Macy turned to Sherri who was standing next to the plane. She yelled over at her, "Sherri, you reserved the video equipment, right?"

Sherri interrupted her conversation with Marcus long enough to tick off the list with her fingers. "Two top of the line Sony cams, extra lenses, extra batteries, solar panel charging device, two light panels, reflectors and night vision. We also have two tablet screens for daily footage reviews. The guide is bringing everything when he meets us at the airport. Don't worry, it's all been arranged and verified." Sounding confident, she went back to her conversation without missing a beat.

"Wow!" Emily seemed impressed that they would have such an extensive list of quality equipment. "That sounds like a lot of stuff to carry!"

"Oh, well. I didn't think the camera operator would be solely responsible for carrying all of the gear. We're going to divide it up among the group and the only thing you'll have to carry is the camera, Emily. Just in case we stumble on something big, I want you to be able to record it."

She looked at the rest of the team boarding the plane, "Besides, it's a very small unit from what I hear. Uses very high capacity memory sticks rather than tape, so you can shoot as much footage as you feel you need to tell the story."

John watched as the group began filing into the cabin of the plane. "Looks like they're ready, Mace. I guess it's time." He smiled and held out his hand to shake hers. "Good luck, commander."

She took his hand with a firm grip, "Thanks, John. And believe me when I tell you, if we encounter what I think we might, we'll need a lot more than luck. We'll need... ah, never mind." With that, she walked toward the plane.

Emily looked at John with an uneasy expression. "What do you think she meant by that?"

Shrugging his shoulders, he responded, "She's just being overly dramatic. If we had the camera right now, we probably should have recorded that. It would make a good start to your documentary."

Twenty-Seven

Fifteen minutes later, the plane was taxiing onto the runway. Mark turned from the cockpit as he maneuvered into position for liftoff and yelled to his passengers, "Everybody, buckle up! We're expecting some turbulence on this trip. Weather decided not to cooperate today." He turned back and shoved the accelerator forward.

As the plane sped down the runway, two men in dark suits wearing sunglasses entered the terminal office.

"Hello, how can I help you?" the clerk asked cheerily.

As if she wasn't already a bit suspicious of these guys wearing stereotypical special agent costumes, one of the men flashed a badge so fast that she really didn't get a good look at it. "We're looking for a woman named Emily Sparks? We have reason to believe she is here and scheduled for a flight to some location in the Northwest."

"I'm afraid you just missed her. See that silver plane out there with the wheels lifting off the ground? She's on that flight." She looked at the men who seemed very frustrated at this point. "Is this some kind of medical emergency or something? Do we need to call the plane back?"

"No!" The men said in unison, and turned and left the building exactly the way they had entered.

When their black SUV had disappeared from the parking lot, the young clerk went to the back room and dialed Mark's mobile phone. She waited as it rang one, two, three times. "Hello, this is Mark."

"Hey, Mark, this is Cheryl. I'm sorry to bother you but…"

"Whoa, Cheryl? Cheryl... from Oakland? This isn't about...? I swear I..." Mark was wracking his brain to remember a Cheryl.

"No, Mark. It's Cheryl at the terminal desk! I'm really sorry to call you, but you know that woman on your flight, Emily?" She picked up a pen from the counter and twirled it in her free hand.

"Sparks? Yeah. What about her?" He flipped a switch on the control panel.

"Well, two guys dressed like Men in Black came into the office looking for her just as you were wheels up down the runway. They flashed some kind of badge like they were for real, but somehow I don't think so."

"What the fuck did they want her for?" Mark sounded frustrated as he banked the plane to the left.

"Well, they didn't say exactly, but I thought you should know. Alright?" She hated talking to him when he was in a bad mood. He always started cursing when he was upset.

"Well, thanks, Cheryl. Maybe I can find out what the hell is going on. I'll call you back if there's anything you need to know." With that he pressed the key on his phone to end the call. "Damn!" he said as he tossed the phone onto the seat beside him.

About an hour and a half into the flight, John was snoring, his head resting on the window of the plane. As Emily turned the last page of the survival document, Macy reached across the aisle and shook John's shoulder. "Wake up, Sleeping Beauty. You said you'd share your toys when everyone was finished reading, and that would be now."

"Nuh..." John wiped a bit of saliva from the corner of his mouth and looked around, "Are we there yet?" he asked smiling.

"No, John," Emily said from across the small aisle. I think we have about fifteen more minutes before we fly over the spot where we will be searching for God knows what." She looked out the window for a second and continued, "You said you were going to show us your toolkit and Macy was letting you know it was time."

"Oh yeah." He unbuckled his seatbelt, and reached down to the floor where he had placed the black case. Pulling it up onto his lap, he unfastened the latch and lifted the lid. The case was lined with a gray foam liner that was customized to fit perfectly around the four instruments it contained. It looked like something out of a spy movie.

Each instrument had a shiny chrome finish and was made with handgrips so it could be easily managed. John moved his seatbelt to the side so he could stand, and getting up from his seat, he turned to face the group while placing the case on his seat.

The ride was a little rough in a plane this small, so he steadied himself against the seat. He pulled the first device from the case and held it up so everyone could see it. "I'm going to tell you about each item and how it is used, and then I'll pass them around so everyone can see them."

"There's an On switch on each of these devices that is right about where the trigger of a gun would be. If it turns itself off while you are holding it, just press this button to turn it back on." He demonstrated by pressing the button with his index finger. The device emitted an audible tone as it was activated, which could barely be heard above the sound of the plane engines, and a small red LED lit up.

"This one is a barometric pressure sensor. It measures fluctuations in air pressure created by any mass displacing any given quantity of air." He held it up and pressed the button.

"Right now the cabin of the plane is pressurized and the sensor is showing fluctuations as the air pressure changes due to natural leaks around the seals." He smiled and handed it to Marcus who was occupying the seat directly behind his.

Marcus began turning the instrument around to look at it up close from every angle as John pulled the next device from the case and held it up for all to see. "This one is an infrared thermographic scanner. On this monitor it shows the patterns of heat and cold." He pointed at the tiny display on the device.

"For example, if I point this at Emily…" He aimed the device at Emily who made a face at him as he spoke. "I can see a large red blob that gradually turns purple as the heat from her body dissipates."

"Theoretically, if there was an unseen object that was colder or hotter than the temperature of the surrounding air, we would be able to see a color representation of that object as it came near." Emily squirmed in her seat when he said this. He grinned at her and pointed the device at the floor adding, "Or not."

John was passing it to Marcus who had already passed the first instrument on. "This is top of the line shit," John boasted. "A lot of paranormal investigators only have laser thermometers, the kind that the heating and cooling guys use." He grinned wide enough to show his teeth in a playful show of pride. Marcus took it from his hand. By now the first instrument was on the return up the other side.

John took the next item from the case and held it up. It looked like a digital music player. "This one is much smaller because it is a digital audio recorder. I don't think I need to pass this one around. I brought this baby with us to record the sounds around us in the woods. There have been cases where recordings were made in what seemed like total silence, but sounds and voices could be heard on playback that had not been heard by anyone present at the time of the recording. I'm hoping we might pick something up with it. In the field, this is a great device to have on hand. It has a high capacity for up to ten hours of recording"

"Record the forest sounds? Like what, crickets and frogs?" Eddie laughed at his own joke, while Karla turned and glared at him. "What?" he asked, a wave of embarrassment swept across his face.

John put the device back in the case and removed the last object, holding it up as he had done before. "Lastly, this baby is called a Gauss meter. It measures magnetic fields and any changes in them. This one is so sensitive that it can find a refrigerator magnet from twenty-five yards away – inside of a house, through the walls!" He turned it in his hand showing the display.

"If we were closer to the North Pole, this thing would give us a massive amount of readings. At night, if there were Northern Lights, since they're caused by fluctuations in magnetic fields of the earth, this thing would just about jump out of your hand." Then he pressed the button on the grip and the object came to life. The meter on the upper face of it was measuring at about twenty percent and the light on the dial was green.

"That's all I have, folks. Take your time checking them out. I'm not worried about the batteries. The case has a solar charger built into the lid, so I can recharge them later." He handed the device to Marcus and moved the case to the aisle floor. "Once again, my name is John, and I'll be here all week!" He grinned and took a bow before sitting back down in his seat.

Twenty-Eight

As the devices made their way around the plane, each person took the opportunity to play with the buttons and use them on the person sitting nearest to them. When Raj got hold of the thermographic device, he pointed it at his legs and saw the two red images that represented them on the small screen. He moved it away and then back again. He turned it toward Sherri who was sitting in the seat across the aisle from him.

The red blob that represented Sherri came clearly into view, but as he studied the image, he noticed two purplish objects moving to either side of her arms. They rose above her and hovered over her head. Initially, Sherri thought Raj was just playing around, but then she became aware of the look on his face. "Raj, what's the problem? You look like you've seen a ghost or something."

"Uh… I'm not sure what I am seeing. There are two purple objects hovering around you."

Sherri seemed startled and waved her arms as if to shoo the objects away. "Are they still there?"

"Yes, they are! You were passing your hands right through them! Hey, Marcus, check this out."

Marcus unfastened his seatbelt and stepped back beside Raj. Taking the device from his hand, he pulled the trigger and aimed it at Sherri. "Holy shit, Spooky! You got two purply blobby things floatin' around you right now! Damn, girl! One just went right through your head!"

Raj unfastened his seatbelt and stood up next to Marcus. He tapped him with the back of his hand. "See, I told you something was going on. Look, they just went through the top of the plane. Now they're back!"

Macy had unhooked her seatbelt and stood looking over their shoulders, "Oh shit, Sherri. I didn't know you could see your..." But Sherri didn't hear the last few words. Instead she heard her great aunt's voice. "Keep your seatbelt on, baby. It's gonna be bad, but don't you worry. You are gonna survive this, so don't be afraid. We are right here with you." She heard her grandmother add, "You might want to tell your friends to sit down."

The blobs on the screen had suddenly disappeared. Marcus and Raj were looking at each other in amazement as Macy grabbed the sensor from their hands, trying to see what they were looking at.

Sherri was looking at her watch to see how long they'd been travelling when she heard the voices. She tried to collect her thoughts, this was totally unexpected. She had to say something to warn the others, so she yelled at peak volume, "Everybody get in your seat! Put your seatbelt on, NOW!"

"Geez, Sherri. What's up?" Raj squatted down so his face was level with hers.

"Gran and Nana just visited me, and something bad is gonna happen!"

"What'd they say?" Macy asked her leaning toward her.

"They said to keep my seatbelt on and not to worry because I was gonna survive! Get in your seat!"

Macy hurried to her seat as Marcus and Raj were buckling themselves in. All of the excitement had awakened John, who had drifted back to sleep. He looked at Emily, his confusion apparent from the expression on his face. "What's going on?" He tried to straighten out his bed head.

"I don't know. Sherri was visited by some purple blobs or something and then she yelled at everybody to put our seatbelts on. I think it's some kind of premonition!"

"Oh shit, something bad is about to happen!" John checked his seatbelt and fastened and tightened it. "Get the pillow from under your seat to cover your face with and prepare to brace yourself!"

"John, what's going on?" Emily was starting to feel panicked.

"Sherri's family warns her when bad shit is about to happen. I guess I didn't tell you about that. Well, we better get ready because obviously some bad shit is about to go down!"

Emily had been holding the device for measuring fluctuations in magnetic fields and, in the excitement, her grip on it was pressing the trigger. Suddenly the device sprang to life with a loud buzzing alarm and the meter on the face of it started flashing.

As she held it out to John, he could see the indicator needle jumping and the light on it flashing as it went past the overload marker on the dial. It pegged at maximum load and stayed there. What happened next seemed to occur in a slow motion time warp.

Twenty-Nine

In the pilot's seat, Mark's flight instruments were going crazy. He was oblivious to the escalating panic behind him. He tapped the dials thinking they might be malfunctioning.

The passengers were anxiously preparing for whatever was coming next. Karla, on one side of the plane, and Eddie on the other were both looking out the windows. So far neither of them could see anything unusual until, all of a sudden, there they were.

"Oh my God!" screamed Karla just as Eddie let out a scream of his own. "What the fuck is tha..." was all he could get out.

Everyone turned to look out the windows now, and what they saw scared the shit out of every one of them. Two flying objects coming in fast from both sides seemed to be on a collision course with the plane. They were cylindrical and silver blue in color, and seemed to mirror the sky and clouds around them making it nearly impossible to spot them.

Seconds later, the two objects struck the plane on either side of the fuselage, just ahead of the wings. They hit the plane at such a high rate of speed that large indentations from the impact could be seen from inside. Everyone screamed and grabbed for the person nearest them.

Somehow the shimmery objects remained attached to the plane and they generated some kind of humming sound that was beginning to rise in volume and pitch to such a level that it drowned out the noise of the plane.

Mark was scrambling. When the plane was hit, he lost control, but could not see what was going on. He switched the plane to autopilot and unfastened his seatbelt. He didn't notice that it did not engage as he removed his headset and got up out of his seat to move back to where the passengers sat staring in terror out the windows. As he realized what they were looking at, three small panels opened on the sides of the objects.

Some kind of probes began extending from inside the objects to the skin of the plane. There was a loud metal piercing sound as the probes simultaneously pushed through the walls and moved into the cabin.

Emily screamed and nearly jumped out of her seat when the silvery rods started thrashing about in the air in front of them. She and John pushed back against their seats as the probes continued to thrust themselves into the space inside the plane.

With a crackling, sizzling sound, three bolts of gold lightning arced across the cabin. The plane's engine died instantly without a sputter. It was as though someone had simply switched it off. The plane jerked, throwing Mark to the floor as they began to free fall out of the sky.

Something kicked on inside the two objects and the humming sound coming from within them gave way to the sound of an engine of some sort. The screams and sobs of the passengers were silenced as everyone realized at once that the plane was not in a free fall at all. Instead, it was being pulled from the sky. Then a second discharge came from the probes. It spread like a cloud of energy that crackled and sizzled filling the inside of the plane like thick smoke.

Heads drooped. The team fell unconscious as the energy cloud spread quickly throughout the plane. Before it could filter down to Mark, who was still lying on the floor, he muttered, "Oh shit!"

Thirty

On the ground, the creature stood before a holograph of the plane being guided through the sky to the clearing. It was a killing field where previous flights had met their demise. Most of the ships he had brought down were smaller craft usually carrying one to three passengers, but he could see that this one was slightly larger.

Many larger ships had flown over in the past few months, all of them out of range and carrying dozens of creatures. He had been frustrated each time since they flew at such an altitude, but this one was flying low enough. His anticipation grew as he could visualize nine life forms on his screen.

This would be more than enough food to ensure the survival of his young hatchlings. He communicated this to the female who was resting in the hammock-like nest he had constructed. She was quickly approaching the time for the evacuation of her eggs.

As the plane descended from the sky, he monitored its progress. He had to make sure it would end up in the clearing where the other craft had been forced down. Here he had set up a harvesting station after his first encounter with the strange creatures. It angered him when they tried to escape, running through the forest screaming. They were often so loud that they scared off other food sources.

He had built a semi-circular barrier with an opening on one side only and designed the walls to curve inward at the top making it impossible for any creature to climb out. Once inside, the only way out was through or past him, and so far there had been no escapes.

After a minute or two, he could see the object in the sky above them and he pulled the control that would slow its descent. Now all he had to do was go to the clearing and harvest the food, a task that would complete his purpose in this life and guarantee that many of his children would survive.

The trap extenders could hold the plane suspended without difficulty but, after the capture, there was no real reason to bring the craft to a soft landing. It hit the ground hard as it came to rest, and the impact was enough to damage the integrity of the fuselage. Landing on a large log of a fallen tree, it cracked open like an egg when it hit.

The break had occurred along the line of panels between the first two rows of seats and the last two. The male creature came upon the scene and could see the strange animals strapped into their seats. Packs and suitcases were scattered about the clearing. They had been dislodged from the storage compartments.

The monster did not care whether the animals were dead or alive. He would harvest them regardless of their condition and strategically position the bodies in proximity to the egg cluster for the coming hatch.

Thirty-One

The receptionist looked up as the young man came up to the counter. She smiled and waved to indicate she'd be with him in a moment as she turned her back and continued talking to the person on the other end of the phone. Assuming she would not be long, the wilderness guide stood and waited. He'd been hired to lead a group up into the forest and he was eager to get it going.

Looking around the small airport, he hoped he could find someone else to help him. He was growing quite weary of the receptionist's incessant chit-chat. She was droning on and on about her boyfriend as she paced back and forth behind the counter.

Occasionally she glanced at the guide. She was gesturing and seemed to be telling him to Hang on a second, I'll be right with you, Please be patient with me, and finally, Get over it! With every nonverbal communication from the otherwise verbose woman, he became more frustrated until finally he broke his silence.

"Miss, I need to talk to you if you don't mind." She replied in sign language by holding up her index finger and mouthing the words, Just a minute.

He walked over to one of the plastic chairs that lined the wall and sat down with arms folded, cursing under his breath and shaking his head. While he was waiting, two men entered the office, dressed well and wearing darkly tinted sunglasses like some kind of government agents.

One of the men removed his glasses and stepped up to the counter tapping loudly to get the girl's attention. He flashed some kind of badge or ID, which finally got the girl to remove the phone from her ear. "How can I help you?" she chirped.

"We are awaiting the arrival of a chartered flight out of San Francisco carrying a team of college students. Do you know when they are expected to arrive?" He looked at his watch, and then the clock on the wall.

The guide walked over and broke in on the conversation. "Yeah, that's why I'm here too. Do you know when they're supposed to arrive? I can't wait here all day."

The girl gave them a blank stare then spoke into the phone, "Hang on a sec, hon. I need to check something." At last, she put the phone down and picked up a clipboard. "It says here a plane arriving from San Francisco was expected around 12:15 to 12:30." She glanced up at the clock and shrugged. "Looks like they're running late."

The clock read quarter past one, and the man in the suit was first to reply. "Right, so they are now an hour late. Is there some way you can check to see what is going on?"

She had already reached for her phone and seemed slightly perturbed by the additional request. "Well, maybe I could call somebody, I guess."

The man, still wearing the sunglasses, stepped forward and barked, "Look, bitch, I suggest you do that. And I mean right about fucking now!" The girl's face turned red, not from embarrassment, but in anger.

"Look, Bozo, I don't care who you work for. You don't come in here talking like that to me and expect me to jump just cuz you say jump!" She put both hands on the countertop and leaned forward, her head punctuating each word as she spoke. "You can just step back and take a seat and I'll get to that in a min…" She stopped midsentence as the barrel of a Glock was pressed against her forehead.

"Pardon me, missy," he sneered. "I said right fucking NOW!"

Caught completely off guard, the receptionist felt the room begin to spin. The guide, who had seen the man reach beneath his jacket and pull out the gun, made a break for it. He was fifty yards down the walkway by the time the girl hit the floor.

"Shit!" The man holding the gun walked to the end of the counter and lifted the panel in order to get behind it. Walking back to where the girl had hung the clipboard, he kicked her limp body as he passed her. "Stupid bitch!" He took the clipboard from the hook and looked at it, then threw it at the girl still unconscious on the floor. "Let's get the fuck out of here," he told the other man.

As they were leaving the terminal, they caught sight of the guide about a hundred yards away near the hangars still running for his life.

Thirty-Two

John wasn't exactly sure where he was or what had happened. He could barely make out the scent of pine through the choking stench of rotting flesh, and for a moment he wondered if he might be dead. He tried to quell his sense of panic as he assessed the situation.

His shoulder hurt like hell and his body seemed to be paralyzed. He tried to move his arms and legs but found it to be impossible. His vision was somewhat blurred but he could tell that he was situated somehow in a large clearing in the middle of a stand of tall trees. Raj was there leaning up against one of the trees, maybe some twenty yards away. John squinted to get a better look.

As his vision began to clear, John could see that Raj wasn't standing next to the tree at all, but was hanging from it, his feet about eighteen inches off the ground. He opened his mouth to yell over to Raj, but found he could only cough. He cleared his throat as best he could then rasped, "Raj! Hey, Raj! Are you alive, buddy?" There was no sign of life.

He turned his head to the left, and blinked several times. Unless his eyes were deceiving him, there was some kind of creature. He had never seen anything like it before and it was standing next to Emily. She also appeared to be hanging from a tree the same as Raj. From this vantage point, John could not get a good look at the monster. He tried to figure out how tall this thing might be. Based on his own height and the distance he guessed he was hanging from the ground, John judged the creature must stand about eight feet tall. It was one of the biggest, ugliest things he had ever seen.

It stood erect on two legs, like a man, but this was no man. John thought the thing looked more like some kind of gigantic bug or maybe a lizard, a hybrid lizard-bug. It was a grayish hue in color that alternated to brown and dark green and back to gray as it moved through the clearing to another tree. It must be some kind of continual camouflaging process he supposed.

Its back had what seemed to be a series of layered, interlocking, segmented, maybe armored plates, each overlapping the one below it. These plates formed a ridge in the center of its body that ran from the top of its head to the end of its tail, which extended to the ground and seemed to stabilize its body weight while it worked.

The creature's hind legs reminded John of the legs of a very large lizard but were segmented more like a grasshopper's. He guessed it to be a four-legged creature that stood upright when necessary to use its front legs as arms. He could see as it moved around an unconscious Emily, that its 'hands' had three large fingers and what resembled a thumb, all tipped with sharp but relatively short claws.

As the monster turned, John noticed some type of appendage, or third arm. It was shorter than the others and positioned near the center of its chest. It bore a foot-long blade-like boney structure that it seemed to be using as a tool. Just now, the monster was using it to apply something to the tree behind Emily's back.

Now John realized exactly what was holding him immobile against the tree. With one clawed hand, the creature held Emily firmly against her tree, while the other hand reached behind its back just above its tail where a thick black liquid oozed slowly from some kind of opening. As it deposited the goo on the tree next to Emily, it used the blade-like appendage to spread it evenly between the tree and her limp body. Was the thing using it's own shit as glue, to bind them?

The creature seemed able to produce the stuff at will because each time it reached back, more of the goo had been produced and was ready to be applied. With each handful of ooze, the creature appeared to be gluing Emily to the tree.

It dawned on John that the forest was eerily quiet except for the crunching sounds the creature made as he moved around the tree. As he strained to see what was causing the crunch, he saw there was a scattered pile of bones surrounding the base of the tree. Most of the bones looked as if they were from smaller animals, but about a yard away there was a human skull which had been kicked to the side.

He felt a shiver of horror throughout his body as his dazed mind began to comprehend that the creature was literally 'putting up' food. His team was obviously not the first group of humans to experience this nightmare.

John's gaze shifted back to his right and another wave of dread passed through his body. He could barely make out Mark lying on the ground in the shadows. His legs appeared to be bent in an unnatural pose as though they had somehow been mangled in the plane crash, or perhaps crushed by the creature.

With all that was happening around him, it was the object hanging above Mark that inspired absolute terror in his soul. It looked like a bunch of translucent grapes about the size of large watermelons. Each greenish globe had dark spots that appeared to jerk and squirm every few seconds. As he scanned the entire object from bottom to top, he realized that it was suspended from some kind of web-like structure.

It hit him, finally, like an aluminum baseball bat to the head. This was a giant cluster of alien spawn and, from the way the things were squirming and jerking, it looked as if they were about to hatch!

Thirty-Three

Commercial airline pilots are in constant communication with the ground as they travel around the globe. When a plane goes missing, there is immediate action taken. Hundreds of lives are on the line and the airlines can't afford to delay a search for a missing plane when possible survivors are awaiting rescue.

The smaller private and chartered planes, on the other hand, can go unnoticed for longer periods, especially when a half-assed cocky pilot does not file an adequate flight plan. Then, if changes are made in-flight without proper notification, a plane could go missing without anyone having a clue as to its whereabouts.

This is exactly the scenario that had played out when Mark Woo had left on this trip. In fact, for as long as he had been flying, he had never been really good at the whole flight plan thing. He had become accustomed to flying by the seat of his pants when he made his trips.

When he had taken flying lessons, he had bribed his flight instructor to keep quiet about his planning skills. A couple of thousand well placed dollars, a few phone calls, and the same instructor covered it over by doing all of the flight planning work for him. Mark considered it to be no worse than paying someone to write a term paper.

So now that his flight had gone missing, no one knew exactly where to look. He had kind of gotten it somewhat close, but even if they had dozens of aircraft covering hundreds of square miles outside of the flight path he had filed, the plane and its passengers might never be found.

If you're searching for a needle in a haystack, you'd at least want to know where the haystack was, before you began the search.

After several hours and the plane had not yet arrived, the required reports had been filed and calls had been made. One of those calls went out to the University and was fielded by Macy's assistant. She was asked if she had been contacted, if any word had been received about the status of the flight. She had not. She was instructed to retrieve any documents which may have been filed containing emergency phone numbers of the passengers. If any documents were located, she was to contact each of the individuals listed on the documents and prepare them for the worst.

The calls were all made before the report hit local news stations. A small passenger flight had gone missing somewhere between San Francisco and Seattle.

Thirty-Four

John heard a cough to his right and, a moment later, a shaky voice called out, "I can't move! Somebody help me!" He recognized that voice. It was Karla and she sounded scared. "Eddie, where are you? Where are we?"

The panic was rising in her voice, and he felt sure she'd be screaming any moment especially when she realized what was happening around her. He tried to calm her. "Karla, be quiet! You'll attract too much attention."

"John! Is that you? Where are we?" Karla's voice continued to rise. "What the fuck is going on?"

He spoke a little louder this time, turning his head as far as he could toward Karla. "Be quiet! Can't you see? There's some kind of monster here and it doesn't look too friendly! Keep it down. We don't want to..." John sensed something moving right next to him as he continued, "attract atten..." He turned and found himself face to face with the alien.

The creature's head was quite wide and, as it opened its huge mouth, John could see its long pointy teeth, rows and rows of them. It breathed out a horrible stench as if it were taunting him, and then closed its mouth again. John stared into the creature's softball-sized black eyes and saw his own reflection there. He struggled to curb the gag reflex.

He made an attempt to remain calm and employ a normal conversational tone as he spoke to the alien captor. "What are you gonna do, you ugly fucker? Eat me?" The creature tilted its head like a dog hearing a strange sound.

"Go ahead, you piece of shit. I hope you choke on my ass!" John raised his voice defiantly. He figured he had nothing to lose since he might be about to die anyway. The creature seemed almost to smile as it turned away and walked out of sight.

One by one, the others were returning to consciousness. John could hear their feeble voices as they tried to speak. "What the hell is this? Where are we?" he heard Macy cry out. Then, a virtual chorus of crying and shouting surrounded him.

"Where are we? Oh my god!"

"What the fuck? Let me go!"

"Holy shit! Somebody help me!!"

"John? John?" It was Emily calling out to him.

"Emily! Are you okay?"

"Sure! Ya think I'm just waiting here for the barmaid to bring me another glass of wine?" she said sarcastically. "What the fuck! No, I'm not okay! I can't move and that – that thing over there keeps looking at me like I'm some kind of tasty snack!" Emily stopped and lowered her voice. "Come on, John, baby, do your rescue thing! Get us outta here!"

There she was calling him baby again. A guy could get used to that. "Give me minute to think, Em. There has to be some way to break loose." He tried leaning forward to pull himself free, but he couldn't move any part of his body except his head and neck.

He could swear he heard Mark moaning. Sure enough, the poor bastard was still alive! Waking up with both legs badly broken, the pilot was lying under the biggest fucking egg sac on the face of the earth. The sound of his groans and the slight movement of his upper body prompted the unwanted attention of the creature.

Mark screamed as he saw it coming toward him and used his arms to try to pull himself away. The creature shook its head and let out a low growl as if to say, "Oh, no you don't," and reached down to grab Mark by his jacket, dragging him screaming back into position below the giant mass of eggs.

The monster demonstrated his familiarity with human anatomy as it held Mark down with one of its clawed hands and surgically inserted its bladelike appendage into his spine just below his shoulders, likely to sever his spinal cord. Surprisingly little blood oozed into a small pool next to his broken body as the creature stepped away.

Mark, wild-eyed, had lifted his head as the blade had penetrated and gasped as the alien withdrew it before passing out from what must have been unbearable pain, or was he was dead now? No, John thought he could make out the shallow movements of his breathing from his otherwise motionless body.

How could the creature know enough to paralyze someone in such a precise manner while allowing them to stay alive? Why would it do such a thing? John looked around. The answer was obvious. Humans and other animals were being stored as food for future meals. It was probably better for the alien hatchlings if the victims were still alive, doubtless more nutritious. Obviously humans were part of the alien food pyramid and the team was destined to be the hatchlings first buffet dinner of fresh meat.

John was more determined than ever to free himself and the others. Like watching a horror film over and over in his head, he kept seeing the replay of the monster cutting into Mark's spine. He struggled against the hardened substance that held him glued in place. He pulled, pushed, squirmed and twisted, but still could not budge.

In the past, even when he had been beaten, stabbed, nearly blown up, burned and left for dead, he had never before felt so defeated, as though there were no chance he'd survive. But this time, it was complicated. This time there were eight other people involved, including a beautiful woman with whom he was becoming more enamored by the hour. No! This was not a good way to die!

"Fuck this!" he muttered as he tried again to break free from the giant wooden skewer that was holding him in place. He strained again, finally letting the air escape his lungs as he gave up one more time. In that split second of desperation, he remembered his buck knife strapped to his belt. He hoped it was still there and he could reach it, then maybe he could cut himself free.

After many attempts at breaking loose, he had managed to free his right hand. He could move it now but only at the wrist, which left him straining to reach what he considered his only hope, the handle of the knife.

The wailing of the team had increased after witnessing Mark spine being severed in such a coldblooded and precise manner. The clearing began to echo with a chorus of moaning and sympathetic pain, and John could hear crying and whispered words that sounded like someone reciting the Lord's Prayer.

He shared their shock, but he could not afford the distraction of grief or fear. He pushed his balled fist against the tree, attempting to get just a bit more room to move. "Come on!" he snarled and gritted his teeth, giving it a couple more tries until he felt something give a little as his hand moved every so slightly closer. At long last, he could get three of his fingers around the handle.

With the alien glue tearing at his skin, John stretched even farther to pull his hand back far enough to unsnap the safety strap that held the razor sharp blade in its sheath and carefully pull the knife out. He would have to take quite a bit of its length into his hand to get it clear of the leather.

John was focused on controlling every movement of his fingers. He was slowly inching the handle up into the palm of his hand when he was startled as someone let out a scream. He lost his grip and let the knife slide back into place.

To his left, he could see the beast eyeing Macy, up close and personal. It was showing its teeth in a wide smile-like expression. It seemed to be trying to provoke her to scream again, as if it found the noise to be entertaining. When there was no reaction, he opened his mouth wider to show the rows of teeth in his mouth in a more threatening pose.

Macy yelled, "Where is she, you piece of shit? What did you do with her?" The beast tilted its head as though it was asking her to repeat the question. "What did you do with my sister? Was it your fucking ship we were taken to? What did you do with her?"

The creature turned its back to her swinging its tail hitting the base of the tree where she was glued as it headed back toward Mark. "I'll kill you, motherfucker! I'll kill you and I'll gut you like a fucking fish!" She was screaming at the top of her lungs at it as it walked away without looking back. From John's perspective, it seemed to be shaking its head and laughing at her.

"John, you used to be a marine, right?" The creature turned to look at Eddie as he spoke. "Oh shit!" His voice was almost a whisper now. "Can't you help us get out of here somehow?" Eddie remained quiet as the alien turned away again.

John continued trying to get a grip on his knife. He had needed the short rest since his hand had begun to cramp before it had slipped from his fingers on the last try. He was hoping to get a better grip but, since his arm was locked into such an awkward angle, it was almost physically impossible and quite painful to reach the handle and pull it out.

Just as he managed to force his hand back into position, John caught sight of the movement to his right. A second creature was moving slowly into view. It was down on all fours, the extra appendage hanging limply to the ground as it crawled. It swayed and staggered as though it was sick. John watched it lumber across the clearing as he began to work the knife little by little out of the sheath. Slowly the second alien moved toward the hanging eggs. It stumbled collapsing with its face in the dirt.

From the look of its stretched, sagging skin John guessed it to be a female. She had most likely been weakened from producing the eggs. The male creature moved to help his mate get to her feet. He walked along supporting her as they moved to the egg sac. She needed to lie down, and did so with help. She positioned herself right across Mark's back!

Thirty Five

The male creature was somewhere out of sight, and John was determined to free his arm enough to get hold of his knife. Marcus was just regaining consciousness. Until now, even Mark's screams had not awakened him, and Mark had screamed loud enough to wake the dead.

Marcus was not sure what was happening around him. Things looked very green, and he could sense that he was somewhere in the woods. He couldn't remember hiking here. Although he realized he had been asleep, he sure as hell didn't feel like he was in a sleeping bag. One thing he was sure of, he was unable to move.

He was definitely hung up on something vertical. Was he tied up? His eyes began to clear. "What the fuck? What is this shit? Where am I? Why the fuck can't I move?" The steady stream of questions did not allow time for a response. "Very funny, guys. Now cut me down!"

A voice beside him spoke, "Marcus, be quiet! It will hear you." He recognized the speaker even though it was more of a desperate sounding whisper than someone actually speaking out loud, and he could hear the fear in Sherri's voice.

"What? Who's gonna hear me?" He blinked and squinted as the scene in front of him came into focus. "Oh shit! What is that? Is that Mark?" He saw the blood that had oozed around Mark's body. He rasped, "What the fuck happened here?" Marcus suddenly became quiet as his vision cleared and he could take it all in.

Sherri whispered, "Hang in there Marcus. We're gonna get out of this." She tried to reassure him. "Gran and Nana said not to worry. We are gonna be freed and then we have to run like hell."

"Are you sure about that, girl? Cuz this looks pretty fuckin' bad," he whispered back. He tried to turn his head, but it was fastened securely to the tree.

"Can you see John from there?" Sherri was even quieter this time.

"No, is something wrong with him? Is he hurt?" He was trying to be as quiet as Sherri. He couldn't remember speaking this softly since the days when his dad would slap him at the dinner table for being too loud.

"Look. I think he's trying to get loose. Looks like he's trying to pull his arm away from the tree and grab his knife." This time she was so quiet he strained to hear her. "If he can get to it, maybe we all can get free. This must be what Gran was talking about."

As she finished speaking, John's forearm suddenly broke loose from the tree, and he was free to grab the handle of the large knife and pull it out of its sheath. Sherri could see him carefully turning it in his hand, bending his arm and inserting the tip of the blade behind his shoulder. The seconds it took to free his right shoulder seemed like minutes.

John continued to work the knife as he pulled away from the tree with his shoulder. Inch by inch he was becoming free! As soon as he finished cutting his upper right side free, he forced himself back against the tree. After putting himself back into place, he turned his hand to hide the knife behind his arm.

Sherri wanted to yell at him to finish it, get loose and save the rest, but she suddenly grasped the reason he had put himself back into position against the tree. The creature was moving around in the clearing now and looking at the humans helplessly hung there.

It seemed to point at Macy as it opened its mouth and let out a high pitched sound that rumbled into a low roar. It was a bone-chilling call as it motioned to each person in turn. Had any of them been able to understand this strange behavior, they would have known that this was a part of the ritual that preceded the hatching.

After completing its circle, the male creature walked toward the bundle of eggs and lowered itself down on all fours. The top of its head came to rest against the lowest hanging eggs and it closed its eyes to rest. It was only a matter of minutes now before his life would have completed its purpose.

In his mind he could hear the chattering of tiny aliens with a near singular voice as they shared one thought. Hungry!

Thirty Six

John had a clear view of the alien creature's back as it knelt below the hanging eggs. He took the opportunity to finish cutting himself free as he grew increasingly concerned that they were running out of time. He sliced through the thick rubbery material that held him against the tree. He thanked God repeatedly that he was fanatical about keeping his blade razor sharp.

Now he just had to get off that tree before the alien became aware. He was suspended off the ground and, with only the right side hanging free, his position was skewed. If the thing turned around it would surely notice that he was halfway to gaining his freedom. That very instant he heard a popping sound and saw a thick clear liquid drip down onto the head of the monster. This was followed by another pop and then another.

The alien's head was dripping with the fluid as three or four, foot long creatures dropped from the egg sac and onto its ugly head. As the tiny ones landed, the monster turned and smiled at John, baring its teeth as if it were enjoying the thought that soon John and his team would be inundated with hungry little copies of itself.

From his perch, John quietly freaked out as the young monsters began eating the head of their still live parent. It let out a hideous howl as the group bit off large chunks of the top of its head, its brain, if that was what it was, and then the head was gone. The body slumped down onto the pile of food below it.

"Time to go!" John said loudly as he sliced the other side of his body free from the tree and dropped to the ground.

He wasted not a moment and ran to free the others. After he cut Emily free, she helped him, pulling each of the others away from the tree while he sliced through the thick substance that was holding them firmly in place.

Now dozens more of the creatures had hatched and they had eaten a large portion of both of the parent aliens. As John was finishing up cutting Eddie loose, he began to freak out. "Did you fuckin' see that? Those things are growing right before our eyes! I swear they take a bite to eat and then immediately grow an inch or two!" He was panicked and his eyes were wide as he dropped to the ground.

By then, the creatures had eaten through their parents and were starting on Mark. John figured he'd be unconscious after the thing had paralyzed him that way. He shrieked and screamed so horribly between rattled breaths and then, mercifully, lost consciousness. It was enough to strike panic in the team.

While John and Emily had been working on Eddie, the rest of the group had gathered just outside the clearing. Macy was talking about what they should do next, but all of the others were arguing about why her idea was not going to work. It was chaotic, and beginning to attract the attention of the creatures. When John and Emily finally joined them, John yelled over their argument, "Those fuckin' things are just about finished eating Mark! We need to GO!"

"Are we gonna try to stick together? Which way are we s'posed to go?" Marcus was looking around, confused.

"We need to get our backpacks. All of our shit is in them!" Eddie was walking around in a circle scratching his head.

"Does anyone have any idea where the plane is?" Macy asked.

They were all talking at once when Karla screamed. Everyone turned to see what was happening. Mark's entire body was gone, nothing but a pile of bloody bones remained on the ground. The little monsters that had devoured their parents and Mark were not so small anymore. They stood up on the ground below the remainder of the eggs, eating other hatchlings as they dropped to the ground, even fighting over them as they gorged themselves, and growing larger and larger with every bite.

Horrified, the group began to move in all directions away from the carnage when John glanced over his shoulder and took control of the situation, "Macy! Everybody! Follow me! We can make our plan when we get away from this shit. This way! RUN! Run like hell!"

Thirty Seven

The aliens scanned the clearing for something more to eat. Creatures of opportunity, the eighty or so hatchlings stood below the remaining eggs ready and waiting to catch and devour their smaller siblings as they dropped from above. The newly hatched beings seemed to be aware of their perilous position immediately. Several stronger ones used their larger hind legs to leap away from the carnage just as they exited their egg. Many were chased down, torn apart and eaten.

The young who were lucky enough to make their way to a place where there was still food began to consume whatever they found before turning on each other. The many rabbits, deer and other animals which had been collected were eaten quickly. The creatures that had moved away from the hatching young to eat, were already nearly two feet long. Suddenly one of them jumped into the air and landed on the clutch of remaining, un-hatched eggs and empty sacs. It crawled to the top of the cluster and began chewing on the thick fibrous strands that held it suspended.

Seconds later, the whole thing fell to the ground trapping two or three of the creatures beneath it. Immediately a crowd of ravenous monsters swarmed over the blob of writhing eggs, devouring them and each other with increasing ferocity eating right down to the unfortunate ones that had been trapped when the mass fell.

This was the hatch day finale. There was no more food to be found inside the clearing. The remaining creatures seemed to be satisfied enough for the moment and the cannibalism had subsided. It was time for them to work together to find more food.

The hatchlings looked at one another as though waiting for something to happen. One of them let out an ear-splitting shriek proclaiming itself as their leader and none seemed willing to challenge it. Heading off into the forest in the same direction as the team, the others followed in pursuit of their prey.

Thirty Eight

About two hundred yards from the clearing, the group stopped to plan what to do next. All of them were winded from running so far, and several were coughing. In that anxious moment, the first one who could speak was Raj.

"We left all of our gear back there, John." He stopped to catch his breath. "Now we have no food, no water, no shelter, and all we have is the knife you used to free us." Again he paused, his chest still heaving. "I don't see how we can make it out here for very long like this, do you?"

"Raj is right. We should circle back and get the gear." Macy was pacing back and forth to try to slow her pulse. "We won't survive in these woods more than a day or two without supplies. If nothing else, we need water."

"But what if those things come after us?" Karla challenged.

Eddie chimed in, "Yeah, those fucking things back there were growing as they ate! Did you guys see that? I'll bet some were already double in size by the time they ate Mark!"

"Yeah, I hear you. All of you..." John started but was cut off by Marcus. "Yeah, motherfucker! You hear, but did you see those things? They fuckin' ate their own parents and they just about finished off Mark in, like, less than two minutes! Man, they was just babies. What're we gonna do when they get even bigger? They could be fuckin' three feet long by now!"

Emily finally spoke up, "Listen, guys. If we stay here, those bastards are going to get us for sure, and if we run, we could run deep into the woods and die from exposure or starvation. I've seen those survival shows where they say to find the water and follow it because streams lead to creeks, creeks lead to rivers, and rivers always lead to civilization. But I don't see any water around here. Not a drop!"

"Or rivers drop off cliffs into waterfalls." John cut her short. "That's television. Who do you think is running the cameras while those people are 'surviving'? I've had some survival training in the military, and we are not going to just find some stream and follow it to get out of here. We need a better plan."

"Does anybody have a compass?" Sherri asked. "I have a friend with a cell phone that has an application that works just like a compass. Anybody have one like that?"

"Hell yeah!" Marcus said, pulling his phone from his pocket. "I got that one - if this bitch is still working!" He pushed the button on the phone to wake it from its sleep mode.

Everyone gathered around him hoping it would work. They waited as he thumbed through screen after screen of icons. As he was searching, they got a good view of the photo of a nude, large breasted blonde that he had loaded as the background graphic for his phone. She looked to be straight out of a Playboy centerfold. "Nice choice! Why don't we just call for help," Eddie suggested with an air of exasperation, "or at least use the navigation app."

Marcus was a bit embarrassed in front of this group who were now eyeing his photo of the perfect Queen. "'Cuz I don't have a signal, asshole!" He scrambled to click the icon and bring up the compass app. As it opened it seemed to freeze. "I have to shake this bitch to wake it up." He was vigorously shaking the phone.

"How 'bout we try it the old-fashioned way?" John suggested. "It just so happens that I have a small compass in my pocket here." He reached into one of the side pockets on his cargo pants and pulled out a small compass. He held it out flat against his palm. Everyone was straining to see where it would point when they let out a chorus of "Oh shit!"

The compass needle was spinning, slowing down, and then spinning in the opposite direction. "We must be in some kind of magnetic field," John said. He looked around as though checking for some sign of it. Sherri looked over at Marcus who was staring at his phone. The compass on his phone app was spinning in the same crazy way as John's, and he held it out for her to see.

"Watch out! Get down!" Suddenly Sherri was hearing a familiar voice warning her. The group had been so intent on looking to the phone, they forgot to keep watch for the creatures that were running silently through the woods and now were almost upon them.

Sherri had become so accustomed to the voices telling her what to do, she didn't question it. She simply dropped to her knees in compliance without a second thought. All eyes turned toward her as she hit the ground. Those who stood directly across from her were stunned when out of the stand of trees came one of the creatures. It was snarling and bearing a mouthful of jagged teeth when it launched itself into the air over Sherri's head.

The monster landed on Marcus pushing him forward into the middle of the group. John reached for his knife as everyone screamed, and the monster scrambled up Marcus' back to take a large bite from his neck. There was a sudden gush of blood as the crazed alien pulled back and ripped out a chunk of flesh. Tendon and muscle made a snapping sound as they tore apart.

Marcus staggered forward with a stunned look on his face while blood sprayed from the severed artery in an arc to the ground. John yelled for Emily to move behind him as the creature took a second bite, sending Marcus' head rolling into the pine needles. His decapitated body crumpled to the ground with the alien still on his back. Drops of blood spattered Sherri as she knelt frozen on the ground, screaming in terror. To the other side of Marcus, Raj wiped the splatter from his face as his knees began to go out from under him.

In shock, the rest of the group began to move like a slow surging wave. Shrieks from the distance signaled the oncoming horde of hungry alien babies. Sherri pushed herself up from the ground, With tears streaming down her cheeks, she followed them pulling Raj along with her. If she hadn't dragged him, his reaction to the horror they had just witnessed might have left him frozen where he stood.

John started to run with the others, then hesitated as they ran on without him. Roaring with rage, he turned back and met the monster head on. He plunged the blade of his knife between the black lifeless eyes of the creature. He twisted the blade as he pulled it out dripping with orange alien blood and shoved it in again.

The dying alien rolled off its victim's body and lay writhing in a pool of its own blood. John shook the slimy mess from his knife sheathing it, as he turned and ran to catch up with the others. He had no idea that behind him in the rotting leaves lay the blood-soaked compass and Marcus' shattered phone.

He found the others travelling slower than he had expected, bogged down trying to navigate thick brush and fallen trees. It was not long before he realized the gravity of the situation they faced. The long tangled vines that seemed to be growing everywhere were covered with sharp thorns all along their stems, and it hurt like hell to move them out of the way with their hands.

"Was Marcus dead for sure when you left him?" asked Raj. His brain had checked out of the horrific scene before his legs had failed him. If he had his senses about him he would have known the answer to his own question.

"You saw him. That fucking monster bit his head off! And that's what they'll do to us if we don't get moving. Does anybody see a branch or a loose piece of wood on the ground?" Perspiration soaking through to his shirt, John was breathing hard and bending over, resting his hands on his knees. "We need to find something to move the brush out of the way."

"Over there!" yelled Emily, pointing to a large branch that had fallen from a tree and become entangled in the vines. John forced his way through to the branch yelling back to the group, "Follow me!"

No one hesitated as they all fell in behind him. He reached the branch and cut it loose, breaking the smaller branches off and leaving two larger stubs that he could use like handles. He took hold of them and turned the thicker end of the branch facing into the tangled mess before him. As he readied himself, he shouted, "Eddie, Raj, get behind me. When I say push, push against my back."

They did as they were told and, when John said push, they began shoving him forward from behind. The way John was holding the branch parted the vines in front of him like a wedge as they forced their way through. It looked good for them to get through this until, with a loud snapping sound, John's makeshift handles broke off.

"Damn, this is bullshit!" He said getting a grip on the main part of the branch, "Fuckin' push! Failure is not an option! Not here, not now!"

Thirty Nine

The group came to a small clearing and stopped for a rest, pulling thorns from their skin and clothing. John pressed a strip of fabric from his shirt against the skin on his right arm to stop the bleeding from the cuts and scratches he had sustained from the brush. He pulled his shirt over his head without unbuttoning it, leaving the cotton t-shirt he wore underneath. Handing her his knife, he asked Emily to use his shirt and cut strips for anyone who needed them.

When she had finished, she handed back the knife and what was left of the shirt. John shook his head and took only the knife from her hands. "Hang onto that, Em. I think we're gonna need more bandages before long, and it probably won't get as dirty if you're holding it." He was still breathing hard as he spoke.

"I hate to say this, but we might need to split up... spread out the group." He looked over at what was left of the team deciding in his head which of them looked like survivors, and which of them looked more like an entrée at an alien buffet.

"What about safety in numbers, and all that shit?" asked Eddie.

"That's usually true, but if we break it up a bit they'll have a harder time picking a target. I'm not talking about going separate ways. I'm talking about spreading out and putting about ten feet or more between us. Maybe that will give us a wider field of vision, and make it easier for one of us to spot them when they're coming."

"Easy for you to say, John. You're the only one with a weapon!" Macy sounded pissed. "Who gets to walk next to you?"

"I might be the only one with a knife," John gestured, pointing at some baseball-sized rocks and fallen tree branches, "but there are weapons all around us. All we have to do is pick them up and use them." He tossed the strip of bloody shirt he had used on his arm aside and made eye contact with each one in the group.

"Those things bleed and die just like we do. I killed the one that killed Marcus. We can defend ourselves if we have to with sticks and rocks, but we have got to keep moving. If we stay ahead of them, they may get tired of chasing us." Even though frustrated, the group nodded their heads in agreement. No one else had any better plan, or any plan at all.

"I'll do whatever you say, John. We'd all be dead right now if you hadn't cut us free back there." Karla moved to stand beside him and put her hand on his shoulder.

Emily saw the game Karla was playing and stepped up as well, brushing Karla's hand away. "I think you, Eddie, Raj and Sherri should spread out on that side and John, Macy and me over there." She glared at Karla.

"But that isn't fair. What if we get in trouble, John? Macy's right, you have the knife! None of the rest of us has anything lethal for defense. That puts us a long way from some help if we need it," Eddie complained.

"Okay, listen. I hear ya, but we need to get a good lead on these things first. Then we'll stop to make you some weapons. I think we should keep our voices down too. We don't know how these things operate." He was scanning the forest all around them as he spoke.

"They might locate us by sound, or smell. They're aliens, and we have no idea how they operate. Come on, let's spread out now. We need to get going." He waved for them to move out in a line. He looked again back at the direction where they had been and didn't see anything, so they pressed on.

The alien creature now leading the pack remained unseen as it leapt onto a sturdy branch of a tree just two hundred yards or so behind them. It seemed to be waiting for the others to catch up. They had been delayed temporarily by eating the sibling creature that had been killed while attacking Marcus.

The team had positioned themselves a short distance apart as John had instructed them, and were walking at a steady pace, something short of a run. Ahead of them the forest was green with the moss that is so common in this region of the country. John thought he might actually enjoy spending some time backpacking up here for a week or so if he wasn't running for his life. In fact, aside from the investigative work he had planned for this trip, he had hoped for just that. Not a life or death encounter with bloodthirsty aliens.

After they had gone about fifty yards, they came upon an obvious trail. "Anybody have any suggestions which way to go? I don't want to be the one to make a decision for everyone, and then have to deal with a bunch of shit." John looked at them, waiting for a moment before suggesting, "Okay then. If nobody wants to take a chance, I say we go…"

"Right!" Emily blurted out, cutting him off. "We go right."

"Why do you think we should go right?" Raj asked. "I think we should go left."

"Then why didn't you speak up in the first place? I think we should go right because I'm sensing it's the way we should go, really." It looked as though Raj was going to back down since Emily seemed so sure.

Eddie looked at the two of them. "This is bullshit, John. Which way do we go? I trust your judgment."

"We go right." It was Macy who answered. "I have to believe that Emily would not have been so insistent if she didn't sense something. We go right. It's time we trust our instincts and our training."

"Training? Would that be our survival training, or our hand to hand combat training? I'm not quite sure what training you're referring to right now, Macy." Eddie glared at Macy, then looked back to John.

"Right it is, then." John confirmed and began walking down the trail. "Look, guys," he called back to them as he went. "We don't have too much more time before it's going to be dark. I don't know if those things hunt at night, but we will definitely be more vulnerable and could get really lost if we try to keep going in the dark. Keep your eyes open for a fairly flat, clear area where we can make some kind of camp."

"What if those things do hunt at night?" Sherri was coming up right behind him and grabbed hold of his arm. She squeezed hard, nearly panicked at the thought. "They caught up with us before... John! You saw what happened to Marcus. We saw how they paralyzed Mark. If they come up on us in the dark..."

"I know, Sherri." He patted her hand and gently pried her fingers from around his arm. "I am well aware of the risk. But in the dark it would be too easy to circle back and run right into those fuckers. Let's face it. If that happens, it's game over." He continued to scan the forest surrounding the trail as they walked.

Eddie moved up next to Sherri. "John's right. I've seen it in movies. People get lost like that even in broad daylight. They go walking along trying to mark their trail with strips of cloth or something. Then all of a sudden one of them notices that their surroundings look familiar just as somebody else finds a piece of the cloth!" He added, "I vote we camp, whatever it takes to find a safe place."

They continued to stumble down the trail, mostly in silence as each one kept watch to the best of their ability. The memory of the unspeakable horror of Marcus' death made them wary of any sound behind them and every movement in the trees kept them on the edge.

"Hey look!" Emily saw them first. The sun was low in the sky and the shadows made them difficult to make out, but there were tents, and some kind of campsite in a clearing on the other side of a stand of trees.

John moved to the front of the group and held out his arm to slow them. "Shhh.., we need to be quiet until we find out what we are looking at here. Look over there." He motioned toward one of the tents. There were gasps as the group realized that one of the tents was partially shredded. Stains from blood spray remained on the fabric hanging from the bent frame of another, and could be seen from where they stood.

John crept closer to get a better look with the others following close behind him in silence, some out of fear, and some out of shock. "Oh shit!" Emily couldn't help the sudden outburst as she realized that what she had thought was a branch beneath her foot was part of a human hand with three fingers still attached.

Feeling dizzy and sick to her stomach, she grabbed John's arm and pointed down at her discovery. Karla nearly screamed in terror at the gruesome sight, but Eddie took hold of her face and looked directly into her eyes, speaking in a low voice, "Don't look, baby." He continued talking to hold her attention while John stooped down to investigate.

Emily backed away and leaned against the nearest tree with her mouth still gaping. John stood and faced the group. "Now, this is what I'm talking about," he said quietly. "We need to be extremely cautious until we find out if the killer is still around. Eddie, you come with me, and everybody else move over closer to the trees. If anything happens to us, run like hell."

"Dude, I don't know about that," Eddie said, hesitating. "Maybe we should keep moving. There might be some place around here that hasn't been hit yet, maybe some people who are alive and can help."

John looked him in the eyes. "Don't be a little bitch right now, Eddie. Grow a pair and watch my back while I look for some kind of supplies. There's got to be something we can use, if not for shelter, maybe as a weapon. Tell you what... if we find another knife or something it's yours. Deal?"

Eddie thought for a second. "Okay, you lead. I'm right behind you."

John cautiously approached the campsite with Eddie so close behind him that he could almost hear his pounding heart beat. Step by step they drew closer to the camp while the sun slowly slipped behind the mountains. Even in the dim light, they could see the large amount of blood on the shredded tent. However, on closer inspection, they found it was dried and brown. Whatever happened here must have occurred some time ago.

Glancing around, they could detect no sign of life. Some of the other tents were intact but were leaning slightly as if someone had run into or out of them in a hurry. A few of the nylon stakes that had held them in place had pulled from the ground and lay where they fell.

John walked over to one of the damaged tents and slowly pulled back the flap that was unzipped and hanging over the opening. There was an odd screech as a startled raccoon scurried between his legs. He was almost sure he pissed his pants right then, but no. He just screamed like a little girl and followed it with a very manly, "Fuck me," as Eddie stood back and let the little looter hurry off into the nearby brush.

He waited to see if anything else was going to run out before he hit the side of the tent with his hand to encourage them to do so. When nothing happened, again he pulled back the flap. The smell of death was strong and he felt his stomach begin to churn.

Inside the tent was a mess. There were remains of a shredded sleeping bag, some scattered clothes, and a very large flashlight, which he immediately claimed. He tried the switch and there was light. It seemed that the batteries were still strong, and he felt a flash of relief that it still worked. Now he could get a better look at the scene inside the tent and it wasn't pretty. Scattered over the clothes and other items were partially decomposed bits of flesh. They were swarming with maggots and it was nearly impossible to identify any real body parts.

"What do you see, John? What's in there?" Eddie caught a whiff of the stench but was still standing watch just outside the tent. He could see the light through the fabric as John looked around.

"Man, you do not want to see this." He started to back out of the tent opening and bumped into Eddie. "Dude, some space?"

He switched off the flashlight as he stood up. "I don't think anyone survived what happened here." He looked around the outside of the tent in the fading orange glow of the sunset. "Let's see if there's anything else here we can use." He flashed the light twice toward the rest of the group still waiting near the trail and motioned for them to come over to the site.

Quickly, they joined John and Eddie as they began methodically searching the other tents and throughout the surrounding area. There were no backpacks at the site. The packs they did find appeared to have been dragged off into the woods and emptied of their contents in an obvious effort to get at the food. There was a small cooler and it had a couple of plastic bottles of spring water in it, but no food.

"Pass this around." John grabbed a bottle and handed the cooler to Eddie. To the rest of the group, he instructed, "Just a few small swallows. Make sure everyone gets a drink. And save the bottles. If we come across a source of water, we'll need something to fill."

He twisted off the plastic cap, took a couple of small swallows, and handed the bottle to Emily. He was watching her as she drank, and she looked at him for any sign that she should stop. When the bottle was nearly half finished he started to move toward her, and she lowered the bottle. "Come on, John! Did you really think I was going to drink it all, or what?"

He brushed her shoulder with his hand and smiled. "No, wild thing. I wasn't concerned about you overindulging. I was just worried about the intentions of that half-dollar-sized spider that was creeping up your shoulder."

Emily let out a squeal as she quickly handed him the bottle. She hopped around brushing off her shoulders and arms, feeling the chills creep up her spine at the thought of the uninvited hitchhiker. "You know, I never thought much about it before, but I hate the fucking forest."

"I'm thinking that spiders are the least of our worries," John answered. "Let's not forget what we've been through today." Protectively, he put his arm around her, and together they joined the others to continue searching the campsite. Five yards from the fire pit, John hit the jackpot. He let out a "Woo-Hoo!" as he reached for the hatchet, half its head buried in the ground.

From across the clearing, Eddie was walking toward John yelling, "The hatchet is mine!" John turned and shone the flashlight in Eddie's face and saw the look of victory in his face, "Damn, Eddie! I guess so. We did have a deal."

"That's right," Eddie replied with a huge shit-eating grin. "We did have a deal." He reached out for it as John unwillingly handed it over, handle first. Although John tried to hide his reluctance, he let out a mumbled warning saying, "Try not to cut your leg off, buddy, cuz I won't be carrying you outta here."

Turning to look at the rest of the group, John was ready to call it a night. He thought how strange it is that people can become distracted with a single purpose and forget about all that's happened to them that very day. He listened as the night settled around them realizing that while they had been searching the campsite, no one had stood guard.

Off into the woods, less than a hundred yards away, the creatures had slid into a dormant sleep-like state as the sun set over the forest. Darkness could be the enemy for humans, as the native creatures that hunted at night stirred from their rest. The alien monsters had their own problems with the dark and were paralyzed as the setting sun forced a loss of consciousness upon them regardless of where they were or who they were pursuing.

Had the team been aware of this weakness, the vicious killers could have been slaughtered while they slept. Survival would have been assured. If only they had known...

Forty

The ravaged camp didn't offer much in the way of protection, but John felt some would not make it much farther. There was no way to know how far away the aliens were now, but there had been no signs of them for quite some time. If they were still in pursuit they could come from any direction. John talked it over with the group and everyone agreed to camp here for the night and take turns keeping watch.

Absolute darkness would be upon them soon. The clouds that had dotted the sky earlier had now merged to block out any light from the moon. There would be no stars to wish upon tonight. The only way they could be aware of any threat would be to build a fire. They would huddle around it as their primitive ancestors had done for light and protection. They would have the comfort of that if nothing else.

When John asked for volunteers to help find some firewood, they argued that he was the only one with both a flashlight and a weapon. Macy suggested that the rest of them should stay together in the center of the camp where they could defend themselves if necessary. John was too mentally exhausted to push them, so he agreed to gather the wood. "Come on, Eddie. Bring your hatchet and help me get the fire going."

Whether the rest of the group was cooperative or not, John was determined to survive, with or without them. As the others began to rearrange the rocks and logs around the fire pit, Eddie gathered some sticks and piled them in the center of the fire pit. Ripping some dried grass out of the ground, he added it to the pile.

The key ring attached to his belt loop, it turned out, was actually a small flint and steel kit. As the others gathered around, Eddie knelt over the small pile of tinder he had gathered. Even John was curious and stopped to watch as Eddie made a motion with his hands sending a bright flash of sparks up into the night.

John smiled as he turned again to the task at hand. Eddie had surprised him, and he felt relief as he realized they would not have to rely on the near empty lighter he had found. There was plenty of dead wood laying around, and John used the flashlight only when necessary. Meanwhile, he could see the sparks continuing to float up from the campsite until finally he heard a cheer as the team began to clap. A small fire had sprung from the fire pit.

Eddie had done well and stayed close to the others who gathered around the growing fire. With John out collecting wood, he felt somewhat responsible for the team and held the hatchet firmly in his white knuckled fist. Each of the others was scanning the surrounding woods which somehow seemed darker and deeper as the flames grew higher.

Raj and the women were jittery and tensed up at every sound and crackle coming out of the black night. An occasional hoot or howl in the distance had them huddling closer together. As Eddie added increasingly larger pieces of wood to the fire, they were forced to back away from the growing heat, putting a few feet of space between them.

Eddie and John had agreed on a whistle system to verify their whereabouts while away from the group. Occasionally a whistle sounded from the woods, and Emily took comfort in knowing that John was safe and would be back sitting next to her soon.

Eddie's mind was racing even as he answered John with his own signature whistle. What would he do if John was attacked and eaten by those things? All he had was the hatchet he was holding. Would this be enough to fight them off if he had to? And if the things charged the campsite, would he and Karla be able to get away? Could he really run away if the others were being ripped apart? Could he leave them behind bleeding and screaming?

He looked over at Karla sitting there in the firelight, and remembered her beautiful naked body lying next to him the night before. Suddenly he was quite sure of the answer. "Yes," he said out loud while the others looked back at him quizzically.

"Yes what?" Emily asked, helping him find some larger pieces of wood to add to the fire.

"Nothing... I was just thinking out loud." He averted his eyes pretending to look off into the woods. His discomfort faded quickly as he reasoned that he probably wasn't the only one thinking about survival. He had no idea how right he was.

Macy was warming herself next to the fire that was growing in the rock lined pit. She was thinking about what they had seen today and what they might face come daylight or, God forbid, sometime later tonight in the darkness.

The creatures that had nearly torn them apart were not the same aliens who had abducted her all those years ago. The monsters that had traumatized her and her sister had seemed more like scientists, coldly conducting their experiments on humans, not devouring them like mindless beasts.

Her memories were quite clear when it came to the terror and pain she had experienced, but she could never remember those who had attended her as anything but hazy figures somehow void of any distinguishing features. The monsters she had encountered today were definitely of a different species and different in a really fucking bad way!

Macy contemplated what she would do if they were attacked again. She recalled an old saying, 'If you and a friend are being chased by a bear, don't worry about outrunning the bear. You only have to outrun your friend.' A wicked half-smile crossed her face as she considered her competition.

If they had to run, she figured John would be out in front. He seemed to be the most athletic member of the team, a survivor and tough as nails. His obvious passion for Emily was his weakness, however, and that alone would be enough to hold him back. If Emily was injured or fell behind for any reason, he would probably rush to save her.

Eddie, well, he was a sucker for Karla and would die defending her if need be. That left Sherri and Raj with no connection to anyone else here now that Marcus was gone. If one or both of them lagged behind, no one would bitch if they somehow happened to end up sacrificing themselves to slow the creatures down.

She knew it was a cold and calculating thought, so she kept it to herself. After all, this wasn't reality TV. This was not a threat concocted by some producer to drum up better ratings. There was no team building, no strategic alliances here. The only connections in this group were natural relationships. She doubted they wanted to play her way or make a plan for surviving that involved sacrificing a few players.

It didn't matter. She had decided before planning this trip that these people weren't all that important. Nothing else mattered but solving the mystery behind her sister's disappearance, and exacting revenge on their kidnappers.

Now she was determined to live. She realized there were not going to be any answers and surely no revenge. There was only a good chance that she and every person with her was going to die if they couldn't get out of here and get some kind of help.

Next to her, Raj sat staring at Karla's gorgeous breasts generously exposed by the low cut of her tight fitting t-shirt and shining like two delicious melons in the firelight. His mind drifted as he dreamed about what he had missed while saving his virginity for marriage. He had decided when he was a teenager that even if his friends were sneaking off to lose their virginity with the whores of his village, he would keep his body clean for his betrothed. What if he died now, a virgin, and never having fulfilled the desires he had saved?

Watching Eddie use his hatchet, he tried to put such thoughts out of his mind. He couldn't help but think about the hatchet he had taken out of his cart at the outdoor store, and how he had worried that he would be sorry he had done so. Well, he was sorry all right. If he had that hatchet right now, he could protect himself if some shit went down, and maybe even save Karla. He would have those huge tits rubbing against him out of gratitude. What a thought!

"It really sucked, what happened to Marcus I mean." Rubbing her arms to warm them, Sherri broke the silence.

"Yeah, but that's what saved us. I wish I could thank him," said Eddie. "If we had gotten to this camp before they caught up to us, maybe we could have fought them off." He eyed the business end of the hatchet turning it from side to side as he spoke.

Karla looked hard at Eddie. "I don't think so, Eddie. You saw how many of those things there were back at that clearing. You didn't find that hatchet right away, and they would have eaten us before we even had a chance to look around."

Eddie blushed a little. "Well, I think he might still be alive if we had made it this far."

John had just returned with a massive armload of firewood and caught the gist of the conversation. He dropped the load to the ground, saying, "Look, even if we had found this place, I don't know if we could have stopped those things without some kind of sacrifice. Old 'Ho-Tep' is with his ancestors now. They're probably laughing at us there in the spirit world. And here we are trying to figure out how to survive." He was now wearing a flannel shirt he had found in the brush. "Eddie, put that thing to some use and chop up some of these branches."

Eddie reached over and grabbed one of the large branches that John had dragged behind him and began chopping it into smaller pieces. John continued, "We need to have some kind of a plan for morning. If those fuckers are sleeping out there, they might wake before sunrise like the birds do."

He took one of the logs from the pile he had just dropped and laid it in the fire pit. It sizzled in the hot flames. Emily added a few more pieces of wood, as he sat down to rest.

"We got lucky tonight." John reached into his shirt and pulled out something that crackled like some kind of wrapper. "There was another backpack out there tangled in the brush. I found this shirt, a couple of energy bars and a bag of peanuts. They seem to be in pretty good shape. Anybody hungry?"

Forty One

"Hey, boss, I don't think this bitch is coming back." The well-dressed man pushed his sunglasses down and massaged the bridge of his nose with his thumb and forefinger. "I ain't seen nothin' here all day. How much longer do I have to sit here?"

The response came quick and loud from the man on the other end of the phone. He held the phone away from his ear as the yelling continued, then put it back against his face as he replied, "Sure, boss. As long as it takes." He pressed the button to sign off and let out a long sigh, banging his head against the head rest.

It had been three days since he and his partner had kicked in the door of that girl's apartment and popped some shots at her from the fire escape. She got away with some man in a car. He had taken a lot of shit for his mistake. Now he was being punished by being forced to sit here staked out in half-day shifts waiting for her to return.

It was unusual for anyone to abandon their apartment and all of their possessions like that. He had expected her to come by to pick up some clothes or something by now, but she had not returned. As far as he knew, she was never coming back.

He had been told that a couple of guys had been sent to stake out the airport. The perky bitch at the airport had told them the girl had probably taken off in some plane. It wasn't clear if Ms. Sparks was going to be gone for a day or a week. The boss clearly didn't give a shit. Until she returned home this was his hell, sitting on some boring street, bored out of his fucking mind, watching a boring apartment building.

The sound of his stomach growling mocked him for not taking time to pick up some food on his way here. It was too late for that now.

Forty Two

The energy bars and peanuts that John had found in the woods didn't even come close to taking the edge off the hungry growls from their stomachs. Divided equally, it had amounted to a small handful of food for each of them. As Emily distributed the snacks, John had reminded them, "This could be the last food we have for the next several days. It would be good to eat half of it now and save the rest for later."

Everyone stared back at him. How could they think of saving something for later when there wasn't even enough for now? John ate half of his ration, returned the rest to an empty wrapper and shoved it into his pocket. He noticed Emily doing the same. She smiled back at him as she realized he was watching. The rest of the team was slowly chewing the remains of their portion, savoring the flavor, and leaving nothing in reserve.

Eddie's fire building skills were well appreciated and a large campfire was still crackling in the pit while the group huddled around taking comfort from the glow. They seemed almost at ease. Perhaps the warmth of the fire and little bit of food had given them some small hope that they might actually survive this ordeal.

John understood that hope and faith were crucial to survival, but he also recognized that he was surrounded with some of the most self-absorbed, unrealistic and helpless people he had ever been involved with. It was, after all, a class from a community college not a crack military unit, and there was still an undercurrent of tension in the group.

"How long do you think it will take before they realize we're missing and start to search for us?" Eddie's question came like a shot out of the dark, breaking the silence.

"Is that all we are? Missing people? I think we have bigger fucking problems than that, jerk wad." Raj's words lashed out, but no one reacted. Everyone was fully aware of the deep shit they were in. No one felt any need to respond to Raj's outburst.

John had been mentally reviewing the events of the day, trying to recall anything that might be important to help them escape the trouble they might face tomorrow. "You know, Macy, I just thought about something from the alien death camp back there."

Macy took offense at the tone of his question. "Oh yeah? What's that, Mr. Hazard? The part where several of us pissed our pants?" She eyed the men and touched herself to draw attention to the fact that she had not.

"No, not at all, Dr. Renner," he sneered back at her. "It was something you said to that fucking alien while I was trying to cut myself free, remember? So I could save your ass?"

"And just what would that be? I don't remember doing much talking. We were all more concerned about dying." She backed down a little.

"Well, you didn't seem to be afraid. In fact, it sounded like you were asking that fucker about someone named... Mary, I think it was." He paused as she sat there glaring at him. "You said something about being taken to a ship? And I don't think you were referring to the Queen Mary. Is there something you would like to share with us, Dr. Renner?"

"Fuck you, John! You wouldn't understand." She put her finger in her mouth and dug something from between her teeth and spit it into the fire. Suddenly, she had shifted from college professor to a streetwise punk girl with an attitude. "You don't need to be all up in my business. You've got your own shit to worry about, Hazard."

"Oh, and what would that be? The fact that we are stranded in these woods with no food, aliens out to eat us, and little hope of a rescue? You're right. I do have my own shit to worry about!" He was getting a bit tired of her smartass comments.

"I guess that's true, what with all your focus on getting you and your... your girlfriend there out of this place without getting your asses eaten, and to hell with the rest of us." She was starting to panic a bit and wanted to keep him distracted. What did he know, anyway? She decided she'd better back off the attitude. She wasn't ready to spill her guts to these people.

"Well, Macy, you do know my background, right? I mean..."

She couldn't help herself as she cut him short. "Oh yeah, John, you were some big detective somewhere and then some crazy shit happened and you don't want to tell anybody the details and blah, blah, blah!" She smiled hoping she was getting the upper hand and distracting the others from the question he had posed earlier. Then John dropped the bomb.

"Yes, Macy. I was a good detective. And once you get the nose for it, you always got the nose for it, which is why I investigated you before I signed up for your course. And you know what I found, Macy? Anyone?" There was no response from the gallery of golden faces who were all waiting for John to give the answer.

"Fucking say it, asshole!" Spit shot out from Macy's mouth as she shouted.

"John, what the fuck is going on?" Emily asked.

He started out slowly. "Remember when Macy told us if we had any weapons, we might want to bring them for protection against the bears, wolves and such?" Heads were nodding.

"Well, when we were stuck to those trees earlier, Macy here was asking that alien fucker about her sister. If you haven't heard about Mary, she was Macy's twin sister. A sister who disappeared somewhere around the age of ten. Isn't that right, Dr. Renner?"

"Yeah, well, that doesn't mean shit! A lot of people go missing every day. Hell, right now, we are missing." Macy was trying to figure out how much he really knew and convince the others that he was way off base.

John set his chin in his hand for a moment and curled his finger up over his upper lip. He took a deep breath before continuing, "You know, I should have put two and two together a couple of weeks ago when you were talking to your assistant about making sure we had a guide who didn't mind if we killed some animals, vicious ones, if we had to. You weren't talking about your regular forest-type animals, were you, Macy?"

"What are you trying to say John? What is this?" Sherri asked.

"What I'm saying is that I think Macy was expecting to find aliens all along. I think her sister was taken by some fuckin' aliens like those when she was a kid. Right, Macy? And she was bringing us up here to help her look for them. This whole class field trip thing was just a ploy." He glared at Macy as he made his claim. "Wasn't it?"

"That's absurd, John. How could I have known anything like that?"

"Yeah really, John. That's a stretch, isn't it? I mean, isn't it?" Karla looked back and forth at the two of them.

"Right, and if that's a stretch, then there's no reason why she was asking that alien where her sister is, right?"

"Did you really say that?" Raj asked Macy in disbelief.

"At this point, do I have any real reason to make shit up?" John brushed a large bug off his pant leg as he spoke. "It was something like, 'Where the fuck is Mary?', or something like that."

"You moron, you don't even know what I said. I asked if it was the one who took h..." She stopped mid sentence and looked down at the fire as some of the others stood with their mouths open. "Shit!" She kicked at the dirt beneath her feet.

"So you did know, you fuckin' bitch!" Emily grabbed a thick piece of firewood and was standing to use it when John rose and put his hand out to stop her. "Out of my way, John. People died here! And I wouldn't even be here if it weren't for this... this...."

"Lyin' bitch?" John asked, finishing her sentence.

"Right, this fucking bitch who lied to all of us and brought us out here to die!" She still had the piece of wood in her hand, her arm cocked to use it.

"Now wait a sec, Em." John was still holding on to her arm. "You were in deep shit at home, remember? You weren't even going to come until those gang bangers came after you!" She closed her eyes and took a deep breath.

Emily's arm had begun to lower when Karla freaked, jumped forward, and grabbed the wood from Emily's hand. She raised her arm and brought it back to hit Macy in the side of the head. The impact landed hard enough that it sounded like the crack of a bat on a baseball.

"You fucking, stupid, ugly whore! I'll kill your ass!" She smacked Macy in the head again before John and Eddie caught hold of her arm on the third swing. Sherri sat with her arms wrapped around herself, rocking back and forth, and crying out, "No, no, no, no! Marcus died for this. And the pilot... No!"

Macy had fallen to her knees and there was a large gash in her forehead. Blood was running down the side of her face. "Ohhh, my head! Please, don't," she moaned holding a hand up to try to protect herself from the next impact.

"Serves you right, you stupid cow!" Raj was livid. "I could be at home with my parents right now where some nice girl is waiting to marry me. Now I'm gonna die out here in the woods like a stupid animal, part of some sick buffet for some fucking aliens! Fuck you very much!" He was hysterical now, walking around flailing his arms.

"Everybody please!" John raised his voice above the rest. "We're stuck here now. We need to figure this out and make a plan to survive. Focus on that." He hesitated a moment, then added, "While I get this bitch tied up." He walked over to the shredded tent and cut a piece of nylon rope from one of the bent poles. "I think we got us a decoy," he said as he came back to the fire.

Forty Three

By the light of the fire, the team was able to forage enough small pieces of wood from the immediate area to keep it going without taking any more chances out in the darkness. Occasionally a coyote could be heard howling in the distance. The discussion around the fire had turned from what to do with Macy to what to do at sunrise and back again to Macy. While they debated, the professor sat tied up in the firelight glaring at them like an escapee from an asylum.

"We could have finished our class with a trip to a haunted house, or some other known paranormal phenomenon," Raj pointed out. "But she had to bring us all here telling us it was some kind of graduation requirement when all the time she had her own selfish motives and was just using us to assist her."

When a vote was finally taken, they held Macy entirely responsible for their current predicament and, because of the danger they believed would come with the morning, they decided that John should lead them and Macy should bring up the rear. Her hands and feet would be sufficiently bound leaving enough slack in the rope to allow her to walk as though she was wearing leg shackles similar to convicts being transported.

That way if the aliens attacked again, Macy would be their first bite and that might give the rest of the team a enough time to escape. Of course, Macy was not too fond of the plan and voiced her opposition strongly as soon as it came up. "You can't do that to me, I'm a human being! I'm a woman! I'm an American citizen, I deserve a fair trial!" She pleaded.

To which John replied, "Shut the fuck up!"

What they needed now was to get some rest or they would not be able to get through the next day, especially if they had to run to keep ahead of the aliens.

"We should sleep in shifts, don't you think?" John suggested. "Two people at a time can stand watch while the others sleep."

"You and Emily can be the first to watch," Eddie said. "Then Raj and Sherri. Karla will take the last shift with me, okay?" He looked at Karla who was already heading to one of the tents that was still clean enough to sleep in. With about two hours watch for each pair, that would just about take them to dawn.

"Fine by me," said Emily.

"I want to be on the move before sunrise," John confirmed.

Macy had fallen asleep before the first watch even started. Her head injury and loss of blood allowed her body to give way to sleep even while sitting tied up. Her hair was matted with blood from Karla's attack and her face was pretty messed up. Sherri had applied some makeshift bandages to stop the bleeding, but other than that no one showed any real concern for her well-being other than to make sure she didn't die before sunrise.

While John and Emily took their positions, the others took shelter in the tent. They grumbled at each other as they packed themselves in like sardines, but ultimately the four of them were able to settle in. It wasn't long before someone inside the tent was snoring.

Macy was tied up tight to prevent her from running off or trying to hurt anyone during the night. They had covered her with some clothes they had found scattered on the ground around the campsite after she kept complaining about being cold. It wasn't that anyone cared if she was cold or not, they just couldn't take the complaining anymore.

Now that everyone else was quiet, John and Emily sat by the fire silently staring into the flames and watching the red hot coals glow. After some time Emily asked, "Do you think we have a chance of getting out of this alive, John?"

He wondered how honest he should be and let out a sigh. "I can't say that I've ever been in shit this deep before, but I'll tell you what, Em. I am not about to give up and die out here." He stirred the coals with a stick.

"What are we going to do about Macy?" She looked over at the woman slumped over on the ground.

"Don't you believe that she knew what she was getting us into when she brought us out here?" He inquired.

"I don't know John. When you stop and think about it, how could anybody have predicted this? It just doesn't make sense."

"Wouldn't you agree that even if she didn't know exactly what would happen, she still knew it was some dangerous shit we were walking into? I mean, she all but demanded that we bring some kind of a weapon."

"Maybe that was only because she was worried about bears and wolves. There are still dangerous animals like that out here, you know." Emily sounded compassionate.

From her place not far from the fire, Macy shifted her weight and perked her ears when she overheard this part of the conversation. She smiled, knowing that the blind compassion of someone like Emily or Sherri could possibly save her. Fools were often convenient pawns.

"So what are you trying to say, Em? You were the one who was going to beat her with that log, remember? Now you want to untie the bitch? Mark and Marcus are dead, ripped apart by those things, and she basically knew that it could happen. She considers us all to be expendable."

Macy started to turn her head to give them a pained look, maybe express regret for what had happened, and to say she was sorry, when Emily continued, "No, John, that's really not what I meant."

"Then what are you saying?"

"I agreed to our arrangement. We should make her walk at the back at the group so if those things come up on us, they'll tear into her first and give the rest of us time to run away."

"Hey! Good thinking, girl." He bumped her on the shoulder playfully. "That is the plan."

"Yeah, but maybe we should break her ankle or something just to make sure it works out that way." She looked at the smile spreading across John's face. "I'm serious!"

"Yeah, I know you are." He shook his head and threw a small pebble at Macy's back while trying to force the smile from his face.

As the pebble landed, Macy jerked in surprise. She resolved to get loose somehow and get away from this group. She'd need a few hours of sleep before she could even attempt it. She would try to make her getaway when one of the other couples were standing watch.

Forty Four

Aside from the howling coyotes, Raj and Sherri's watch was uneventful. Nothing moved in the forest, not even a breeze. Sherri knew that she'd hear the warning voices if anything was coming. She stirred the fire once in a while and watched the sparks float up to the sky.

Raj didn't feel much like making conversation. He just sat and made promises to the universe about what he'd do if they got out of here. Sherri could see his mouth moving and decided to leave him alone with his thoughts and prayers, if that's what they were. She couldn't help wondering how Shandre was doing. She hoped she could count on her Gran and Nana to get her home safe. "I'll be back with you as soon as I can, little man," she whispered to herself.

Eddie and Karla were awakened when it was time to take their watch. Karla started complaining about being hungry, cold, and tired. They sat down together next to the fire. It had burned low and Eddie threw another log and a couple of smaller branches on it. This caused a flare up and lit the clearing around them.

Karla snuggled up to Eddie, put her head on his shoulder and hugged herself while she fell asleep. Eddie, now nice and warm with her up against him, felt relaxed and it was only a matter of minutes before his eyes were closed too.

Macy had every intention of waking in the night to try to escape on her own, but she was lost in her nightmares of abduction and horror. Though she screamed in her dreams, she remained silent and very much asleep.

Just as the sun began to reach for the horizon, when the line between darkness and daylight began to blur, no one was awake as the deer came wandering into the far side of the campsite. Eddie and Karla were snuggled next to the smoldering ashes of the fire. They were laying on some material from one of the damaged tents, completely oblivious to anything happening around them.

The deer quietly grazed on some young grass and paid no attention to the three people sleeping out in the open. However, the rustling sounds coming from the tree line nearby got their attention and they lifted their heads. They stood like statues except for the twitching ears. After a moment, they resumed grazing in the dewy grass nearest the trees.

The next time there was a noise from the woods, the deer ignored it and continued to feed. There was no chance for them to react when the attack came. Two of the aliens came from the shadows and bounded toward them. Finally alert, the deer raised their heads and turned to run. Behind them were more than twenty monsters, and when they bolted, they ran directly into them.

Each animal fell in a showering spray of their own blood, and the carnage that followed was a hellish scene. The team woke to the screaming sounds of the terrified deer and crazed shrieks of the aliens. Eddie and Karla jumped to their feet just as John and Emily ran from the tent. Raj and Sherri were right behind them. John swerved past a tent he had dismantled during his watch and grabbed the four aluminum poles that had been supporting it. He tossed one each to Raj, Emily, Karla and Sherri and yelled "Run! Get out of here! I'll get Macy!"

"No! John!" Emily tried to call to him to leave the professor behind. When she saw him motion to her to get out of there, she ran for her life along with the others.

Macy was already struggling with her bonds, her eyes bugging out in fear. "Please, John! Oh my God! Don't leave me here." She pleaded with him as he was pulling his knife out from its sheath. With one movement, he cut the ropes that bound her ankles and lifted her to her feet. "You might be a lying bitch, Macy, but I'm gonna give you a chance to run for your life. Try not to lag too far behind." And with that, he broke into a sprint after the others.

He quickly began to close the gap between himself and the crew. The bizarre screaming, slurping, and bone cracking sounds of carnage at the campsite grew more and more distant as he ran. He could see them just ahead while Macy tried to keep up, her own thoughts rushing back to haunt her. All John had to do was run faster than her and she would be the one to be sacrificed. The distance between them was growing by the second.

Even with her feet unbound, it was difficult for her to run and keep her balance. She never realized how important the arms were when running and how they served to maintain a center of gravity. With her hands tied, she had to be cautious of every step while she ran. She wondered how much time she had before the deer would be completely consumed and the monsters resumed the hunt. It seemed she was about to find out.

About a hundred yards behind her a screeching howl cut through the quiet of the forest, and then a chorus of chilling sounds came from the blood drenched camp. The creatures were coming, and judging by the way they continued to grow as they ate, the deer had been a mere appetizer for their breakfast.

The noises of the monsters behind her were getting closer, and the pounding of her heart in her ears nearly drowned them out. It sounded as though more than fifty creatures were in pursuit, the same number of ravenous mouths screaming for more food. They were screaming for Macy's blood.

Forty Five

When John caught up to the group, they were standing at the edge of a very deep and narrow ravine. The distance across was only about thirty feet at that point. It was too far to jump and John could see why they were not moving forward. That sucker was really deep, maybe a hundred yards, with a lot of sharp rocks jutting out at the bottom.

"Now what, John?" Emily was looking at him anxiously. He turned, shouting, "Follow me!" and began running along the rim of the deep chasm. The group fell in behind him, trusting that he would have some kind of plan. The truth was, he had no plan. He was hoping for some kind of a break and he had no idea how they were going to cross.

Running along the edge over the rough terrain was nearly impossible. Outcroppings of rocks and fallen trees were scattered along the cliffs and the group was becoming quickly fatigued from climbing over them. Macy was trailing about fifty yards or more behind the group and was growing hoarse from yelling for them to wait. No one was paying attention. She really wanted to stop and somehow free her hands, but every second wasted put less distance between her and the creatures chasing her.

Up ahead, John noticed a tall, nearly dead pine leaning halfway over the gap. A lot of the dirt had washed away from the roots leaving them mostly exposed. He ran to get a better look at it and called to the others behind him, "Give me a hand with this tree. It looks like we could push it over and use it for a bridge!"

He began pushing against the trunk trying to rock it back and forth. As each person caught up, more hands pushed at the tree trunk and it was beginning to sway under the pressure. "Push!" Together they rocked back and forth against it. "Again!" The ground around the roots on their side began to rise a bit higher.

At last, the tree roots broke free, allowing the tree to fall over and land with a crash on the other side of the chasm. Some of the large branches cracked and broke off, spiraling down to the jagged rocks below. John grabbed the back of Raj's shirt as he started to scramble up on the fallen tree. "Not so fast, cowboy. Give it a few seconds to settle or you might get halfway across when it all lets go."

Raj stepped down and inspected the roots to see if they were shaking loose. The others stood and looked across to the other side waiting to see if the tree would stabilize. Karla was pacing back and forth. She was saying that she wasn't sure she could get across the makeshift bridge. "Sure you can, baby," Eddie assured her. "You sure as hell don't want to stay here and face what's coming."

They heard yelling from behind. "Somebody help me! I can't keep up! Please! Get these ropes off of my hands!" Macy was about thirty yards away and trying to climb over a large log. Just as she topped it, she fell face first into the dirt.

"That's the idea," Eddie said under his breath. "You lying bitch."

Macy managed to stand up and wipe her face on her sleeve. She glared at them and spit out some dirt that had gotten into her mouth as she began to stagger forward again in an awkward run. She got about three steps when Sherri gasped, "Oh my God!" She pointed to the trees behind Macy. They could see the creatures coming, darting from tree to tree in hot pursuit.

"Cross! Now!" John said forcefully. For a moment, they stood paralyzed, then Raj was up. The lower trunk of the tree was virtually free from branches, but spotted with slippery moss. Raj took very tentative steps as he tried to balance himself. He found his footing and slowly placed one foot in front of the other to inch his way across.

Eddie was already losing his patience and called out to him, "Drop to your knees and fucking crawl! You are gonna get us all killed!"

Raj did as he was told and managed to get across the log without slipping. He held onto some branches and scrambled up to the other side. "It's safe, come on!" He motioned for them, but Emily was already up on the log.

"All of the girls go next!" John directed them. The look of concern crossed her face as she turned her head and looked back at him. "I'll be all right," he promised. "Go now." She turned and began crawling. Before she reached the other side, Sherri was up and crawling. Karla was next and nearly fell to her death when Macy let out a blood curdling scream.

They could see her with her back to a tree. She was surrounded and waving a large branch, holding the monsters at bay with her hands still tied. "You motherfuckers get away from me! I'll gut you with this stick. Get the fuck back!"

She swung the branch at a couple of them to her left and they began backing up. They turned as if to leave when one of the creatures to her right shrieked and lunged at her. It was a coordinated attack, the ones that had pretended to retreat jumped into the air closing the gap and landing on her, knocking her off balance.

Eddie didn't stand around to see what would happen. He scrambled onto the log and crawled across without looking back. "John!" Emily was screaming for him to hurry. The others who had been watching the attack on Macy now realized that John was still standing on the other side. "John! Hurry! You can't help her!"

Macy's arm was lopped off just above the elbow by a single bite. She shrieked in agony as it dropped, then hung there swinging, suspended by the other arm. Her hands were still bound at the wrists. She had so much adrenalin pumping through her veins, at first she attempted to use her severed arm to swing at them and defend her self. Finally, she began to sway and slumped to the ground. The group of monsters swarmed on her and began to tear her apart.

John had stood mesmerized. He had only known Macy for the couple of months he had been in her class, but he had never seen anyone try so hard to fight their way out of such a dire situation against such overwhelming odds.

"John!" Emily's voice finally got through to him. She was jumping up and down on the bank on the other side of the ravine trying to get his attention and yelling at him, "Get your ass moving!" He started across the log, trying to run instead of crawling like the others. A short way out, the slippery moss under his foot sent him sprawling face first. "Oh shit!"

Forty Six

John scrambled to grab hold of something as he started to roll off the log. He managed to find a handhold on the stump of a branch sticking out from the trunk. He tightened his grip and pulled himself back up. He wasted no time crawling to the other side.

Now Emily, Raj and Sherri were crouching behind some of the tree branches. Emily leapt out to throw her arms around John as he was standing up. "Why didn't you guys run?" he asked. "Where's Eddie and Karla?" He looked around expecting to see them nearby.

"We didn't know which way we should go. They bolted in that direction." Raj said in a low voice, pointing off into the woods.

"I wasn't about to leave you, John." Emily hugged him again. "Shouldn't we push this log off to slow those things down?"

"I don't think the four of us can move it. Besides I have a better idea," said John. He pulled a lighter from his pocket and began setting fire to the dead pine needles. "I found this at the campsite last night." He lit as many branches he could before the lighter gave out. Some were beginning to burn, and he hoped the whole thing would be in flames soon.

"Come on!" He grabbed Emily's hand as he took off. He made a slight turn to the left and broke into a fast paced jog with the others following. "Eddie and Karla went the other way." Emily said between breaths as they ran.

"'We can't worry about them. They made their choice." He caught his breath and continued, "To tell ya the truth, I'm not sure we're headed in the right direction anyway." He paused to breathe again. "Eddie has his hatchet, so good luck to them and God help 'em. They may end up saving our asses, you know, if the monsters go after them instead of us." He kept his pace and grabbed Emily's hand as they jumped over some smaller, fallen trees.

Meanwhile Karla and Eddie were over a hundred yards away and headed in the opposite direction. They had come across some kind of a trail, and Eddie slowed to let Karla catch up. "Are you sure we should be going off by ourselves?" Karla asked as she ran up next to him.

"I figure we have the lead. Those things are behind them, and they are behind us. No matter which way they go, the bastards will follow them. I think we have a better chance on our own." Eddie slowed to a walk and was breathing hard. "I think we should follow this trail. I have a good feeling about it. Probably leads right into civilization."

"That's why I love you, Eddie. Sometimes you are so smart." She forced a smile and kissed him on the cheek. At least he is useful!

He was taken off guard and stopped to look at her. She had never said she loved him before, and it was the only thing he had wanted since he first met her. Now in the midst of this crisis, she had said it! Did she really mean it or was it the crisis that compelled her to say it? "Damn." He let it slip from his lips out loud. Why did she have to tell him under these conditions when their chances of survival were slim at best?

"What's wrong Eddie? Why'd you say that?" She looked out across the woods and then turned to see if anything was following behind them.

"Nothing, baby. I think I have a rock in my shoe, that's all." Eddie pulled off his shoe and shook it upside down to convince her that what he was saying was true. Then he dropped it on the ground and slid his foot back into it.

"Oh my God! What's that over there?" She pointed off into the woods at a dark shadow that seemed to be moving toward them. Eddie looked in the direction she was pointing. He wasn't quite sure what to look for. The shadows from the trees made it difficult to tell if something was moving toward them, or were his eyes just playing tricks on him?

"I can't make it out. It can't be one of those fucking monsters or we'd know it for sure, they make that shrieking noise when they're excited. Let's just get going." He began walking down the trail. Karla didn't follow. She stood there troubled by whatever it was that was moving their way. It appeared to be a very large animal with a vaguely familiar gait. Then it hit her.

"Eddie!" She was trying not to be too loud, but he hadn't heard her. She tried again a little louder. "Eddie, I think it's a bear!"

This time he stopped to look as Karla moved to try to hide behind a tree. "Oh shit!' Why did she have to be right? It was a fucking bear and it was headed right for them! Eddie felt a rush of panic. His mind was reeling. He tried to come up with some way out of this, but his brain was frozen.

"Run! No, wait!" He ran back to where Karla was clinging to the tree. He tried to remember everything he had ever seen on TV about bears. Wasn't there something about bears on those papers Macy had given them? Should they run?

By now the bear was nearly upon them. "Get behind me Karla!" Eddie said, taking a stance, holding the hatchet up preparing for what might be a charging wall of a bear. The damn thing looked bigger than anything he had seen on television, this one probably weighed eight hundred pounds.

The bear slowed and Eddie thought it just might turn and leave them alone after all. No! All of a sudden it reared up on its hind legs and tilted its head in a loud roaring growl. Long trails of drool flew from its jowls as it established its dominant position preparing to charge.

Eddie held his position gripping his hatchet with both hands like a baseball bat, ready to swing with every ounce of strength he could manage. Karla was whimpering behind him, or maybe she was praying.

Eddie slowly backed away, keeping his eyes riveted on the bear. He was afraid that he would be attacked and dragged from behind if he tried to run away. Visions of bear attacks he had seen on television and in movies flashed through his mind while he tried to figure out what to do.

As he backed up, he bumped into Karla who seemed frozen in place. He nudged her to move back. "Back up Karla," he whispered over his shoulder, "this fucker is not going away." The bear roared again, but Karla was not moving. Eddie had to push hard against her to get her to move.

Suddenly, the bear howled and jerked as though it had been struck from behind. Its arms flailed wildly while its head twisted around trying to reach its back. Karla shrunk back against the tree in a futile attempt to make herself invisible. She pressed her face against the rough bark and squeezed her eyes shut.

"John?" Eddie called, but it was not John who had come to the rescue. "What the hell?" Eddie's mouth gaped open as a clawed arm burst though the midsection of the bear. The giant bear dropped down on all fours and rolled violently to one side. Eddie realized they were in deep trouble. Two aliens were clinging to the bear's back, one chewing a mouthful of bear guts and the other biting off huge chunks of meat and swallowing them whole.

In all the excitement and confusion, they had somehow missed the possibility that the bear had been charging toward them because there were monsters chasing the bear. Now several more of the aliens piled on as the bear roared in pain and rage. It twisted its head back and grabbed one of them in its powerful jaws throwing it to one side. From behind the tree, Eddie got a view of raw bone and internal organs as hot blood gushed from the wounds.

The bear made a futile attempt to stand. It thrashed about for a moment before falling back, smashing the four bastards on its back as it fell. There was a cracking, squishing sound as they were crushed by its weight. Like a pack of wolves, more blood-spattered monsters were closing in from the side. Larger than the first who had attacked, they obviously had been feeding well that morning, and had now grown to nearly five feet tall.

Eddie was spellbound. By the time his brain registered Karla's scream, he had already wasted any chance he'd had to escape. "Stay back, you ugly motherfuckers!" He swung the hatchet back and forth at the three advancing aliens while four or five more were busily tearing into the bear.

From the encounter with the deer earlier that morning, Karla understood that when these monsters were busy devouring their catch, they were fully occupied and didn't chase after anything else until they were finished. The tiny gears in her brain were churning as she sized up the situation. If they turned and ran away now, neither of them would stand a chance. She had a choice then.

She could leave Eddie there and try to save herself, or she could stay and fight with him. Yes, Eddie had been good to her, but she knew that was because he was totally obsessed with her. Though his courageous attempt to protect her now was rather admirable, if they somehow got out of this, she would owe him a debt that she might never be able to repay. He would expect something in return – something that she really did not want to give to him, a real relationship or even marriage. Her mind was reeling with the possible price this rescue would demand from her.

"Fuck that!" She yelled out as she checked out Eddie's wide stance as he braced himself for an attack.

"What?" asked Eddie as he continued swinging the hatchet, afraid to turn his head to look at her. Steeling herself, she used the self-defense moves she had learned to manage unruly men at the club. Bringing her foot up in a swift arc with all of the force she could muster, she made a direct hit between Eddie's legs, kicking him squarely in the balls.

"Aarrrgh! What the fuck!" Eddie didn't go down immediately, so she kicked him again. This time he dropped the hatchet and went to his knees grabbing his groin and doubling over in agony. He turned to look at Karla searching her face for a reason for her betrayal.

Wasting no time, she snatched the hatchet off the ground. "Sorry baby," she said, and ran in the opposite direction as fast as her shapely legs could carry her. Behind her she could hear the shrieks of the creatures as they dove down on Eddie. He screamed his last words, "You fuckin' whore!" as thousands of razor sharp teeth ripped him to bloody shreds.

Karla was running for her life at top speed by then. The wheezing of her lungs as she gasped for breath was loud enough to block the sounds of Eddie screaming. Eddie… she had just lost her ticket to a new future… but would there even be a future for her

Eddie's screams had been silenced when she'd heard a loud cracking sound like a baseball bat slamming a ball to a home run. Karla shuddered when she thought that it might have been the sound of his skull being crushed. Could it have really been that loud or was she beginning to imagine things? Cold shivers of fear and dread crept up her spine propelling her on. It would not be long before the alien creatures would be after her, and fearing the same fate as Eddie, she ran like the wind.

Forty Seven

Karla had run for survival before. There had been many close calls to escape the trouble she had gotten herself into, and she had always managed to get away. But never had she faced anything that came close to the blood thirsty enemy behind her now. The trauma of the mayhem, or maybe just the physical exhaustion caused her mind to slip back in time as she ran blindly through the trees. It was as though she was searching for something... something she could apply to save herself once again when it was her turn to face the aliens... alone...

The bright rays of the mid-afternoon sun shone through the window of the plush hotel room as Karla dialed the number for room service. She felt pleased with herself after a long week of hustling stooges at the club. She had actually made enough cash in the last two days to catch a flight to Vegas for the weekend.

Sometimes these little trips were just a bit of rest and relaxation, and other times she would end up with some rich businessman, fresh from the tradeshow floor looking for a bit of fun before he returned home to his wife and kids. This had been one of those trips.

At this very moment, she was plotting to increase her stash of hard-earned cash. The fool in the bathroom was whistling as he washed himself in the sink. He had left the door partially open and she could see him, through the gap, with his pants around his ankles, scrubbing his balls with a washrag. As far as he knew, he was preparing for an afternoon of wild sex with this hot babe. She knew better.

Right about then there was a knock at the door and Karla walked across the floor dressed only in her black lacy lingerie, which made her look especially alluring. She opened the door and allowed the young man to push the cart into the room. He couldn't help but stare at her, slack-jawed, as she gave him a tip and ushered him out the door.

She worked quickly then as Phil, or Paul, or whatever that asshole's name was, finished cleaning up. From her bag, she pulled a small plastic zip-sealed baggie of white powder and poured it into one of the wine glasses on the cart. Lifting the bottle of wine from the chiller, she poured some into the glass, stirring the powder with her finger until it dissolved. She wiped her finger on the underside of the cloth that covered the cart, and poured a second glass of wine.

Just then, Phil, now she remembered his name, emerged from the bathroom. Except for the monogrammed hotel bathrobe, he was naked and obviously ready to go. It was time for her to take control of the situation.

"Let's have a couple of drinks, shall we? Before we get down and dirty." She handed him the drugged wine before holding her glass up for a toast. "Here's to everything you've ever fantasized, baby, right here, right now."

"I can drink to that," answered Phil, raising his eyebrows in an attempt to look sexy. He chugged down the entire glass of wine and made a face as he tasted the bitterness of the drug. "Wow, that is the worst wine I think I have had in a long time. Reminds me of some shit my dad used to make. It has a terrible aftertaste."

"I guess it's that cheap Vegas stuff. I think they take an empty bottle from some expensive well-aged wine and fill it up with cheap shit," she said in her most sultry voice. "Let's have one more."

She filled his glass again, but didn't top hers off because she had only drunk half of it on the toast. She raised the glass again. "To us!" She smiled as he clinked her glass against his.

"To us." He smiled back at her and chugged the second glass. "I guess it's like anything else. Once you get used to the taste, it's not too bad. That one tasted better."

When she finished her glass, she told him "I need to go freshen up. Why don't you sit out on the balcony and soak up a few rays while you wait. I'll only be a few minutes." She winked at him.

"Sure, sweet thing." He smiled and stroked her cheek before walking toward the sliding glass door.

As she walked to the bathroom, she stopped and pulled her lipstick from her bag, then went on in and locked the door behind her. She had placed her clothes carefully in the bag earlier and got dressed slowly to pass the time. After the requisite twenty minutes had passed, she checked herself in the mirror, wiped some stray lipstick from the corner of her mouth, and unlocked the door.

To her surprise, she found two men standing there in the room. One of them was standing in the doorway to the balcony and was talking to someone outside. The other was holding her large handbag and rifling through it.

"What the fuck! What are you doing?" she yelled when she realized what was happening.

"Here she is, guys! We can go now!" The guy closed the bag and put it under his arm. He stepped toward her, announcing, "I'm Officer Wilkins, and this is Officer Jackson, Vegas P.D." The other cop nodded and smiled. He stepped forward in her direction as the first cop continued, "And you, Missy, are under arrest. Please put your hands on top of your head."

Out of the corner of her eye, Karla noticed the door to the room standing slightly open with no one guarding it. She didn't think about it, she just reacted. Snatching her purse from under the cops arm, she ran out the door and bolted for the stairwell with the two cops in hot pursuit.

She ran then as if her life depended on it... She turned the corner and saw the red EXIT sign above the stairwell door. She was almost there ...

Ooomf! Karla stumbled and slammed to the ground. The fall snapped her back to reality like a slap from one of her abusive ex-boyfriends, and she quickly stood up and got going again. She was clutching the hatchet in her hand so tightly that her knuckles were turning white and her fingers were numb. The weight of it was slowing her down making it harder to keep her balance. There was no way in hell she was going to get rid of it to be able to run faster.

The small branches whipping into her face kept her ducking to avoid them when she could. Something was moving to her left, just past the trees ahead of her. Instinctively, she began to slow her pace. What was that? Her body did not react to what her mind was beginning to take in as she stumbled on past the tree that had been blocking her view.

Too late, she saw the three aliens just as they saw her, about a half second before the collision. They were moving toward her at least as fast as she was moving toward them when she slammed into the two in the lead. The impact sent them tumbling into a mound of moss and grass. She lost her grip on the hatchet and it flew a few yards beyond her reach.

The third creature had time to adjust and avoid the impact. It stood looking at all of them with a strange expression as though it were laughing at them.

Karla got to her knees, frantically looking for the hatchet that had been knocked from her hand. There it was, lying in the dirt about fifteen feet away. She made a mad scramble to retrieve it pushing the dead leaves and dirt before her while she crawled. As she was about to close her fingers on the handle, she turned to see if the monster had noticed what she was up to.

Time slowed as the alien sprang over the two others she had toppled. With its razor tooth rimmed jaws open wide, it seemed to be coming at her in slow motion. She instinctively held up her arm attempting to shield herself.

They say that when you are about to die, your whole life flashes before you, that you see all of the things you could have done better, and the opportunities you missed when they were presented. You remember the mistakes that caused you and others to suffer as the circuits fizzle and fade. Karla recalled this stupid concept. She instinctively squeezed her eyes shut. As the thing landed, she said the last words she would ever utter, "Oh Shit!" and realized what a load of crap it all was – everything about her entire life.

In a shower of crimson mist, the gruesome beast closed its jaws, jerked back and cleanly ripped off the top of her skull. The clean cut of its many sharp teeth exposed the hidden curves of her still intact eyeballs. Her lifeless body swayed, and then slumped forward to the ground. One of the other monsters slammed into her knocking her on her side, laying her out like a buffet for the ravenous aliens. They pounced, their teeth grinding her flesh into hamburger. In a few gore drenched minutes, she was gone.

Forty Eight

"How long do we have to run?... Are these things... going to keep chasing us forever?" Sherri hollered as she followed wheezing behind the others, trying not to trip while jumping over the logs and rocks beneath her feet. They had been running for some time now and everyone was fatigued.

Raj was just ahead of her, and although he realized that John and he could probably move faster if it were not for the women, he had a sudden rush of concern for Sherri. Even now, she remained strong and sweet. He knew her question wasn't meant to complain, but he could see she was growing tired. If there was anything he could do about it, he would make sure she made it out of this.

"I have no fuckin' idea... I figured our asses... would be overrun by now... Can anyone see... if anything is coming behind us?" John breathed hard between his words.

Raj turned his head to look behind them just as his foot hit a pile of leaves and sunk into a hole in the ground. He felt his ankle snap as he fell. "Aaarrrggghhh! Fuck!" he wailed. He felt as though he might pass out from the pain. Sherri turned back to help him. "Oh shit! Raj, what happened? John! Emily! Help!"

"Fuck! Oh my God, it hurts! Fuck! Sherri, help me get up. I can't stay here!" The excruciating pain was evident. Tears streamed down his face as he raised his hand for Sherri to help him. He tried using his other arm to push himself up.

Emily had heard the commotion behind her and turned to go back. The shadows made stripes through the trees making it difficult to distinguish what was happening from where she stood. "John, help! I think Raj is hurt!" she called out as John continued to run.

"Damn!" He knew there was no way to convince Emily to leave them, so he turned back. Together they ran to find Sherri trying to help Raj walk. His arm draped over her shoulders, she was straining to hold him up. "Shit! Arrrh! God it hurts so bad!" he groaned at every step he took.

Emily knelt down beside them trying to assess the extent of the injury. "I think it's broken, John. Do you think we could make some kind of stretcher? There's no way he can walk on that."

John was not happy and quickly weighed their options. "We'll have to leave him," he said somberly.

"No! You can't be serious, John. I think he broke his ankle, not his back! He'll be okay, won't you Raj?" Sherri pleaded.

"Don't you understand? He's already dead!" John barked at them shaking his head. He understood how they felt. This wasn't easy, but it didn't make sense for them all to die out of sympathy for one. He held out his hand to Emily. "Come on, he'll never make it. Even if we try to splint it or carry him, he'll slow us down enough for them to catch us."

Raj screamed in pain. "I'm not dead! I can walk! Look!" He pushed Sherri away and tried to take a step. Immediately he fell to the ground in agony.

"I'm sorry, Raj. I hate to sound like some kind of fuckin' beast, but there is no way you'll be able to run, and we can't carry you and still get away. We don't have time man, game over. We have to go." He squeezed Raj's shoulder and said again with more empathy, "I'm sorry, dude."

Emily protested, "John, we can't just fucking leave him. Those things will get him!" She was crying now and struck out at him as she spoke, narrowly missing his jaw with her hand.

"Em, we gotta buy some time." He put his hand on Raj's shoulder and looked into the tear-filled eyes of his injured classmate. "Raj, you can be a hero, right here right now, maybe save lives."

"What if I don't want to be a fuckin' hero, John?" Raj grabbed a handful of debris from the ground and threw it at John.

"We can't leave him!" Sherri was trying to lift Raj to his feet again, but there was no way he could put any weight on his ankle.

Emily had an idea and asked, "What if we cover him with some leaves and branches, you know, hide him?"

"Don't just leave me! Fucking please don't leave me." Raj was trying like hell to stand on his own. "Give me your belt, or wrap something around it!"

"Come on, Raj. A belt is not going to help a broken ankle." John was shaking his head.

Sherri looked at him sternly, "I thought you were a Marine, John. What about all of that 'hoorah' shit and 'no man left behind'? What about that?"

John matched her glare saying, "Listen, that shit is for the battlefield, and the saying is, No marine left behind, and Raj is no fuckin' marine!" He had a flash of remorse as he said it, and looked at Raj. "Sorry, buddy."

"Buddy? You gotta be shittin' me!"

"No Raj, I am not shittin' you." John turned to Sherri. "Look, I'll help you cover him up, but that's it. No carrying, no carving him a walking stick, no lean on my ass and we'll get through this together." He looked around to his right and left, then pointed at a low spot in the bank. "Get him over there! Then, Raj... Lay the fuck down!"

"But John…" he sputtered.

"Shut up and lay down over there, or I'll knock your ass out!" He pointed again.

Raj moaned as he crawled to where John had directed while Sherri tried to help him. He reached the low spot on the ground and lay back huddling himself into it. Sherri and Emily began gathering branches while John dropped to his knees and began digging up large handfuls of partially decomposed leaves and sandy dirt, throwing them on Raj.

"Cover your face now. We gotta get out of here, and I don't have the time to be careful about where I'm throwing this shit." John was scooping up large handfuls off the forest floor. "The rotting smell of this stuff might cover your scent."

Sherri and Emily brought quite a few branches and laid them over Raj while John brushed the dirt around to try to make it less obvious that something was hidden there. By the time they were finished, it was hard to tell there was anything there but a pile of dirt and branches.

"You're going to have to stay there for as long as you can, Raj. Try not to piss yourself, because if you do, it will give those fuckers something to smell. When we find our way out of this mess, we'll send somebody back for you. Okay?"

John knew that there was only a minute chance in hell that they would ever find him. If they were able to get out of this alive and sent a search party back, it was highly likely that wild animals, exposure to the elements or even the bastards they were running from would have already killed him.

"Sure," came a muffled response through the leaves.

"Bye Raj. Just do what John said, and you're gonna be okay. Stay still." Sherri looked for his hand or a shoulder or something she could touch to reassure him, but there was nothing left exposed. It gave her some small comfort that she couldn't see him as she stood beside Emily.

"Good luck, Raj." Emily said as she and Sherri turned and walked away. Like John, she figured they would never be able to find him again and a tear rolled down her cheek. She understood why they had to do this, but she hated that there wasn't a damn thing she could do about it. John was right, just as he had been all along, and she wasn't about to start doubting him now. Raj could never walk out with a broken ankle. If they had taken the time to build a stretcher or even tried to carry him, they wouldn't be able to get away.

They picked up their pace and caught up to John, who was quickly walking away. As the two of them came up beside him, he turned to them and asked, "Are you able to run some more? We need to regain our lead on those bastards. We lost a lot of our advantage helping Raj. I just hope it doesn't get us killed."

Still conflicted, Emily didn't feel like talking. She just nodded and began jogging out ahead. Sherri was trailing behind John silently praying for Raj. They ran for about a hundred yards before Sherri finally spoke up. "Hey, John... Emily..." and she slowed to a stop. "I can't leave him alone like that. I'm going back."

John stopped and snapped at Sherri, "Don't do it! If those things find you, you're dead. Raj is hidden, and he'll be okay."

"I'll cover myself too, John. They won't find us." She started to head back.

Emily heard the discussion and came back to intervene. She caught Sherri by the shoulder. "Look, Sherri, John is right. You don't have to go back."

"Yes, I do. I'm going, and don't bother arguing with me. Just go get us some help!" The tears were streaming down her face as she turned to run away.

John shook his head and took Emily by the hand. "Come on, Em. Let's go. Good luck, Sherri! We'll send somebody back when we get out of here." To find the bodies if there's anything left to find, he thought as he pulled Emily along behind him. Reluctantly, she followed.

Forty Nine

Raj lay very still as he sensed someone or something nearby. He was very well covered and outside sounds were quite muffled, yet he had the feeling he was not alone. His ankle was throbbing and it made no difference whether he moved or not, the pain was excruciating.

"Raj? I'm back." Sherri nearly passed him by as she looked for the mound they had made to cover him. This looked like the right spot and she patted the top of the mound to let him know she was there.

Raj jumped and the branches covering his head slid away enough that she could just make out his face. Muddy streaks across his face made it clear that he had been crying. "Why did you come back? You should have stayed with them." He was both surprised and dismayed.

"I just couldn't leave you like that, Raj. It didn't seem right." She tried to wipe the dirt from around his eyes without getting it in them. You hold still now, I'm going to cover you back up then I'm going to cover myself too." She put the branches back over his face and wedged them against each other so they would stay in place better than before.

"Okay, Raj. I'm going to go get some branches for myself. Hang in there, I'll be right back." She walked into the wooded area where she and Emily had found the other branches. Her mind wandered to thoughts of her son as she pulled some dead branches from a tree. She hoped she hadn't let him down by coming back here to stay with Raj. She wondered if anyone had yet reported them missing. If Shandre had heard about it on the news, she knew he'd be worried about her.

She had a good armload of sticks and branches, which she carried over and dropped on the ground next to Raj. "First load, Raj. One more and I'll be good to go." Raj mumbled something in response and she headed back into the nearby trees.

She was reaching to pull a low leafy branch from a tree when she saw a movement to her right and turned to look. "Oh God," she whispered out loud, "please let it be a rabbit or..." Then she saw them.

Four aliens were standing nearby, and they looked hungry. They always looked hungry, and they were even bigger now, standing nearly five feet tall. She was so startled, she let out a scream. For a moment, they just stood looking at her.

With no time to think, she had to decide what she should do. It was obvious that there was no way to hide herself now. If she ran after John and Emily, she would lead these bastards right to them. What should I do? Gran? Nana?

Finally she yelled out, "Raj, they're here! Don't move! I am going to draw them away from you. I'll circle back after I lose them." With that, she started running. She ran away from the trail and deeper into the trees as fast as she could with the monsters in hot pursuit.

She was not sure how she could be running with such speed and agility - she should be exhausted by now. They had been going hard at it all morning, but somehow with every step she found more energy. She was running for her life and she knew it. She was putting distance between herself and the creatures and she was running uphill!

She could see the top of the ridge and those snapping jaws were now far behind. If I can keep up this pace, I might be able to outrun them, she thought as she jumped over a fallen tree like an Olympic runner.

Meanwhile, Raj was lying as still as he could under the pile of debris. He could feel his heart pounding in his throat, and he was having trouble breathing with the branches covering him. He figured Sherri must have gotten away. If she hadn't, he should have been able to hear her screaming by now. There was no way to tell how far away she had gotten or if she was even still alive.

Raj tried to suppress the feelings of panic that were growing inside of him. What if I just can't hear anything under this mess? What if she let them get her to save me? He thought about it. She may have actually saved his life. She might be sacrificing herself for him right now, something he had never thought possible, never expected such a thing from anyone. He knew he didn't deserve this, and again the tears started to stream.

Calm down, Raj. Don't think about the worst that could happen. It's going to be okay. He fought the feeling of his throat closing off the way it does when someone is about to begin sobbing. His mind was racing but he tried to reassure himself and slow his mind to a state of calm.

He was so focused that he hadn't sensed the two aliens walking up to his hiding place. They stood directly above him staring down at the pile of leaves and dirt, flexing muscles as their skin was stretching with new growth. They raised their heads and smelled the air around them. Something was not right. They sensed that food was very close by, but nothing could be seen.

One looked at the other and tilted its head as if gesturing at the pile of leaves. Then, without a sound, they dove onto it together, clawing the branches and dirt away. Raj began screaming uncontrollably, and suddenly his bladder let go.

He felt the spreading warmth of his urine spreading across his lap as his mind snapped. He screamed again and again realizing full well that he was about to die.

A clawed hand hit his stomach with incredible force, ripping it wide open. Raj was frozen with fear and agony as he watched his small intestine being ripped out and thrown a few feet away. It landed with a wet 'slup' sound on a patch of pine needles. He passed out, and was spared the torture and butchery that ended his short life.

Sherri was coming up to the ridge and her heart was pounding in her temples, her lungs burned, and she could swear that she tasted blood in her mouth. For a moment, she thought she heard screaming, but she felt sure it could not be Raj because all four of those creatures were still behind her. No, she must be hearing things, she was sure of it. Maybe it was the shriek of a hawk. She reassured herself with that thought and kept on running.

Suddenly she topped the ridge and, breathless, stopped in her tracks as she nearly fell forward. This was no ridge, but a cliff, a very high cliff overlooking a large valley and a craggy, rocky drop below her. A river trailed through the center of the valley, the swift running water frothing white as it crashed against the rocks. There was nowhere to go. She looked to either side for an escape route but the brush was too thick to run through.

Sherri could hear the things coming. It was as though they were communicating with each other in scraping, shrieking sounds that made her blood run cold. They were getting closer and closer. She looked around on the ground nearby searching for something to use as a weapon. Maybe a branch, but then again, she realized that hadn't worked for Macy.

Maybe somehow she could manage to lure them to jump off the cliff. After that she could run back the way she had come, check on Raj, and hopefully meet back up with John and Emily. Scanning the area, she could find nothing but a few small sticks lying around. It was just her luck that this part of the trail was mostly dirt and rocks. Rocks, that was her only choice!

As she picked up a couple handfuls of medium sized rocks, she saw a pair of the creatures coming over the ridge right at her. She started throwing the rocks to try to slow them down. "Stop! Come any closer, and I'll kill you with my bare hands if I have to!" She said a quick prayer and threw one of the rocks narrowly missing the head of one of the aliens. Immediately, she threw the next missile and managed to hit the other one directly in the eye.

It roared as it reached up and clawed at its injured eye. Orange blood began to run down its neck. She had put out an eye!

"Yeah, come on! I'll put out both of your eyes and throw you off the cliff!" Defiantly she yelled, her voice faltering with false courage. The injured alien was obviously enraged, though somewhat stunned. Arms flailing, it continued to grab at its eye. The other one had slowed its advance. It seemed more cautious, seeing its partner's eye oozing blood. It shrieked at her and stood sizing her up.

The monsters were closer now, standing no more than ten feet away. They seemed to be weighing their attack strategy as they clicked and growled to communicate to each other.

Sherri stood clutching the remaining rocks in her hands. She had never been so frightened in her life, and she quaked to her very core. There was no place to run, no place to hide. In that desperate moment, she heard her Nana's voice.

"You've done well, child. Now there's nothing more we can do. You can't hold them back much longer." Her grandmother sounded calm and seemed close as always when she spoke. "Jump, honey. You have to jump."

"I can't survive that, Gran. There's no way!" she argued.

"We know honey, we know. Don't be afraid, we will be right here with you." The voice was soft and reassuring.

"I can't! Shandre is waiting for me to come home! Who will take care of him?" Sherri was crying as she continued to argue.

"Shandre's grandma loves him very much," Nana responded. "He'll be well taken care of, you'll see. Come on, honey. There are more of those monsters coming for you, and it will be a slow, painful way to go. Don't let them take you, child. I promise you won't feel a thing if you do as we say."

Gran added, "When I say jump, don't even think about it, just do it." Her voice was calming to Sherri.

"Okay, Gran, okay. I know you love me and have always watched out for me. I have to believe there is no other way. Just tell me when to jump."

The creatures suddenly broke free of their confusion. They closed ranks and began their attack with one leaning forward much farther than the other, turning its head and opening and closing it's jaws as if taunting her. They were so close now that Sherri gagged as she caught a whiff of their stench.

"Jump now!" and without hesitation, she jumped as far out over the edge of the cliff as she could. The creatures charged and jumped right at her. Since she had jumped just before them, they misjudged the distance and began to shriek as they fell with her over the edge of the cliff.

As they fell together, the seconds seemed like forever. The monsters writhed as their fate became apparent to them. They were clutching at the air, but Sherri felt at peace somehow. A smile appeared on her face as she crashed against the rocks and the aliens splattered next to her.

Back in the neighborhood, Shandre had been begging his grandmother to let him ride his bike on the sidewalk. After his relentless tirade, she had finally agreed — if he promised to wear his helmet and stay off the street.

She helped him unlock the chain on his bike and carry it down off the porch. "Okay, Shandre. Stay on the sidewalk right here in front of the house until I get back out here."

"Okay." He put his helmet on and fastened the chin strap that held it in place, then jumped on the seat and began riding down the sidewalk toward the corner.

She'd made a nice glass of iced tea and left it on the kitchen counter while she helped Shandre with his bike. He was a good boy and she figured he would be okay by himself for a few minutes.

Shandre loved the feeling of freedom he had when riding his bike. For a boy his age, this was as good as it got. He had promised to stay in front of the house, but when he reached the corner, he forgot all about it and made the turn. A few houses down the road, his grandmother's words came back to him and he swung wide up into someone's lawn and made a U-turn. He pedaled back toward the corner hoping to get back home before his grandma came back out.

As he came up to the turn, he thought he saw some money blowing across the street. It could be a dollar bill, or maybe even more. It made his heart race thinking about what he could do with that money. Quickly he calculated his options. Could he ride out there, grab it, and get back on the sidewalk before his grandma could see him? Or should he let that money just blow down the street for someone else to pick up?

It didn't make sense to leave it. He would just have to be quick and then explain to his grandma that the money was on the sidewalk. That's right, it was on the sidewalk and all he had to do was pick it up! He had one wheel over the curb when he heard a voice yell, "Shandre! You stop right there!" Was that his grandmother?

"Dang!" He was gonna be in trouble now. Immediately, he rolled to a stop just before his back tire came off the curb and onto the street. No sooner had he stopped than a large cement truck came around the corner and blew past. The driver was blowing the horn and driving faster than any vehicle should have been going through this neighborhood.

Shandre could feel the stiff wind as it ruffled his shirt. He looked around for his grandmother. He knew he was in for a tongue lashing. He sheepishly looked up to face her, but she wasn't there.

If it wasn't her, then who was it? Maybe his mom was back! She must have come home from her trip earlier than she expected. A big smile spread across his face until he realized that now he was really going to catch it for almost riding into the street. But no one was there. Shandre didn't see his mother, or his grandmother.

"Shandre, baby, don't be afraid. Something has happened, and I won't be coming home." This time he was sure that it was his mother. He could feel her love radiating through his body like he did when she was hugging on him. "Honey, I want you to know that I'll always be with you. I'm with my Nana and my Gran, and we will all be here to protect you. Now get on home, honey, and stay off the street!"

Shandre was confused and he looked around. "Mama?" He took off his helmet. What did she mean? She wasn't coming home? He felt confused, but the voice was gone.

A wisp of perfume, the kind she loved to wear, drifted by in the soft breeze. He hung his helmet on the handlebars of his bike and pushed it in the direction of his grandmother's house. She was there, frantically calling for him.

Fifty

Emily was exhausted. Her mouth was parched and her body was screaming for rest. They had not had a drop of water since early in the morning, but they didn't dare to stop knowing the aliens were still in pursuit.

John was determined to get Emily back home safely. He would lay down his life to do so, and this came as a surprise to him. In just a few short days, he had grown more than fond of her. She was so different from every other woman he had ever met. It seemed that protecting her might involve standing between her and the gnashing jaws of certain death.

For all he knew, the rest of the team had already been eaten. He couldn't worry about it right now. Instead, he stayed focused and alert, prepared to kill or be killed, if they were attacked.

The well-travelled trail they were on appeared to be headed down to the river below, and John was thinking if they made it there, they would be close to finding their way out. "You see that river... down there... Em? I'm thinking... it might lead us... back... to civilization."

"But you said... we shouldn't follow the water... I'm confused," she commented between breaths.

He was short of breath too, and speaking was difficult. "I know... but I was talking about streams. Large rivers like that... almost always end up passing through a city or town." It was likely the river could lead them to some inhabited area, reservoir or at least a ranger station. Hope seemed within reach, and he caught his second wind.

"I hope so… I can't go… much farther… My chest… is going to burst!… At least… there's water!" Emily's voice was raspy, and she was having trouble getting her words out.

Suddenly, out of the trees came a howling shriek. John felt his heart drop into his shoes, and he paused to look back. About a hundred or so yards behind them, he could see more than a dozen creatures coming through the tree line. They must have stumbled across some kind of animal because they were beginning to circle something intently. From his vantage point it was hard to tell what it might be.

Several of them began fighting over something, rolling on the ground. Perhaps they were eating one of their own. John could only hope they had resorted to such cannibalism.

"We gotta push it, Em! We might gain a little time cuz it looks like they are turning on each other, but those fuckers are almost on us now at that distance. I just can't tell." He was still scanning the wooded area up the hill from them and stopped to take a large gulp of air. "We gotta make it to the river!" He turned to her then and found that he had been talking to himself. He wasted no time catching up to her.

Emily hadn't stopped to see what was behind them. She was desperate for a drink and stayed focused on the water ahead. She was steadily jogging her way to the river. When John reached her side, he could see how tired she was. Her face was red with exhaustion.

"They stopped fighting amongst themselves and they're gaining on us! We gotta get out of here! Come on, Em, let's get to the water." If she could just keep going, they still had a chance to survive. "They're catching up!" he repeated.

She was too winded to respond but gave him a look that seemed to say, 'As if I'm not trying!' and he reached for her hand and kept running.

"Just... tell me... you have... a plan!" He could hear her wheezing with every breath. Without hesitation, he squeezed her hand and nodded affirmative, knowing full well he had no plan.

They forced themselves to pick up the pace, which was much easier now that they were running downhill toward the river. As they stumble down the bank, it wasn't long before Emily was kneeling down at water's edge guzzling the water she had cupped in her hands.

"I'm going to see which way is best. You keep an eye out for those things behind us!" John set about looking for some place to cross to the other side while Emily watched the hill behind them, scanning for the oncoming aliens.

It was hopeless. There was no way to cross the river and John felt sure that running down the bank would not get them away from the aliens far enough or fast enough. He picked up some rocks and thought about throwing them at the bastards. Tossing one up at the hill to see how far he could reach, he doubted he could hold them off for very long. He was tired as hell.

He searched the brush a short way downriver, looking for a tree branch to use as a club. "Yes, there is a God!" he called as his eyes landed on their salvation. "Canoe! Emily!" He ran to the aluminum canoe resting upside down on top of the paddles that stuck out from underneath. "Give me a hand, Em!"

Emily ran to him as he was grabbing the underside of the canoe. She helped him roll it over and flip it upright. Brushing aside the spider webs, they made a cursory examination of the inside of the canoe and found it to be in excellent condition. Even the paddles looked fairly new and unused.

"How do you think this got here?" she asked breathlessly tucking the paddles up under one arm. "You think this thing belonged to somebody at that campsite?"

"I have no idea, but I don't care! Let's get it in the water!" John said, already dragging it to the edge. "Pull!"

Both of them were exhausted and weak. They hadn't eaten except for a few morsels back at the camp. Emily strained to manage the paddles and help John pull the canoe, so she tossed them into the boat and pulled as hard as she could. Her hand slipped as her foot lost traction sending her nose first into the sandy gravel. "Damn!" she exclaimed as she stood back up and got another grip.

"You all right?" John kept pulling and waded into the fast running water until the canoe was half way in. He went to help Emily steady the canoe as she climbed in.

A quick look over his shoulder let him know the fuckers were coming over the last hump of the downhill grade. They were staggered in a line that stretched out about twenty feet wide. They had to go now! He gave the canoe a hard shove and jumped in as it glided out onto the river and was caught in the current. Quickly, he steadied himself and sat down as Emily handed him a paddle.

John had only been in a canoe once before so he only had his instincts to go by. Steering was definitely more difficult than he remembered, but he'd never tried it in the rapid water of a river. His previous experience was on a private lake with no wind, no waves, and no current tossing him around. That was recreational. This was survival.

The creatures at the front of the pack were at the shore now, soon to be followed by the others. They seemed to be in a frenzy as they pursued the canoe, running down the along the rocky shore. As they caught up even with the boat, at least five of them charged into the water at full speed.

Even in the heart pounding heat of the moment, John found it to be interesting, satisfying, and hilarious at the same time to watch them trip and sink like rocks. Even though the water wasn't over their heads they flailed and drowned, not knowing they just had to stand up to save themselves.

Obviously, they had no concept of water, and no ability to swim. He could see their mouths gasping and the water filling them as their heads went under. Flailing arms tried without effect to claw their way back up to the surface as the swift current swept them downstream.

"What's a matter, bitches?" John yelled at them. "Forget to wear your floaties?" Two more jumped in and sank straight to the bottom as the canoe floated away.

All of a sudden the others stopped as if they had learned from their lost siblings' mistakes. One closest to the water let out a shrieking squawk, and the others turned as if in attention. Now, instead of charging into the river, they began following their prey along the shore once more.

"What are they doing, John?" Emily's newly found hope reverted again to fright. "Do you think they are smart enough to figure out..."

"I don't know," John interrupted. "They must be intelligent to have gotten here in that ship. They created and used whatever that thing was that ripped our plane from the sky. I think right now they are in a crazed frenzy from their hunger and we are the only food on the menu!" He used his paddle to guide the canoe as the current carried them on.

He watched as the creatures followed along the bank of the river. He was hoping they would give up and turn back. There was a bump as the bottom of the canoe scraped across the top of a rock just below the surface, and John turned his attention back to the river. "I only counted about eight of them. Do you see any more?"

"No," Emily was holding her hand above her eyes and squinting to get a better view. "Those eight are all I see."

"Are there any more coming down from the woods?" John didn't want to risk a spill in the river by looking for himself.

"No, I'm pretty sure there are only those eight."

The monsters seemed to be communicating to each other, though the noise of the river and the bumping of their paddles against the canoe were enough to drown out the sounds they were making. The river was carrying them around a bend and they seemed to be headed into some kind of a valley. The creatures followed along, continuing to climb along the steeper banks while constantly monitoring the progress of the canoe.

The water was faster here and the aliens scrambled around trees and brush trying to keep up, but remained relentless in their pursuit. Perhaps they were waiting for an opportunity to strike. Maybe they were waiting for the food in the boat to become tired and pull up on shore. John was getting worried that they might not be able to travel fast enough to escape. "I need you to paddle, Em!" he called up to her.

"What if we just paddle into shore on the other side of the river and head into those woods?" Emily pointed at the shoreline where the river bank was more level than the one where the aliens continued their chase.

"We could do that, but I'm afraid those things will figure out how to cross. I'm not sure if we have the strength to run much farther if they do. It seems a little too narrow here to try it." He worked his paddle to maintain their position in the center of the river.

"We need some kind of a plan, John. They seem to be up to something. One is running ahead and moving around in circles like it's trying to figure out the best way to get to us." She shifted uncomfortably in her seat as she tried to keep watch on the cliff above them.

Emily planned ahead, envisioning a worst case scenario to figure out how she might react if somehow those monsters got into the boat. Just ahead of them, one launched itself into the air to do just that. It arced out over the water in line with the canoe.

Reflexively, John brought his paddle up from the water to try to deflect it should it successively manage the attack. Emily reacted quickly and shoved her paddle into the water to create some drag to try to slow the canoe just enough to make it miss its mark.

They watched holding their breath as the creature overshot its target and landed in the river. Water splashed about three feet up in front of the canoe and right into Emily's lap. She squealed as the cold water hit her and turned her head around to look at John, hoping he was flashing a triumphant smile, but he looked terrified.

"Behind you!" he yelled.

There was the clawed hand of the alien hooked over the front of the canoe. As it attempted to pull itself up, the bow dipped from its weight. Unwavering, she lifted her paddle in a single motion, splashing water into the air as she swung. With a loud crack, she brought the paddle down and hit the monster in the side of its head. Spot on, it was a world class swing. A large gash opened across its face splitting its eye on impact and covering the end of the paddle with yellow and orange goo.

The canoe was rocking and Emily was losing her balance as she drew back and swung again. Another slash opened above its mouth spraying sticky orange blood at her as the creature lost its grip and slid into the water. There was a thumping sound as it passed under the canoe. John could feel it in his feet as they ran it over, and when he looked back, he watched the wounded creature thrashing around as it sank into the grayness of the water.

"Ho-ly shit! That's my girl!" John shouted and began paddling again reinvigorated. The river widened as they rounded another bend. John maneuvered the canoe to stay as close to the lower bank and as far away from their pursuers as possible.

"Those fuckin' things never give up, do they?" he commented as they continued to float downstream.

"They must be starving all the time. It's probably been a while since they've eaten." With that, she started paddling to help John keep the canoe on course.

"I think they ate one of their own just before they headed down the hill toward us. They can't be starving already, can they?" John twisted his paddle in the water to keep them floating in the right direction. "Is it my imagination or are we moving faster now?"

"Ahem, could it be because one of us is paddling? Hmm?" She was being a smartass and he loved that about her.

"Oh really." He made a face at her. "I don't think that's the only reason. Do you hear that?"

"I don't hear any…" and then she did hear it. The sound of rushing water was growing louder with every passing moment.

The river took them around the next bend, and they were soon faced with the terrifying truth.

Fifty One

Macy's assistant had followed instructions upon hearing that the flight had gone missing. She had made calls to the people on the emergency forms. Still, she felt useless where she was, so she had gone home, packed a few things and hit the road for Seattle. The least she could do was to go there and help in the search. Without Macy, there was no department, and without the department, no job for her. She didn't care too much for Macy – her career was on the line.

A search team had been assembled out of the small community airport near Seattle. It consisted of two small civilian aircraft and a helicopter that was leased to the forestry service by a company that used it to inspect high voltage electrical lines.

Yesterday, a pilot had volunteered to assist in the search and had flown for about six hours before packing it in. Today, the helicopter had been hired by a lone citizen for the same purpose, but the guy was searching for an old friend who had been lost with the flight. That friend was John Hazard.

Now they were well into the second day of searching along the flight plan filed by Mark Woo. The two small plane pilots had given up the search for the day and headed back to base. They had logged about eight hours in the air, and were tired. Even though they knew there were lives at stake, they were merely volunteers. Not only had they sacrificed their time, but they had sacrificed their fuel and wear and tear on their planes. In these tough times, neither could afford to continue any longer without compensation. They would take it up with the head of the local FAA office first thing in the morning.

The helicopter team, on the other hand, had started the search well before dawn and the pilot was in his tenth hour. The chopper was carrying Frank DeMint, a friend of John's from his military days.

Frank had been contacted by Macy's assistant who had used emergency information that had been collected weeks earlier. The simple release form was meant to list family, but John had filled in the blank with Frank's name. After all, if some shit went down, would his younger pot-smoking brother even bother to take a minute to care?

As soon as Frank had heard that the plane had gone off the radar, and John was missing somewhere in the forest, he gathered up his gear and hightailed it to Seattle. He had arrived at midnight on the very first day of the search. Once there, he used some of his connections to grab a seat on the search chopper. Now here he was, hanging out the side door with his hi-power binoculars, scanning the land below, looking for his friend.

"Frank, how much longer are we gonna stay out here today?" He heard the pilot's voice through the headset. "This shit is wearing me out."

"I want to stay out till just after sunset if we have the fuel. Every minute is critical if there's any injury, and I don't want to miss an inch of this place if John is alive out there." He lifted the binoculars back up to his eyes. "Hey, you say we've covered the whole flight path. How wide was the sweep this time?"

"We've been crisscrossing at about five to seven miles out."

"Let's go to fifteen. I have a gut feeling that the pilot didn't follow his own flight plan. I know you aren't getting much for this gig, so I promise I'll make it up to you when we find 'em. Trust me."

"And if we don't find them?" The pilot shot a concerned look back at him.

"Dead or alive we're gonna find that bastard, and that's just the way it is! No Marine left behind!" he barked into the mike.

"You got it, sir!" and the pilot banked sharply to extend their range.

"Where the fuck are you, John?" Frank muttered to himself as he resumed scanning the endless green canopy below.

Fifty Two

John and Emily were sizing up the rapids ahead of them. They were still maneuvering through the slightly choppy water, but farther out, they were definitely headed into trouble. To one side of the river bank, there were a half dozen creatures doggedly running along beside them. They remained trained on the canoe, even as they stumbled along the rocky embankment.

On the other side of the river, where just moments before had been a flat sandy beach, was now a steep rocky cliff. This would allow them no opportunity to get the canoe out of the river and onto the shoreline. They were going to have to ride out the rapids.

"I'm going to steer us through this, Em. Sit on the floor and hold on. It will help with our center of gravity and maybe keep us from tipping over." He dug his paddle into the water, testing his steering acumen in preparation for rapid water.

"John, I just want to say… if anything happens to… well, I just want to say thank you… for saving me and keeping me safe the past few days… I.."

"It's okay, Em. It was worth it. Every bullet, every crazy minute and every raging alien… I'd do it all over again." He smiled because for the first time in his life, he really meant those words.

The water was lapping hard against the side of the canoe now and they had gained speed as they hit the first leg of the rapids. A series of loud, roaring shrieks came from the creatures who were being forced to climb yet higher by the rising, rocky river bank.

"I think they're getting a little tired of how much work it is to chase us." John had to shout now that the water was beginning to churn up. "Serves the bastards right! I hope they bust a gut trying to keep up." John maneuvered to the right, narrowly missing a boulder that jutted up in front of them. "Damn, that was close!"

"They seem really pissed!" Water splashed over the side of the canoe as Emily shouted back to John. "Just pay attention to the river. I'll keep an eye on those fuckers over there!" She shifted sideways so she could see them better. She was glad to ignore the shit storm they were now headed into.

At one time, she probably would have closed her eyes and hoped for the best in a situation like this, but those things on the shore forced her to keep watch. Moreover, all of the things that had happened to them in the past few days had strengthened her, hardened her into more of a badass than she had ever thought she could be.

The canoe bobbled in the rapids as they were carried along. Water splashed up over the sides again getting her wet and forming a small pool where she sat on the floor.

"Keep that paddle ready, Em. I might need some help with this. Just don't get back up on that seat." John steered hard to the left to keep the canoe in the deeper flow of water and ended up going farther than he wanted. They brushed past a rock that was just below the waterline.

"Shit!" The impact made a loud thud and then a scraping noise as the side of the canoe rubbed its entire length against the rock. The canoe began to turn sideways while he struggled to correct their position. The wider profile must have seemed like an invitation to the predators on the cliff as another one launched itself like a snarling missile with snapping jaws.

"John!" Emily's warning gave him just enough time to see the creature falling toward them while the vessel continued to spin in the water. At the last second he was able to hold them steady, but they were turned around completely and beginning to drift backwards.

The alien's trajectory remained true as John raised his paddle to try somehow to deflect it. His movements seemed sluggish and poorly timed and his stomach was in his throat as he braced himself for the impact. He brought the paddle up from his right and the delay caused by the drag of the water allowed the monster a chance to be slightly ahead of his swing.

When the paddle connected, the force behind the strike boosted it past the canoe slamming it into a large boulder about two yards away. There was a cracking sound as its skull collided against the rock. In an instant, the writhing alien slipped into the water and disappeared beneath the rushing current.

John was freaked out as well as relieved, but there was no time for celebration. Emily was on her knees gripping the gunwales of the canoe as they continued down the river backwards. John was frantic to get them straightened out, and he dug his paddle into the water pulling back hard.

"Stay down, Em! I think we got it!" After five or six hard strokes, the front of the boat was again headed straight down the river. The water was rough, but there were no visible rocks.

"Keep watch. Those things have not given up and we're not in the clear yet!" John was working hard to stay as close to the center of the river, in deep water, as possible. He was doing a fine job of maneuvering through the rocks and whirlpools until the next monster launched itself.

"It's coming!" Emily yelled back. It was aimed for the center of the canoe. Regardless of how hard he tried to maneuver out of the way, John judged the trajectory to land right in the middle of the canoe between them. He fell forward on his knees, crouching down as the thing landed. Straightening to get a clear swing, he brought the paddle back behind his shoulder. Emily braced herself for the impact and readied her paddle in case John needed help.

The creature tried to steady itself as it moved to attack Emily. John did not give it time to get its footing before letting loose with a major league swing that caught it from behind just below its skull. "You... son of a bitch!" he yelled as he hit it.

The canoe began rocking and the monster lost its balance. It managed to grab hold of the side as it flipped into the water. It shrieked at them as it struggled to climb back in. John expected them to roll any moment as water started pouring in. A second chopping swing to the monster's clawed hand caused it to release its grip and slide beneath the surface.

"These fuckers sink fast once you get 'em in the water," John said breathlessly as he regained his seat. "How many more are up there? Can you see?"

"Maybe four, but it's hard to tell. They keep running behind the bushes," Emily shouted back. "Rock!" she added, bracing herself for the hit.

The front of the canoe banged hard throwing John forward onto a cross beam and knocking the wind out of him. He was struggling to breathe as the canoe began to spin once again. The current was taking them downstream sideways, then backwards again.

"Fuck this!" John finally caught his breath and got to his knees. He began paddling furiously to try to turn the canoe back around, but they were traveling rapidly and he was fighting to regain control. Emily tried to help him and made an effort to push against the rocks below with her paddle. Out of the corner of her eye, she saw two more of the creatures jumping off the ridge.

"Two!" was all she had time to scream as both of the aliens landed squarely in the center of the canoe. There was no time to react as their killer jaws came at them wide open and the canoe was rocking wildly. John yelled as loud as he could. "Jump!" and he shifted his weight to try to fall away from the boat as he flipped it over.

The alien that landed near Emily was snarling and snapping at her as the canoe rolled. Just before they hit the water, the creature managed to reach out his claws and grab hold of the tail of her shirt. The one nearest John was sent splashing into the water where it sunk beneath the surface in front of him as they both washed downstream.

"John... Help!" Emily was flailing, her arms wildly grasping for something to grab on to. She struggled to keep her head above the churning water as they were all being rushed downstream. John was swimming desperately to get to her. Regardless of how hard he tried, he was having trouble closing the distance between them. When her head went down, he kicked even harder and dove down into the cold rushing water in hopes he could grab hold of her.

He forced his eyes open to try to see, but it was nearly impossible through all the bubbles. Suddenly, he caught sight of her. The creature had a tight grip on her shirt, but appeared to be lifeless, dragging along behind her, holding her down like an anchor. Her eyes were widened with panic as air was escaping from her nose and mouth. She was reaching for him and he tried to grab her hand as the current drove him on just past her and out of reach.

John's lungs felt as if they were going to explode. He needed to get some air or else he would not have the capacity to rescue her. He broke the surface and sucked in as much air as he could, then plunged right back in. He lost her! Under water, he turned himself to fight against the current. What have I done? He was overwhelmed with grief and guilt as he continued desperately seeking for some sign of her.

He surfaced again to see if she had somehow broken free, but there was no sign of her. One more gulp of air and he went down again, and suddenly there she was behind him! The alien was still dragging along behind her, bouncing along the bottom. He summoned every bit of strength he had to go back to her. She was no more than five feet away, but in the cold rushing water it might as well have been fifty.

Kicking and reaching as far his arms could, he strained to get to her. He was determined not to lose sight of her again. When at last he was close enough to grab her, she was limp and unconscious. He took hold of her arm and pulled her hard toward him. He felt some resistance as he yanked her free of the alien's death grip. The last he saw, there was still a torn shred of her shirt clutched in its claws.

His lungs were burning and his heart pounded in his head as he pulled Emily to the surface. His fingers were numb and he prayed that he would not lose his grip as he tried to get his bearings. Propelled along by the strong current, they scraped against the rocks more than once as they were rushed along. He looked to the cliffs above and there was no sign of the aliens as he kicked toward the bank on the opposite side of the river. Ahead of them, the canoe was floating partially submerged as it banged along from rock to rock.

The riverbank had transitioned to a tree-lined slope and they were not far from it. John tightened his grip around

Emily and kicked for shore. Finally, he was able to get a foothold and pull her out of the water. She was bruised and scratched, and John took great care as he lifted and carried her limp body in his arms. He moved as quickly as he could to get to dry land, gently laying her on a flat rock.

"Don't you fuckin' die on me now! Not after all of this!" he yelled. Kneeling beside her, he added in a softer tone, "You hang on, Em. I need you."

There was no feeling at all in his fingers making it useless to try to feel for a pulse. He tilted her head and checked. There seemed to be nothing blocking her air passage, so he pinched her nose and placed his mouth over hers to give her a couple of breaths. "Come on, honey, breathe."

There was no response from her lifeless body. John applied his hands to her chest and pushed to compress it. "Emily!" Anguished, he yelled at her. "Em! You are not going to leave me! Not today, baby, not today!" He covered her mouth with his and pushed the air into her lungs. Again, he began compressions. Then, just as he placed his mouth over hers for the third attempt at resuscitation, she jerked and began coughing up water.

He rolled her onto her side and rubbed her back. "Thank you, God!" he said, tilting his head toward the sky. Now feeling the exhaustion, he collapsed beside her. He pressed in behind her and wrapped his arm around her for warmth. She eased over to face him as he cradled her head. "It's gonna be okay. I think the worst is behind us now."

"What happened?" she said feebly, as she looked into his bloodshot eyes.

"I think you... died," he said quietly.

Fifty Three

They rested there on the rock, warming in the bright sunlight. John wanted to give Emily some time to regain enough strength to get moving again. She coughed from time to time and complained of the burning in her chest, but John was doting over her like a nervous mama and assured her she was doing fine.

It wasn't like him. He had never felt like this before, and it was more than unsettling. He didn't want to leave her side, but he felt like he needed to get some distance for a few minutes. This… woman was making him feel as weak as a schoolboy and it wasn't a feeling he was comfortable with.

When he was sure she was okay, he excused himself by saying, "I'm going to go up to the tree line and check out our situation."

"Be careful," she answered. She wasn't fully aware of the situation around them. After what they had been through, she had a reason to be concerned for his safety.

John walked away and headed up the incline into the tall trees. After a few minutes, he walked back down the slope to stand next to her.

"I didn't see any sign of those bastards anywhere. We should get going while it's clear. Can you walk?" He knelt down and rested his hand on her back.

"Yeah," she nodded, "John, I just want to say…"

"You don't have to say anything," he interrupted, touching his fingers to her lips.

Pulling back, she said, "No, John. Really, I do. I just want to say that the next time you save my ass, could you make it just a little less exciting?" She smiled wide. "I mean, I'm just sayin'..."

"You think that was exciting? Hang around a while, I'll show you exciting." He smiled back at her and offered his hand to help her get to her feet.

"I'm ready to go home now if you don't think that would be too boring." She took his hand and pulled herself up.

"Can you walk?" She was taking her first unsteady step as he asked.

"I'll be fine, Mom. Let's go." She smiled at him again and the two of them began walking slowly up to the tree line. They entered the woods hand in hand.

John was thinking about everything they had been through to get this far. It was a miracle that they were still alive. The attacks, the people who had been lost... Were Karla and Eddie gone? Did Sherri and Raj manage to stay hidden? Could he have done something different and saved them all?

There was no way to know, and he would have to live with that. One thing he knew for sure. If Macy had not brought them here under false pretenses, they would probably all still be alive and well. They might even be laughing over a drink while discussing some haunted house project they could have worked for their final grade.

It was that conniving bitch who would have to carry the blame all the way to hell for this, not him. Unfortunately, he would probably be the one who would have to explain this to the families of the others if they didn't make it home. He had been through this kind of thing before, and it weighed heavily on his shoulders as they walked on.

The stand of trees was only a narrow strip that stood between the river and a large clearing. They could see the open area through the shadows when they were about halfway through. They walked faster, hoping they might actually be on the edge of a populated area, and that hope gave them the renewed energy to keep going.

John stopped walking and listened. Emily stopped next to him and turned, trying to read his face. "What is it, John?" She stepped closer.

"Listen, do you hear that?" He turned his head like a directional antenna, "I don't... wait, I do hear..."

"Helicopter!" she squealed.

"Run, Em, run!" He grabbed her hand and took off for the clearing with her dragging behind him trying to keep up.

As they broke through the trees, the helicopter was just entering the airspace above them. The whoomp-whoomp of the chopper blades was really loud now, and they were both running to the center of the open field waving their arms screaming, "We're here! We're here!"

Frank had glanced away from the ground to the fuel gauge as they passed over the clearing. It was only seconds before he looked back, but long enough to pass over the desperate couple on the ground.

"Wait a minute! What was that? Go back!" He thought he had seen something out the corner of his eye. His instincts told him that John was around here somewhere, he could just feel it in his bones.

"Did you say go back?" asked the pilot through the headphones that were now hanging around Frank's neck. Setting them back on his head, Frank leaned forward to repeat what he had said. "Go back! I saw something in that clearing," he yelled into the mike.

"I didn't see anything. Man, are you sure?" The pilot sounded skeptical.

"Fuck, yeah! I'm telling you I saw them! Go back!" Frank yelled. "Come on! Get this thing turned around!" Reluctantly, the pilot pulled controls to swing the chopper into a banking curve and headed back to the clearing.

John wasn't sure if they had been seen. He was looking for some way to signal the chopper, even if it meant setting the field on fire. He thought about how unpredictable the wind here could be. He might start a fire and burn them both to death if it shifted, so he quickly gave up on the idea.

Emily was devastated. The helicopter had flown right over them. She was starting to have visions of them collapsed in the woods, unable to go any further, emaciated by starvation, being fed on by wolves! They were going to die out here after all!

"It's coming back!" John yelled. "It's coming back. Let's get to the center of the clearing so they can see us this time." He grabbed Emily's hand and they hauled ass toward their best chance at being spotted, directly in the center of the open field.

A roaring shriek, the sound they never wanted to hear again, came from the trees behind them, snuffing out the spark of hope that had fired in Emily. She could feel her heart breaking.

The chopper continued in their direction while they turned to see three aliens bounding out of the wooded area. "Look for something to fight with!" John shouted as he scrambled to find anything he could use. He was hoping for rocks, or branches, or anything to use as a weapon.

He had checked his belt for his knife, but it had somehow been lost, perhaps in the river when they had flipped the canoe. Now they were totally unarmed, out in the open, and unprotected. He felt a cold wave of dread creep up his spine. This seemed almost unreal, like some fucked up sci-fi movie and they were about to experience a really bad ending.

The monsters were raging across the clearing at top speed, but then slowed and spread out to surround them for the attack. The loud noise preceded the chopper as it again entered the airspace above the clearing. The aliens stopped their advance for a moment and shrieked at the aircraft coming in above them.

Frank saw John in the center of the clearing. "There!" he called to the pilot who had already seen them. Three creatures appeared to be moving in for the kill. They had John and the woman with him surrounded.

These aliens had grown nearly to their full size and were almost as large as the creature that had taken their plane from the sky, the one that had fastened John and his classmates to the trees. They stood up on their hind legs as the helicopter approached, howling at the intruding aircraft. While they were distracted, John was getting a closer look at them. He was checking for any weakness he might exploit.

"John, take this." Emily thrust a large pointed rock into John's hand as he kept his eyes directed at the monsters.

"What the fuck are those things?" Frank yelled into his mike as he reached for his rifle. "Get me in closer. I gotta take a shot and I can't wait until we land!"

From the ground, Emily tried keeping her eyes on the aliens while looking out for John. She was waiting to see what would happen when the chopper landed, if they would make their move. Her mind was racing and her breathing quickened sending her into a coughing fit. "Be careful, John! We're so close..."

John was holding the rock in his hand like a dagger. He stood with his knees slightly bent to gain more stability.

"When they touch down, fuckin' run for the chopper and don't look back! I'll be right behind you, I promise."

"No, John." She set her hand firmly on his shoulder. "I can't leave you... I don't want to go without you. Not now."

He saw tears in her eyes, and told her, "Just do it, Em. I got this."

That's when the shot rang out. The high caliber slug from Frank's rifle slammed into the head of the alien closest to them causing it to explode in a cloud of orange mist. It flipped backwards and hit the ground. The other two monsters let out a blood curdling scream. They looked toward their fallen brother, shrieked in unison, and leapt for John, their razor filled jaws open and ready for the kill.

A second shot rang out, and another of the creatures slammed to the ground. A hot hunk of lead had blown a fist-sized hole clean through it. While it thrashed around screaming in a pool of its own blood, the other monster rammed head-on into John.

John had lunged forward to meet it with the rock in his hand. He brought his arm up and deflected the protruding bony blade of the alien. The impact somehow stunned the creature. It had not expected to be counter-attacked and the two of them tumbled in the grass, tangled in a struggle of life and death.

From the helicopter, Frank was freaking out, yelling for John to move out of the way. The wrestling match on the ground made it impossible to get a clear shot. He could draw a bead on the thing, but one quick move as he was pulling the trigger and John could go down instead.

Emily hadn't run. She meant it when she'd said she couldn't leave him. Beyond being grateful that he had saved her ass several times, she had grown extremely attached to this man. In fact while they had lain on the riverbank together she realized she'd fallen in love with him and now was not the time to run away.

She felt helpless as she watched John squirming to avoid the alien's slashing teeth. Its claws and the bony bladed arm thrust at him as they struggled, rolling over and over. Frustrated and frightened, she turned to the chopper and yelled at Frank, "Shoot the motherfucker! What are you waiting for? Shoot it!" She saw him shake his head and realized his desperation. He couldn't risk the shot.

From behind her came a loud 'Kraack!' as John landed a lucky blow to the joint on the monster's bladed appendage, breaking it off clean. It lay there on the ground, and as Emily saw it, she thought how much it looked like an ancient stone dagger. The kind you might see displayed in a museum. She looked at John, and then back at the creature, and she knew exactly what to do.

She dove for the blade without considering any possible consequences, and grabbing it, she rolled and ended up on her feet. From somewhere deep inside, her pent up rage exploded as she screamed, "Now you die, you son of a bitch!" and she launched herself into the air.

With all the fury inside her, she landed squarely on its back. She wrapped her legs around its midsection while grabbing one of the scaly layers with her free hand. She held on while raising the blade above her head. With all the strength she could muster, she brought the thing's own fucking blade down, plunging it deep into its fleshy neck.

Pulling it free, she turned her face as an orange fountain of bloody gore sprayed in her direction and into the air behind her. The creature jerked back and let out an agonized shriek as she slammed the blade down again. It scrabbled, trying to reach around and throw her off, but she wasn't about to be tossed.

The stench of alien blood was overwhelming, and burned her eyes as she struggled to hold on and keep from vomiting. She pulled the blade up and jammed it in again.

"That's right, motherfucker! You die now!" she screamed continuing to stab it again and again. Her body was covered in slimy orange and greenish goo as the monster howled in agony.

Still, it tried to grab John who was fending off clawed hands, gnashing teeth, and an occasional slap from its tail. He was exhausted beyond comprehension. Every second seemed like eternity, and he was fighting for his life.

All it would take was one mistake and he would be gutted right there on the ground. He could hear Emily's war cries and knew she was attacking it. The thing kept howling in pain and orange blood was gushing out of it and falling all around him.

The beast lurched one last time and gave up its struggle as she drove the blade into the back of its head. It fell to the ground away from John, tossing its enraged rider into the grass beside it. He was incredulous as he saw her roll away, covered in slop.

"I thought I told you to run, wild thing," John called to her as he was getting up from the ground. Winded and bleeding from a wound on his head, he limped over to her and extended his hand to help her up. "Please tell me you're not hurt." He grasped her arm and helped her to her feet.

"Oh, I'm just fine." She spit out some slime that had dripped onto her lips. "Was I supposed to run off and leave you here to get ripped apart by that ugly bastard? No fucking way, John! I hope it's okay if I say that I care way too much about you for that!"

"I'd kiss you if you didn't have that orange shit all over your face, but how about a rain check?" He put his arm around her as they heard Frank yelling at them. "Hey, you two, I'll get you a fucking room. Now get your asses over here! Let's go home."

"Yeah, let's get the hell out of this place," John said.

"You don't have to ask me twice! Let's go!" and they limped toward the chopper.

Frank had jumped out and was standing there wearing a huge shit-eating grin. He gave them a hand as they stepped up into the chopper. Yelling over the noise, he asked, "So what the fuck were those things?"

"Remember that shit I told you about, the thing that happened back in Idaho?" John looked at him directly.

"Yeah man, that was some weird shit too." He slid the door on the helicopter closed for take off as he climbed in behind them.

"Remember I told you we couldn't tell anybody about it because they'd think I was crazy?" He twirled his hand next to his bloody head making the crazy sign.

The chopper engine revved as it lifted off the ground.

"That's why I don't tell anybody about it either." Frank replied handing a headset to Emily.

"Well, Frank, you can add this one to the list of 'no fuckin' way can we say what really happened'. Unless, of course, I need a witness when I have to explain why me and Em here are the only ones who made it out alive." He looked at her and added, "Oh, by the way, Frank, this is Emily. Em, this is Frank." He was putting on his headset as he spoke.

"It's nice to meet you, Frank. Thanks for the backup!" She held out her hand to shake his.

"My pleasure," he said as he reached out to shake it until he saw the orange slime. He grimaced and grabbed a rag from a storage bin and handed it to her instead.

"Nobody is going to believe this." Emily shook her head as she tried to wipe some of the sticky goo from her face and arms with the rag.

"I know, babe, story of my life. Now that we have more in common, I think we should spend a lot of time together talking about it." He smiled at her.

"You betcha, my alien-wrestling super-marine detective! A lot of time!" She wiped her lips with the rag and planted a big one right on his mouth.

The chopper lifted up out of the clearing and swung wide on a flight path toward Seattle. Behind them lay the three dead aliens where they had fallen. The sound of the engine faded away and the sun was low in the sky. The birds and the rustling wind were the only sounds to be heard, and all was peaceful.

Suddenly, from a nearby stand of trees, came a horrific howling shriek...

Families of Hikers Silent As Search Abandoned

Umatilla National Forest
Wednesday 6:30 PM PDT

After a small chartered plane went missing several days ago over the Umatilla National Forest, a search was initiated for a group of students from a San Francisco Community College. Unnamed sources revealed that the group was alledgedly destined for a two week field trip to complete their class.

Local pilot groups and forestry officers launched a massive search covering 1200 square miles of rough terrain. With no sign of the students, the search has been abandoned.

Names of the missing have been withheld pending notification of family members and forestry officials have been reluctant to discuss details of the incident.

Family members who have already been notified have begun arriving at the Umatilla National Forest Supervisor's Office in Pendleton, Oregon. So far the group has remained sequestered from all media outlets and have offered no comment on the missing students or the mysterious details surrounding the nature of their disappearance.

College officials have declined all requests for comment or interviews.

Watch for The Next Episode of
"The Paranormal Adventures of John Hazard"
"Send No Angel"
Visit www.JHGlaze.com to stay connected.